UNPARDONABLE SIN

To Mary Catherine —
I hope you enjoy this.
Be afraid... be very
afraid.

Michael Potts
June 19, 2019

UNPARDONABLE SIN

BY

MICHAEL POTTS

Unpardonable Sin is a work of fiction. All references to persons, places or events are fictitious or used fictitiously.

Cover design by David Warren
Cover photography by Kenn Stilger

Sweet Hour of Prayer by William W. Walford, Public Domain
All Scripture quotations from the King James Version of the Bible, Public Domain

Published by WordCrafts Press
Tullahoma, TN 37388
www.wordcrafts.net

DEDICATED TO

KAREN BOUVIER (1964–2010)

A Dear Friend
A Fine Writer
An Irreplaceable Loss
Requiescat in pacem.

AD MAIOREM DEI GLORIAM

CONTENTS

The Mantra 1
Zeke, Andy, and Azathoth's Servant 22
The Storyteller 26
Joy in Chaos 31
The Lie 34
The Art of Temptation 46
The Baptism 48
It's Only Temporary 56
The Bike Ride 58
Frustration and Satisfaction 72
Uncle Irwin 75
The Challenge 86
Worries 100
Uncle Frank's Advice 102
Good Ol' Uncle Frank 113
The Reprieve 115
The Demon 125
The Possession 132
The Urn 134
The Increase of Sin 143
The Girlfriend 145
More Joy in Azathoth's Realm 164
The Heretic 166
The Church Split 176
A New Strategy 185
The Teacher 187
Not a Good Day for Zeke 198
The Battle 200
Going Back 213
The Wrap Up 215

CHAPTER 1
THE MANTRA

Jeffrey Conley sits on a pew at the Farris Road Church of Christ and slides his right hand over the slick pine surface. That moment takes his mind off the sulfuric yellow schoolhouse lights on the white ceiling that burn like Hell's flames. He sits beside Aunt Jenny at the Sunday evening service. For Jeffrey, the hard benches serve as security in the midst of chaos. He is home again, to a land of loss - parents and grandparents gone, twin brother dead two hours after birth, great-aunts, great-uncles, and Uncle Lawton, Aunt Jenny's husband, decaying in their graves. Less than a quarter mile down the Old Randallsville Highway stands the Benson house where he had lived until his first year at David Lipscomb College in Nashville, Tennessee.

That morning Jeffrey drove past that log house, now covered with vinyl siding reflecting the summer sun. He took a left on Bramble Road to get a better look. Ancient and bent, sugar maples remained in the back yard, covered with pale green leaves. The trees brought back old memories of a swing where his boyhood self flew back and forth across the gravel drive.

Halfway between the church and house stood the spot where Jeffrey's white Spitz, Fuzzy, died when Jeffrey was nine - pickup vs. dog. Even after Jeffrey had seen the blood encrusted body, he expected Fuzzy to come home, but death's finality refused to relent. Somehow that same summer slowly grew idyllic - that is, before the agony of Jeffrey's losing his granddaddy at the end of summer.

Every trip home is a laser playing disks of memories, Jeffrey's heart a collage of desires to re-live the good, forget the bad. Bad hangs around, an unwelcome guest, so now, at age fifty, it forces him to focus on misery. He fights the urge to sink into sticky sorrow, glances at his beloved aunt, examines the familiar spaces of the church he visited often over the years.

The song leader's announcement of the next hymn startles Jeffrey out of his trance. The song is one he has known all his life: "Sweet Hour of Prayer." Not a bad song, but easy for church members to drag, especially given the a capella singing of the Church of Christ. As soon as Jeffrey joins in singing, a mantra invades his mind - for the millionth time, it seems:

Dear God, give me peace, don't let me think about blaspheming the Holy Ghost. The unpardonable sin. Haven't I already committed it more than once - if I'm going to be damned no matter what, what good is overkill? Oh God, not those thoughts! "The Holy Ghost is good. The devil is bad. Damn fool Devil, but the Holy Ghost is good." Don't think that thought again, don't let it interrupt, God, no - but the voice in his mind says, *"Damn fool Holy Ghost." No, I didn't mean to think that, God forgive me, I'm damned to die in sin and to burn for eternity with a laughing demon licking my face with its forked tongue.*

The mantra begins again. Jeffrey's heart races and his eyes burn with the heat of new tears, tiny Hell-flames rolling down his face. His aunt can't see him crying - if she did, she would ask about it, and he would have to lie again, as he had lied to his granny when the unpardonable sin filled his heart with Hell. His face burns as if seared by a hot iron.

God, let that slow song end so I can focus. Please God. One more stanza. Thank God this church only sings the first and last stanzas of every song.

Jeffrey concentrates, squeezing out every drop of will power remaining to squelch his itch to bring the mantra back. Somehow he survives the service and drives Aunt Jenny home without getting them killed. He has an extra incentive to avoid an accident - he knows the moment he dies will be the moment of his eternal damnation.

His gut tightens but the familiar curved arms of the street lights of Randallsville cheer him and he finds the strength to make small talk.

"Brother Elliot had a good sermon tonight."

"Sure did," Aunt Jenny says. "He's been a great preacher. Takes time to see people when they're in the hospital. Saw him when I was in for my legs."

Jeffrey tries not to think about Aunt Jenny's legs - the atherosclerosis blocking blood supply, starving her legs of oxygen, exposing a strutting bone in the foot. Jeffrey must help her keep her balance when she walks. Everyone and everything in his home state of Tennessee is aging, dying, decaying. If only there exists more than memories. An afterlife? He believes in one - intellectually. Yet those 2 a.m. doubts whisper into his ear and say, *One day your dying brain will make you think you're floating to a tunnel to Heaven. When Jesus' arms pull you out of the tunnel and into the light, your mind will blank into eternal blackness. All you were will be annihilated. If you're not annihilated, God will cast you into outer darkness after you die. A lose-lose situation.*

"What's in that big notebook you brought?" Aunt Jenny interrupts his thoughts as he makes a left turn onto East Main Street. Shop windows cast a glow that reminds Jeffrey of a warm house and hot chocolate, and his mind starts to wander. He recovers his bearings and answers his aunt.

"I found it at home, hidden under my bed. It's an old journal of mine. I'd forgotten all about it."

"How much time does it cover?"

"The first entry is from July 1971 and the last is from December 1975 - ages eleven to fifteen."

Jeffrey pulls into Aunt Jenny's drive. When he stops the truck, Aunt Jenny gives him a long look and asks, "How did you forget having a journal?"

"I have no idea. Maybe I'm just getting old, or maybe there is something in that journal that I don't want to re-live. But if that's the case, I would probably have thrown it away. Guess the only way to find out is to read it."

"Hope everything you read in there is good," she says.

They get out of the car, and Jeffrey helps Aunt Jenny inside the small, 1940s-built, white wood frame house. *Quaint*, he thinks, *what real estate people call 'a cottage.'* Yet he always feels safe when he stays overnight in the tiny guest bedroom, like a cat sleeping inside a warm, cushioned box.

Aunt Jenny is ready for bed early, so Jeffrey brushes his teeth, showers and leaves the bathroom to Aunt Jenny. He walks through the hall to the guest bedroom whose blue walls add to the dollhouse-like feel of the place. A perfect spot for a man diagnosed with high-functioning autistic spectrum disorder to stay. He was diagnosed six years before with Asperger's Syndrome. That was before the psychiatrists revised the name for his condition in the DSM-V, the diagnostic manual for psychological *'disorders.'* Jeffrey's case is mild, but he becomes annoyed at people's ignorance - after the tragic Connecticut school shooting, ignorant Internet trolls said that all autistic spectrum people should be locked up. *Yeah, right*. As if autism had anything to do with why Adam Lanza killed twenty children and six adults.

I may be odd, but by God, I'm not mad.

Jeffrey lays an old spiral notebook on the bed, adjusting it as if it is lying in state. The loose cover hangs on the notebook with the aid of a few frayed cardboard strands. Jeffrey checks the clock by the bed. It is 8:15. He thinks he can finish reading the journal before his usual bedtime of 11 p.m.

He lies on his side, folds the pillow in half to support his head and turns to the first page. As he begins to read, his head hurts, and he closes his eyes as he leans forward and places his hands on the sides of his head. Lights flash in the grey darkness of his visual field. The lights coalesce into pictures, which stay still for a few seconds, then start to move. Jeffrey's life beginning at age eleven, between fifth and sixth grade, commences replaying. As memories drag the past to the present, the unpleasant ones overpower the pleasant, and he comes to understand why he forgot about the journal. With the hideous ghosts of those memories flooding his mind, Jeffrey decides to face them head on. His left hand grips the sheet as he returns to the day that started his journey to darkness, a day he had forgotten - or buried. Now it raises itself like a vampire from its coffin, its Nosferatu face filled with sharp teeth, eager to strike. Jeffrey says in a low voice, "Okay, Nosferatu, show me what you got."

In the summer of his eleventh year Jeffrey begins reading the New Testament, having finished the Old Testament the previous year. He loves the stories of David and Goliath and the Joseph story, especially the part when, as second ruler in all of Egypt, Joseph reveals his identity to the same brothers who sold him into slavery years before. Most of all, he loves the stories of the kings in the books of Kings and Chronicles.

The preacher at the Harrell's Corner Church of Christ, Brother Richard Noland, is in the middle of a Sunday evening sermon series on the kings of Israel and Judah. Jeffrey can't wait to go with his Aunt Jenny, Uncle Lawton and Granny to church to hear those sermons. Whenever Brother Nolan preaches on those Old Testament stories, Jeffrey feels as if he is living in ancient Israel in the land of good and evil kings. He pictures the Temple at Jerusalem, shining in the morning sun, priests busy with sacrifices, their knives slicing lamb's flesh to release the blood, the life. A great army leaves the city under the command of King Hezekiah, who is mounted on his chariot. Another battle comes to mind: Good King Josiah, fighting Pharaoh Necho of Egypt. One of Necho's archers shoots Josiah, who leans over in his chariot, bleeding to death, dying too young. Jeffrey cries at the end of that story. A prophet warned Josiah not to fight. King Josiah disobeyed God. *Did he go to Hell?* Jeffrey wonders. *Were the years King Josiah spent in goodness wasted?*

Jeffrey obsesses over Hellfire. He imagines burning sulfur, especially after Aunt Jenny bought him a geology set for Christmas. He plays with it in the garage that his late granddaddy built. He lights the alcohol lamp from his chemistry set and burns the yellow stone, sulfur, that he took from his geology set. The bright blue flame flickers, mesmerizing Jeffrey. The odor, however, is more rancid than a rotten skunk. So Hell is pretty, he thinks, though he doubts that people burning in the hot flames, smelling that sulfur-stench, being tormented by hideous demons, care that much.

Jeffrey also suffers from doubts about life after death. When he was a small child, he watched the Easter episode of the Claymation show, *Davy and Goliath*. The death of Davy's grandmother in the episode threw him into a panic. He ran into the kitchen, turned on the bright schoolhouse light, and asked over and over again, "When will I die?" He imagined death as nothingness, a state in which he would not be aware of anything - dead like Rover, dead all over.

Jeffrey would rather die and go to Hell rather than be annihilated. However, Hell holds a strong second place on his list of fears. He fears it more than Granny's switch. He fears it more than the next door neighbor's fierce German Shepherd. A dog bite can heal. The pain of Hell never heals but continues on and on, never stopping, people screaming, cursing God, cursing demons, cursing one another. Hell is full of bad people - people who beat up kids - or kill them. Jeffrey hates the thought of being around the worst murderers in history, and imagines them leering at him as flames torment his naked skin, their hot hands reaching for his body, grabbing him, grasping his neck and squeezing, with Jeffrey knowing the choking will only hurt - not kill. Still, better to be aware than not to exist at all.

Salvation is on his mind. He has not been baptized and plans to wait until he turns twelve, the age when preachers say a child knows right from wrong. Before he turns twelve, Jeffrey has a few months of real childhood left. He fears that he will die after the age of accountability and before he gets baptized - if that were to happen, he would roast in Hell for sure. What is scarier is that now, at age eleven, he senses that he already knows right from wrong, what sin is, and God's judgment to punish sinners. How much longer can he wait before he is baptized? The risk of dying and being eternally damned grows every moment. Each passing day is a gift - with the deaths of his loved ones, some unexpected, this truth cuts to Jeffrey's heart. If he miscalculates the day of his death and fails to be baptized, when Jesus opens the Lamb's Book of Life on Judgment Day Jeffrey's name will be missing. Then Jesus will say, *Depart from me, ye cursed, into everlasting fire, prepared for the devil and his angels.* The flames of Hell will roast his body, and demons will whip it and lick it with their seared, forked tongues that have the texture of rough sandpaper.

The worst night of Jeffrey's pre-pubescent life arrives - the night he reads chapter twelve from the Gospel of Matthew. In that chapter the Pharisees accused Jesus of casting out devils by Beelzebub, the prince of the devils. Jeffrey is fascinated by any reference to devils or demons – he has loved horror stories from the time he first read the stories of Edgar Allen Poe. He also loves stories involving ghosts, demons and monsters. As he reads the passage in Matthew, a surge of interest fires through his body like liquid lightening, and he raises his upper body with his elbows, his eyes eagerly scanning the page in his King James Bible.

Jesus tells the Pharisees that a house divided against itself cannot stand. Jeffrey recalls social studies class in which he read Abraham Lincoln's Second Inaugural Address. Lincoln had used that phrase, and Jeffrey is proud to have found the source of Lincoln's words. Maybe he can show off to one of his teachers in the fall.

His good feeling sinks into the pit of his stomach, moves down to his groin, and kicks him as he continues to read.

Wherefore I say unto you, all manner of sin and blasphemy shall be forgiven unto men: but the blasphemy against the Holy Ghost shall not be forgiven unto men. And whosoever speaketh a word against the Son of man, it shall be forgiven him; but he that speaketh against the Holy Ghost, it shall not be forgiven him, neither in this world, nor in the world to come.

Jeffrey re-reads verses 31-32 of Matthew 12. He lies down, struggling to keep his nausea in check. Before he read this passage he assumed God can forgive any sin. He can forgive lying. He can forgive theft. He can even forgive murder. Why is God not able to forgive someone who speaks a word against the Holy Ghost? Could one small mistake, one slipped word, damn a person to eternal Hell and place that person beyond all hope of forgiveness and salvation? One slip of the mind and an old man who has struggled all his life to obey God, has been faithful to his wife and kind to friends and strangers, will spend eternity with the Devil and his angels with their fiery sandpaper tongues grating his bare back? A serial killer who slaughtered one hundred people can get off scot free if he repents. Someone who dies for his faith, eaten slowly by lions, or who suffers greatly via illness or injury, but who by chance combines the wrong word with 'Holy Ghost' will be damned forever? God suddenly seems a cruel, arbitrary tyrant, a being who will allow a word-trick to send someone to Hell.

Jeffrey marks the place, closes his Bible, and walks outside. The warmth of summer grass recalls lost innocence, and a fluttering monarch butterfly reminds him of times he chased butterflies on sunny afternoons filled with childhood joy. Now his heart races, and his mind outpaces his heart. Can he damn himself this very moment by using a curse world right after saying 'The Holy Ghost?' He begins to walk in circles around the back yard. Neither the bright sun nor the sight of the monarch butterfly cheer him up or throw him off his train of thought. In school he read a story version of *Hamlet* in which Hamlet seemed to make his own decisions, but all along Fate was in control. Is Jeffrey in the same state, with Fate leading him to eternal ruin?

Jeffrey opens the gate to the field, steps through, and sits on the ground by a salt lick. The curved shapes where cows licked the salt lend an odd elegance to the scene. Jeffrey's body shakes, his heart races, and his face flushes with searing heat. He starts a strange chant: "The Holy Ghost is good. The devil is bad. The Holy Ghost is good; the devil is bad." The chant kidnaps his soul, steals his will. Thoughts claw the back of his mind like the sharp spikes of Satan's fingernails. What if Jeffrey says, "The Holy Ghost is stupid?" Will that damn him to Hell forever?

He keeps repeating his original mantra. Five minutes pass. "The Holy Ghost is good. The devil is bad." Another five minutes pass - then he slips. "The Holy Ghost is stupid."

No! he thinks, the weight of damnation drawing his body to the ground. He swallows the hot sour liquid welling up inside his mouth. By the old bathtub used to hold water for the cows, long strands of dead grass sway in the breeze. Jeffrey pulls some of the fescue grass, drops it, its blades whirling to land in a patch of red clay dirt. He puts his hands on his head and cries out a soft wail of despair - "Ahhhhhhhh noooo, O God, no no no no." It does not matter that he is not yet twelve. He knows right from wrong, he really has reached the age of accountability and he has committed the unpardonable sin. He is going to Hell and there is nothing he or God can do about it.

I should have seen this coming, he says to himself through sobs. Earlier that year, in the spring, he sensed something was wrong. With fifth grade coming to an end, the stability of having the same teacher all day in class would change. Earlier in the year, Aunt Jenny told him "In sixth grade you start changing classes." The idea of having different teachers every hour frightens him. Change is bad. Later in life he will discover the reason for his dislike of change - his Asperger's Syndrome. As a child he always assumed he was like everyone else - they would not like change, either. Now, in the spring of fifth grade, Jeffrey feels his childhood slip away into the abyss of the past.

Jeffrey faces changes he cannot understand and will not until Uncle Lawton explains the *facts of life* to him in the middle of sixth grade. In the back yard of Granny's place where he lives stand two sugar maples that provide ample shade in the hot Tennessee summers. One tree is easy to climb - a large, low branch a perfect target around which Jeffrey can wrap his arms and legs and pull himself up to climb higher. At a point where the main trunk branches off is a little "room" where he likes to sit and read. His first introduction to reading *The Hobbit* was in that room. He remembers thinking how fitting that in the middle of the maple he read about Middle Earth.

One spring day, after daffodil blooms have given way to Iris and the chill of March has moved into the warmth of early May, Jeffrey runs out the back door, abandons the screen door to slam and crosses the yard to the tree. His heart pounds, and he feels energized by a strange warmth filling his body. With a running start he grabs the maple's low branch and tries to pull himself up with his legs. His legs slip, as they often do on a branch worn slick by climbing, but it is easy enough to re-wrap his legs around the branch. He senses something good, a warm glow that spreads from his lower abdomen to his chest, and it burns his heart. The branch rubs against his groin and the good feeling grows stronger. He lets go and wraps his legs again, repeats, his heart beating faster and harder and warmth overwhelming him until he feels something give way inside his jeans and warm liquid spill into his underwear. The feeling of release makes him lightheaded and his arms slip. He falls straight down like a cat and lands on his feet. He staggers to the tree swing and sits down on the wood seat, having no idea what happened. Whatever happened felt good except for the shame of the place from where the warm liquid flowed. *Is this as bad as bed wetting? What will Granny think when she does the laundry?* What secret power does Jeffrey's body have that it lacked before?

Why is that part of him standing straight up and hard, hot and hurting? His body is betraying him, behaving in ways his child's mind is not ready to accept. He bows his head in shame that his hidden parts have suddenly become all too visible.

What makes it worse is that whenever Jeffrey sees Sharon, the blond, slender girl in his English class on whom he has a crush but is too shy to tell her how he feels, he experiences that terrible heat and hardness in his groin. Those feelings must be wrong. How can something good come from disgusting body parts? How can such feelings not be sinful? He senses a serpent growing inside him, striking him whenever it wills.

It is only a small step from such shame, such sin, to the unpardonable sin. From the shame Jeffrey felt when Sharon looked him in the eye one day, when the heat in his groin moved straight to his face - and she laughed - to the pleasure tree where innocence was first lost - to dreams of female flesh - Jeffrey's soul is soiled by guilty knowledge.

It is Uncle Lawton, his cool uncle who wears sunglasses that make him look like a spy, who explains to Jeffrey *the facts of life*. One Sunday afternoon, Uncle Lawton walks to the maple trees where Jeffrey sits on the unpainted wood seat of the swing, his hands gripping the links of the chains on each side.

"Jenny says you ain't actin' right lately. You've been moody, really down, and that ain't like you, 'specially during Sunday dinner. Anything botherin' you?"

Jeffrey struggles to calm his breathing, but blurts out, "What is that hot stuff that comes out down there?" Jeffrey points to his groin and continues. "It happens when I wrap my legs around the tree? Why does my peter stick up in the bathtub? Am I sick? Am I bad?"

Uncle Lawton places his hand on Jeffrey's shoulder, looks him in the eye. "I'm gonna tell you some things - some secret things - that you need to keep to yourself right now. Don't tell your Aunt Jenny anything about it. I'm gonna 'splain everything to you."

When Uncle Lawton describes the act of sex, Jeffrey's stomach turns and he retches, but he manages to get himself under control. "That's so gross!" he says. "That's what you pee with. That's crazy."

"It ain't crazy. When you're married to somebody it ain't wrong - it's a beautiful thing. God made sex - stop looking like I've said a cuss word - He made it so it can't be bad. Don't do it with anybody before you're married. That's called fornication - and that's a sin. Don't 'spose it's worse than other sins, but it can get a woman pregnant - with child. Knock a woman up like that - stop laughing - it ain't funny - you're responsible for that child. Even if the woman ain't with child, some women have diseases. Hopefully you'll never get one, but you can get them from sex. They hurt like Hell."

Jeffrey wonders how Uncle Lawton knows that, but he ponders his uncle's lesson. He had been thinking about what was happening to him before he'd read Matthew 12 and damned himself to eternal fire. Now he is sure that sex, death, sin, blasphemy against the Holy Ghost are somehow related. His obsessions grow. He undresses Sharon in his mind, imagining her bare breasts underneath her top and bra. Whenever he does this, he feels good and guilty at the same time. Jeffrey rests his chin in his hand and considers whether he should feel guilty. After all it is not fornication to imagine Sharon naked since they never had sex. How can thinking about it be so bad?

That's what Jeffrey thinks until one Sunday morning when Brother Noland preaches on the Sermon on the Mount. "Jesus said if a man looks on a woman to lust after her, he's committed adultery with her in his heart." After church in Uncle Lawton's old Plymouth, with Aunt Jenny driving, Jeffrey asks Uncle Lawton, "What does 'adultery' mean?"

Uncle Lawton tries to answer, but Aunt Jenny interrupts him. "Lawton, stop that. He's too young to know all that stuff."

"Guess you're right," Uncle Lawton says, and he turns to Jeffrey and winks with his right eye. When they get home,

Uncle Lawton has Jeffrey sit on a chair in Granny's bedroom. The remnants of talc from two years ago when Jeffrey's granddaddy was alive waft through the air. Uncle Lawton tells Jeffrey what adultery and lust are.

Darn, Jeffrey thinks. He can't think about sex or think about Sharon's bare chest without sinning. How many times can he be damned in one day?

At church on Sunday Brother Noland preaches about levels of reward in Heaven and levels of punishment in Hell. Outside his house after church, Jeffrey walks underneath an overhang of pine trees and bushes. He sits on dry pine needles and cries, knowing that after he dies he will burn in the hottest part of Hell. Even if God spares him the worst pain and puts him in a higher level of Hell, it will still hurt forever and ever and ever.

Jeffrey prays to God for mercy, to spare him from further evil thoughts so that he can avoid the lowest level of Hell. He prays for a break from change in this life, since every change in his life thus far has been a nightmare. What is worse are his obsessions with death and the heart.

The following week Ann Curtis, a friend of the family and a nurse, visits for Sunday dinner. Jeffrey's Great Uncle Frank has problems with high blood pressure, so Ann checks his on the Sundays she visits. She brings a stethoscope and a blood pressure monitor. Jeffrey hides in the back bedroom and waits for her to finish. Ann steps into the same bedroom to put her stethoscope and sphygmomanometer, or what Jeffrey calls a blood pressure cuff, in her purse.

Jeffrey's identical twin brother, Michael, died two hours after birth. Jeffrey believes that is the source of a fascination he has with death and causes of death. When he was nine, Granddaddy took him rabbit hunting in the field behind the house. A rabbit jumped from behind a brush pile encircling a sinkhole, and Granddaddy fired his .20 gauge. The rabbit ran about twenty feet, fell, and lay still. Jeffrey wondered how the rabbit's heart could keep beating for twenty feet and stop so suddenly. The situation turned more intriguing when Jeffrey sneaked outside to examine the rabbit's heart. The shot missed the heart! How could such a powerful, muscular organ stop beating so quickly when it had not been hit? Jeffrey cut the heart open with a sharp kitchen knife, but nothing in the strong strings of tissue and powerful muscle revealed why it failed. He ran to his hiding place in the bushes between the gravel driveway and the field and cried.

The heart, life and death are connected in Jeffrey's mind - and now, with the pubescent changes in his mind and body and how he thinks about girls, sex mixes into the brew. Jeffrey checks out as many books from the library about the heart as he can. He wants to listen to his own heart.

With women, however, he has a new problem – sex and the heart have become dance partners. When Ann walks into the house, a wave of heat spreads over Jeffrey's heart, his face, and down to his groin. It is the most intense heat he has felt thus far, so intense it seems to flow out of his toes to keep him from catching on fire. Ann is blond, slender, in her mid-thirties, and Jeffrey cannot understand why the heat inside him burns more when he views the curve of her breasts. Suddenly he imagines her strong heart beating inside her chest, and the hardness in his groin tightens. He gasps with pain and desire. He swoons and claws the wall to keep himself from falling. Ann hears the scratching and turns around. She puts the sphygmomanometer away and holds the stethoscope in her hand. She asks, "Jeffrey! You okay?"

His heart pounds with jackhammer force in his chest, and he swallows hard, working up his courage. He tries to look Ann in the eye, but cannot - he focuses on a spot in the center of her forehead. He struggles to avoid staring at her breasts. If he thinks about the space between her breasts and what lies underneath, he knows he will faint. A few seconds pass. Jeffrey swoons, but he catches himself in time. After what seems to be an hour he asks, "Can I see your stethoscope?"

She smiles and says, "Sure. Come over here. Have you ever listened to your heartbeat?"

Hearing the word "heartbeat" makes his heart pound harder. He wonders if it is strong enough to beat that fast. Maybe it will stop like the rabbit's heart. He mutters, "No, ma'am."

She places the stethoscope's earpieces in Jeffrey's ears and the diaphragm against his shirt. His heart pounds as loud as Granny's new washer sounds when it runs on spin cycle. The thought of listening to Ann's heart rushes through his mind like some fiery tongue that makes him so hot in that devil-cursed spot between his legs that he swoons again. "It sounds strong," he says.

Ann smiles, and Jeffrey asks, "Can I listen to your heart?" She laughs, picks up the diaphragm of the stethoscope and says, "I bet one day you'll be a doctor. Here, listen." She slips the stethoscope under her blouse, and the strong "lub-dup, lub-dup," perfectly regular (*like you're perfect, Ann*, Jeffrey thinks, and he pushes his legs together to hide his throbbing hardness). When her heart begins to beat faster, the lightheadedness overcomes Jeffrey, and he falls toward the bed. Ann catches Jeffrey in her arms and lowers him to the bed, pulling his legs onto the mattress. His head starts to clear, but she says, "You're looking flushed. Let him check you. Pull your shirt up."

If he had died that moment he would be happy. He hopes she will think his heart is strong. Will she think he looks good, too? Jeffrey knows someone Ann's age couldn't...but her listening to something so central to his life, so intimate...

"Your heart is beating fast and you're feeling faint because you've been breathing too fast. Slow down your breathing. Good. Your heart's slowing down. Keep breathing normally. There you go!"

She smiles, tousles Jeffrey's hair, and puts her stethoscope in her purse. "Thank you," he says, and gives her a hug. She helps him up, has him walk a few steps, and says, "I guess you're good to go." He steps toward the back door, tells Granny he is going outside, and races to the maple tree. When he reaches the bottom branch he stops and thinks, *I can't do this here. There are too many people inside for Sunday dinner.* He crosses the gravel drive to the line of bushes on the other side, crawls into his secret place. A small oak stands nearby, and there is a branch low to the ground, but high enough to wrap his legs around. Jeffrey twists his right leg to wrap around the branch, and there is an immediate flush and flow of warmth. He crumbles to the ground in a swoon.

When he wakes up, he cannot tell how much time has passed. He feels the wetness in his groin and touches the sticky dampness on his jeans. Despite a strong breeze, the odor, musky like a wet dog, wafts through the air. There must be some way to hide the shame. Jeffrey crawls out of the bushes, sneaks to the front of the house, peeks in the front door to make sure the coast is clear, and climbs the stairs to his room. He prays that no one noticed the odor when he walked inside. When he reaches his room, he takes a towel from a drawer, strips off his jeans and underwear, cleans himself off, and changes into a set of jeans identical in appearance to the first pair. After his old clothes dry, he will throw them in the laundry basket Granny leaves him to fill every week, placing the offending clothing at the bottom. No one will notice the difference.

Jeffrey's stomach twists into a knot, and he retches. He lies down on the cool floor, feeling air flow from an old window air conditioner and is barely able to avoid throwing up. He turns over, lies on his stomach, wraps his arms together, rests his head on them, and cries. Tension eases as tears wash away stress. He stops crying and peeks through a crack on the floor to see what is going on downstairs. Dust specks shimmer in sunlight as they drop toward the top of the antique piano by the back door. Jeffrey shifts his eyes to the wood stove. In the winter Granny burns coal in it - hotter than wood - and cheaper. He imagines himself inside the stove, orange flames biting his back, blowing bubbles on his skin, forcing his nerves to face the height of pain. His skin will heal, slowly, itching as he were bitten by a thousand mosquitoes - but then the flames will burn him again.

Jeffrey deserves God's judgment in Hell. First, his body betrays him on a tree, something that seems blasphemous as he thinks of Jesus' torment on the tree of the cross. Then his dreams betray him. Finally, his mind betrays him, causing him to blaspheme the Holy Ghost, to commit the unpardonable sin.

Anger strikes him like lightening, and his feelings about God change from love to hate. He is furious at God for making it impossible for him to be saved. Who knows how many others are damned because of how He makes human bodies, how He twists human minds to trick them? The Bible may say that the devil does all those bad things, but God's the one who created the devil and set the world up so the devil will win. The reason is so God can torture people in Hell. Jeffrey hisses like a serpent. "Damn the Holy Ghost. Damn the Father. Damn the Son. Damn God to Hell." He pictures punching Jesus in the balls, enjoying his pain, piercing him with a knife to avenge for the suffering Jesus inflicts on people in Hell. Jeffrey realizes that Jesus is bigger than he, but this means that Jesus has more power to increase Jeffrey's ability to feel pain so God can torture him more. God the Father. God the Son. God the Holy Ghost. The Divine Bully, three-in-one.

Anger cools into guilt, and regret swells inside Jeffrey until he runs to the upstairs bathroom and throws up, hoping that he expels sin from his body, but knowing he has blasphemed the Holy Ghost worse than ever. He flushes the toilet, washes out his mouth, and wets his face with cold water.

When he looks in the mirror, a white shape appears in the distance. Jeffrey has seen that figure before, in an old farmhouse where he had once lived that burned down when he was three. That memory is one of Jeffrey's earliest. Not long before the fire, he approached a mirror. A figure of light moved toward him. As it approached, a skull-shaped head appeared, cartoon-like, its face mouthless, eyeless, its nose two black holes, its body with thin limbs of light extending toward him, long fingered light-hands crossing from mirror to room. Jeffrey ran to Granddaddy and Granny, told them a monster was in the mirror.

"Ain't nothin' there," Granny said, taking him by the hand and guiding him back to the mirror.

"Yeah, light plays tricks on your eyes sometimes," Granddaddy said. "Look! Nothin's there."

It took all his strength for Jeffrey to keep his eyes open. All that was in the mirror was the reflection of the wall, a chair and a coffee table. Jeffrey trusted Granddaddy and Granny. If they said the monster was not real, they must have told the truth. In the years since then Jeffrey's doubts grew, and his fear of mirrors remains.

That day haunts him, upstairs at Granny's house, as he stands in his own bathroom. The white shape floats closer, its skull-face growing until it overwhelms the mirror. Jeffrey stands frozen in place, his heart thudding like a car engine with a knock, skipping a few beats like a car's backfiring. Skeletal hands made of white light pour out from behind the skull and stretch, breaking the plane of the mirror. They grope for Jeffrey's throat. Jeffrey slips and falls on the slick floor, and tendrils of grey-white light, the color of a corpse's skin, lunge to touch Jeffrey's neck. He rolls away and stands up, his body swaying. The being's hands are still less than a foot from Jeffrey's shoulder. He remains frozen. A clawed finger touches him. He screams as searing pain runs up his arm. He twists, writhing in the grasp of demon-arms. An oversized mouth suddenly appears, and the skull-jaw opens, the lower jaw stretching to the floor. A tongue of yellow light touches Jeffrey's lips, tries to force them open. Jeffrey twists away and flies out of the room and downstairs.

He reaches the bottom, unhooks the door, and Great Aunt Susan stands outside. "What in the world were you doing up there? You 'bout scared me and your granny to death."

Aunt Jenny and Granny come around the corner.

"I'm okay," Jeffrey says. "I was playing and running, but slipped down and fell on my... you know."

Granny laughs a little and says, "Fell on what? You know them floors are slick up there. If you want to run and slide, do that inside when I'm watchin' you and other folks aren't around. I ain't seen the like..."

Granny walks back into the kitchen where she was helping put food in the refrigerator. Aunt Jenny stands in front of him, and Ann comes over. *Why does it have to be her*, Jeffrey thinks. She says, "You okay? Overheard you say you fell."

"I'm fine." Jeffrey manages a smile. "My butt hurts some."

Aunt Jenny says, "Just be glad your butt ain't hurting from a whipping. Be more careful next time. Go outside and talk to the men. Those lazy bums are sitting in the gliders under the pear tree as usual."

"Thank you," Jeffrey says, and he opens the screen door into summer sunlight that pushes aside thoughts of Hell - and that...death's head...for the moment.

The revelation of the thing in the mirror throws Jeffrey back to the present, and he sets the journal on the bed, lies back and closes his eyes, trying to sharpen faded memories. He read once that memory is a construction, that false memories are easy to create. The risk of accidently fabricating events is real. Perhaps some truth will seep through, some sense of what he really saw - and kept seeing year after year - in that mirror. He wonders why he forgot everything about the monster other than dreading to look in a mirror. Has his imagination run past reality all these years? Is he schizophrenic? No strange voices talk to him, and unlike some of his colleagues at the university, he believes that his office desk is real. Could Death's image be a trick of the light? If so, why does Jeffrey continue to see not one, but two figures over the years? If the thing is real, then, like Horatio, Jeffrey's "heaven and earth" would expand, perhaps beyond what any human mind could take.

Did Jeffrey see a demon? A being from another dimension or universe? Some versions of quantum theory say there are an infinite number of universes, but they are causally closed to this one. What if a tear in space and time were to allow something trans-dimensional to slip through? If that were true, why would it (or them) want to follow Jeffrey around? Why was it skeletal in form and associated with death? Jeffrey considers the image of the death's head. He has read Karl Jung's work on the collective unconscious and the universal images that appear in all cultures – the skeleton as a symbol of death is universal. That makes sense given that only bones remain after the flesh decays. Jeffrey chills as he remembers paintings from the plague years of the fourteenth century showing hideous skeletons, slivers of skin hanging onto their dry bones as they harvest the dead.

Could the beings that haunted Jeffrey have been good rather than evil or neutral? Something should be said for human intuition, that instinct that knows a threat is present before the threat is perceived by the five senses. Jeffrey's intuition is going off like every Christmas tree light in the world on Christmas Eve, telling him that what he saw in mirrors over the years is malevolent – and it is real. Jeffrey feels as if ice is falling on him, freezing his skin. He climbs under the covers, pulls them over his head and slides the journal toward him.

That chill he feels reminds him of an older woman who tried to split the church that he had attended as a child, a woman with a rattlesnake's venom worth of spite. She gossiped and stirred up people who had been lifelong friends to hate one another. Jeffrey sensed similar feelings of spite in the mirror beings. The feeling becomes so overwhelming that Jeffrey slams the journal shut. Jeffrey wonders if spite for spite's sake has come to life and reached out with icy, thin, tentacled fingers to grab his throat. He swallows with difficulty, gently rubs his hand over his throat. *Anxiety, that's all*, he thinks.

As for the heartbeat fetish, Jeffrey had no idea as a child how a fascination changed into a fetish. As an adult, when he had wandered through Granddaddy's field on a cold November day after his granny had been buried, he grew to understand that the fetish is about life. Having been so fascinated with death because of its ability to change a living unity into a pile of stinking chemicals, the heart, as the organ of life and death, is a natural interest for Jeffrey. When puberty arrived, it was a short step for Jeffrey to become turned on by a female heartbeat. Of course as a child - and even as a younger adult - he considered the fetish creepy and weird. However, his guilt over sexuality in general was as crazy as a cockroach in heat, since sex is only human - to despise a God-given function and basic part of bodily life as evil is wrong. His rule-oriented religious training in a Fundamentalist framework affirms the goodness of sex in marriage, but it also makes sexual sin into the worst of evils - to the point that Jeffrey had associated all sexual feelings with evil.

The blasphemy against the Holy Ghost – now that is the real rub. How could Jeffrey have wasted good years of life, with most of his relatives still living, with splendid Sunday dinners at home with Granny and aunts and uncles and cousins, of learning so much at school - by being obsessed over a so-called 'unpardonable sin?' Why is he still obsessed? Why is progress in reason not matched by progress in emotion? As a child his problem was taking the Bible in a strictly literal sense, but he has no excuse now. How did the unpardonable sin and his sexual struggles at puberty relate to the experiences in the mirror (if at all)? Jeffrey decides he must continue to read the journal. As he picks it up, he senses someone else was involved in his journey, someone whose actions were hidden, who appears in his journal sporadically but who protected him from...what? Is his mind fading from exhaustion? The story of his early adolescence suddenly seems larger than a journal can contain.

CHAPTER 2
ZEKE, ANDY AND AZATHOTH'S SERVANT

Zeke Harris tosses and turns on his narrow bed in a back room of his convenience store. He wonders why sleep escapes him. *It's not President Nixon keeping me awake*, he thinks, *so it must be somethin' else*. Something clutches his heart, and he springs up, holding his hand to his chest. *Dear God*, he silently prays, *please, not a heart attack*. The pain subsides, and he clicks on the light. The dusty wood floor looks the same. As he starts to close his eyes the room disappears, and in its place is a dirt basement. A boy sits on the basement steps and cowers at a figure in front of him. Zeke gets up, stands between the boy and the figure.

Zeke screams, praying his heart won't stop from what he has seen. A demonic being, scaly, with a mouth straight from Hell, smiles like an ancient Greek actor's mask. The boy turns toward Zeke, says in a deep voice, as from a recording that is too slow, "Help me. My name is Jeffrey Conley." The demon opens its mouth unnaturally wide and hovers over Jeffrey before sinking down to swallow him. Zeke tries to talk, finally wheezing, "No, God, no." The demon fades away, and his bedroom replaces the vision of the basement. Zeke runs out of the bedroom, flips a light switch, revealing the interior of his store and a counter with an old-fashioned cash register and an ancient black rotary phone. He opens a small notebook on the counter and dials.

"Eh... Hello?" a sleepy voice answers.

"Andy, this is Zeke. We got trouble."

"What are you talking about?"

"Remember Charlie Branson?"

There is silence on the line for a long moment. A quivering voice answers, "Yeah, I remember."

"I had a dream tonight. Not about Charlie – he's beyond any help, God rest his soul. Another boy, looks about the same age. Name's Jeffrey Conley."

Zeke hears a gasp and something fall to the floor and break. "You all right," he asks.

"Let me pull myself together." There is a long silence, then Andy speaks. "See, Jeffrey is a cousin of mine. I knew his granddaddy, Bud Wilson, well."

"Bud! I used to talk to him years ago when he lived on the Preston place that burned down in '63. Didn't know he had a grandson."

"You say he's in trouble," Andy asks.

"Same trouble as Charlie was in, I reckon. Maybe worse. What got to Charlie didn't look half as mean as the thing I saw tonight in a dream. Sometimes I wish God had never given me my gift."

"There must be a good reason He did. Pray that Jeffrey won't harm himself. You got any ideas on how to help this boy? Any intuitions, if you know what I mean?"

"My sense is he'll be coming here, by the store. That wasn't part of the dream, but that voice in my head is pretty loud right now."

"That voice ain't lied yet. For now, we'll wait and see, I suppose. If you figure out a good way to help him, call me and we'll meet. Another boy committing suicide would kill us both."

"Ain't that the truth."

Zeke hangs up the phone. *Hangs,* he thinks. An image of a bare, dead oak, a rope, a twelve-year-old boy, face swollen and black, the stench of shit and rot in the air invades his mind.

It was a crisp October in 1947. Zeke farmed thirty acres off Allenville Road, and Andy, his friend dating back to first grade, lived in a small farmhouse on Bramble Lane. Zeke visited Andy on the Ides of October after dreaming about a boy named Charlie who called to him for help. They both knew Charlie from church, so they stopped by his house and asked him if he needed help. He spilled out an experience with a demon who told him to blaspheme the Holy Ghost. They visited Charlie at least every other day, trying to raise his spirits and reassure him. Just as Charlie seemed to be in a better mood, he was found hanging in the tree, a suicide. Zeke saw the demon in another dream howling with joy and satiation and saying they would see him again in a quarter-century and that they will not be able to stop it then. Zeke's guilt haunts him in a dark night of his soul. Charlie's swollen, blue-black face appeared to him over the years in nightmares. Now the damn thing's back again attacking another teenaged boy. Zeke bangs his fist on the counter saying, "Why? Why? Why? God!"

For years the Antibeing waited, patient as time's passage, to find a gate inside the world of Its dreams. Over twenty-five revolutions of the third planet around a pathetic star passed before he once again slipped through. It tried times innumerable to break through the barrier between spaces and times, but the Enemy blocked the way with the help of those inferior beings the Enemy calls Messengers. In Its past journey to the third planet, It found easy prey, the human boy's despair and death-agony enough to feed it many years. *Ah, the pleasure of eating pain!*

How It has studied the strange religion of that region, Its dread of those inferior beings who fight against the Enemy. The Antibeing took on the form of one of those beings that humans call *demons*. After the Antibeing feasted on Its first human and enjoyed the boy's delicious despair, It perfected Its demon-form. Now It knows better than before how to frighten and drive a human child to madness. The Jeffrey-child will give in quickly to despair and destroy himself.

Two pitiful humans tried to stop the Antibeing long ago in Its quest of creating despair in a human child. They failed, and the Antibeing smelled the beginnings of their conscience-pangs before the Enemy forced It back across the barrier to Its home universe.

In the Antibeing's universe, Azathoth, the Blind Chaos god, underlies all. The Antibeing cannot understand how Azathoth's servants who dance in madness around the eyeless, insane god have failed to bring absolute chaos to Its world. Perhaps the Enemy in the third planet's universe has interfered with Its own. He seems to meddle everywhere, as if He thinks He owns all dimensions. *The arrogant ass*. Soon, however, the Antibeing will defeat the Enemy and stop this meddling deity. Enough food, enough despair, enough death, and It will conquer every dimension, every world; and great Azathoth will be all-in-all.

CHAPTER 3
THE STORYTELLER

Lives are stories, and telling stories reveals their secrets. In sixth grade, stories are the weave that holds Jeffrey together in the midst of change. When he was nine, before Granddaddy became ill, the old man took Jeffrey to a flea market between Randallsville and Morhollow. There were only two items Jeffrey could afford with the small change he carried: coins, mainly old pennies, and books. Most tables charged a quarter for paperbacks. One paperback intrigued him - *Eight Tales of Terror by Edgar Allen Poe*. When they returned home Jeffrey devoured the stories, especially *The Tell-Tale Heart*.

Yeah, that's the surprise of the year, Jeffrey thinks.

Jeffrey re-reads the book in sixth grade, and the story that intrigues him that year is *The Fall of the House of Usher*. The description of desolation at the beginning of the story – the dark sky filled with gray clouds blocking all signs of sunshine, the ruined path ringed by trees decaying from a hundred-year death, the house beginning its terminal crumble into dust – these images stay with him throughout the school day. After school in late fall when the last leaves of deciduous trees dot the ground, Jeffrey walks in the field on a windless, soundless day and watches tree branches reach out to grab corpse-cold air.

With Jeffrey's imagination duly stimulated, the timing of Mr. Trammel's announcement in English class that the class's assignment is to write a story a week could not have been better. He says that volunteers can read their stories in class. Jeffrey relishes the challenge and writes his first story about a World War II skirmish. Three of his great-uncles served in World War II, but Uncle Rick was the only one willing to talk about it. He was in vehicle repair in the Pacific Theater, but he knew soldiers who had been in combat with the Japanese, and he knew military terminology. Jeffrey asked him how to tell the story of a battle in which a platoon of Japanese troops is surrounded and killed or captured by American soldiers. "Figure out a way that the American platoon outflanks the Japanese platoon," he said.

"What does 'outflank' mean?"

"A 'flank' is a side. If a group of American soldiers outflanks the Japanese, that means they outmaneuver the Japanese soldiers so that the Japanese unit is effectively surrounded. You don't have to have American soldiers surrounding them on all four sides – if there is a barrier of rocks on two sides, then the Americans would only have to surround the Japanese on two sides."

Jeffrey writes a story using that terminology in which a good soldier, Bob Moony, in his first battle, is the only American killed in the skirmish. He describes Bob Mooney's widowed mother, his farmhouse, his brothers and sisters counting on him getting home safely. Jeffrey hates killing Bob off, but figures if the class cares about Bob Mooney the story will affect them more.

Jeffrey volunteers to read, his sense of self-pride overriding shyness, and by the end of the story some of the boys say, "Yes, we kicked butt!" but some of the girls are crying. Mr. Trammel said it was the best war story he has heard by someone Jeffrey's age.

Jeffrey decides to emulate Edgar Allen Poe and write a horror story. When Mr. Trammel requires the class to draw a picture of a favorite writer, Jeffrey traces a big photo of Poe from a biography he checked out from the library. The result is not bad at all and is unique enough that Jeffrey considers it to be his own work.

Now Jeffrey writes a story about a murder in the style of *The Tell-Tale Heart*. This time, a man ties down a woman because he likes her heart, not because he hates her eye. He unbuttons her dress at the top, takes a knife, slices open her chest, and watches her heartbeat slow down and stop. Then he cuts her heart out and holds it up while it is still quivering to candlelight and says, "My bride! My bride!"

This time the class's reaction to Jeffrey's reading is silence. A pin drop would sound like a hammer blow. Mr. Trammel's eyes are wide. Then he asks, "Any other volunteers?" and Will Nelson reads his story about summer vacation in Florida.

After class Mr. Trammel tells Jeffrey to talk with him in private. Jeffrey thinks he will praise the story. Instead he asks, "Do you feel okay?"

"I feel fine."

"It is disturbing for someone your age to write a story that, er, graphic. I understand you are living with your grandmother?"

"Yes sir," Jeffrey says, thinking it is good to write such a disturbing story at his age and that Mr. Trammel is going to phone Granny to tell her what a great story he wrote. She will be so proud of Jeffrey.

When Jeffrey gets home Granny meets him at the door. "Your teacher called today. He wants me to give a story you wrote to your doctor."

Jeffrey scrunches up his face. "Why would he want Dr. Landau to read my story?"

"I don't understand what your teacher said. Too high-falutin' for me. Smart aleck thinks he knows everything. Do you want Dr. Landau to read your story?"

"I don't know. I guess it doesn't matter."

"Don't worry 'bout it. I sure ain't going to ask Jenny to mail it. Stamps high enough already."

"Fine with me," he says.

After that day some of the students avoid Jeffrey – even those he usually hangs around. Jeffrey wonders why his story makes people nervous. To him it is a cool, creepy story about murder, with the heart element thrown in for fun.

Before gym class starts one day Ricky Jones tells Jeffrey that he likes his story. Jeffrey asks, "Why are people weirded out about it?"

"I think it's because you had this crazy look in your face when you read it. Like you'd get off if you really held a woman's heart. Martha Allen and Sharon Smith tell me they are afraid of you. They said if you liked readin' so much about killin' that woman you might like killin' them."

"Oh no!" Jeffrey says, and his heart collapses into his stomach. "I'll have to talk to them."

"Don't think you should. They'd run away or tell Mr. Trammel about it, and then you'd be in deep do-doo. Tell me what you want to say and I'll talk to them."

Jeffrey tells him to let them know that his story isn't real and that he would never hurt them or anybody else. Since Jeffrey's classmates soon start to talk to him, he assumes that Ricky passed the word. Jeffrey reckons he owes Ricky one.

Jeffrey is obsessed with stories – how words that are not true can make people think he is some sort of crazy killer, how he can get lost in a Poe story or read E. F. Benson's *The Monkey's Paw* and get so scared he cannot sleep at night. A preacher's words can make some people so nervous they shake when they come forward to be baptized after the preacher gives the invitation. The Bible's words – *God's words* – torment Jeffrey with the thought he has blasphemed the Holy Ghost and is going to Hell. Words equal magic, but words are not tricks. Somehow they are real. *Maybe some day,* Jeffrey thinks, *I will read this journal again and these words will mean something, maybe something different than what they mean now. Maybe somebody else will read it and get something different out of it. Maybe nobody will read it again, and these words will stay around, even if the journal rots away, until the Lord comes on Judgment Day.*

CHAPTER 4
JOY IN CHAOS

The Antibeing, beyond good and evil, smiles as It dons Its cloak of darkness and moves to and fro on the third planet. A perfect meal is so rare, and the lure of the hunt improves the flavor. The human child called Jeffrey, fearful, despairing, never fitting into his world – will soon magnify his despair, with the Antibeing's help, and hasten his death by his own hand.

The mantra about blaspheming the Holy Ghost was the Antibeing's idea, and It is proud of its success. The last time the Antibeing was on the third planet, It studied the primitive cultures, their backward science, and, most annoying to the Antibeing, their primitive religions. The worst of the religions worship the Enemy, and whatever weakens them pleases the Antibeing.

The human child Jeffrey is infected by religion. That infection will add flavor to his flesh, and soon the Antibeing will savor the soul of another suicide. The scent of despair is so powerful that hot acid runs down the Antibeing's mouth. It wipes away the acid with its tentacles and sucks the acid off one of them with Its oversized tongue. This child Jeffrey should satisfy the Antibeing's appetite for at least fifty revolutions of the planet the primitives call *Earth*. If Jeffrey's despair grows stronger than

It expects, It may be able to stay indefinitely, gain more power, and bring more Its kind back to the planet They once ruled.

Unfortunately the child Jeffrey is different from others of his kind. Something in his brain changes his behavior. He focuses on single interests and refuses to budge. He focuses on the blood pump in the human body, is driven toward its sound in a female body. The Antibeing is already putting that fascination to good use to damage Jeffrey's will and destroy his sanity.

Reproduction drives humans like cattle, a great source of chaos. The Antibeing is learning how to exploit that drive in Jeffrey. It almost has him in Its grasp.

In the meantime, the Antibeing must take care of an annoyance who desires to help the human child. That annoyance is a mere mosquito compared to the Antibeing – yet an annoyance can interfere with Its enjoyment of Jeffrey's flavor. The annoyance is the human called Zeke. Long ago the Enemy gave him the ability to see into the future and discern names. Even the Antibeing cannot yet read the future when it is in this particular universe. *All in good time*. Zeke works with the human Andy, but Andy is only the body, the go-fer for Zeke. As the Antibeing knows so well about humans, a body without a head is dead. Zeke and Andy think they can help save Jeffrey from the Antibeing. *What delusions these humans hold!*

Zeke wheezes as he awakens from another dream. His heartbeat is an irregular drumming against his chest wall. *The best advice*, he thinks, *I can give to young people is this - don't grow old.* In his dream, the demon that haunted him before held Zeke's head and pulled him close to the demon's face, its claws forcing Zeke's left eye open. The demon smiled a rictus into its face and laughed, a grating laugh like thousands of thumbnails scratching chalkboards. A voice escaped the demon's mouth, high-pitched, cartoonish but poisoned with spite. "Hey, Zeeko. You're going to die soon. Ain't that grand? You'll go to Hell, too. You couldn't save the other boy who came to you for help, and you won't save this one, either. Ahhh. One hung from a tree and the other... Wanna bet on how he'll off himself? Wanna bet, Zeeko, Zeeko, Zeeko..." The demon repeated the name until Zeke cried out and awakened.

Zeke continues to gasp for air. *What must God be thinking to choose two old coots past their prime to help save a boy from something none of them understands?* He drops to the floor on his knees, prays as he remembers the prayer his mother taught him as a child: "Lord, help everybody, help me to be good, forgive the bad. Thank you, Lord for everything. Help me sleep, to wake again."

CHAPTER 5
THE LIE

A middle-aged Jeffrey gets up and stretches. His eyes ache from an hour of close reading. He sits on the bed, picks up the journal, cradles it in his lap, and glances at the clock on the table next to the bed. 11:30 p.m. He hopes the journal will continue to draw his attention from sleep so he can finish reading before the night is over. His new goal is to finish reading by 2:30 in the morning, but it appears this will be an all-nighter. *So be it*. He sighs and opens the journal.

When he begins reading again, however, most of the remaining account of his sixth grade experience is benign. There is an entry on the rumor that school cafeteria hamburgers were made of horse meat. Jeffrey believed it, and when the hamburgers served at lunchtime tasted like paper mixed with glue, he knew the explanation. That was the only reason the flavor could have gone so bland in one year. Horses taste like crud.

Another entry concerns playing flag football at play period. Jeffrey was overweight and slow, so no one picked him until the very end. One talent he had was the ability to catch a pass. When three completed passes make a first down, as in the rules his sixth grade class followed in flag football - that is a useful ability. When his team was close to the goal line, no one guarded him because he was slow - so the quarterback threw the ball to him. Jeffrey scored five touchdowns in two days - the height of his athletic career.

The journal becomes darker when describing the late fall and winter of sixth grade. At that time Jeffrey lost his faith for the first time. The account of that loss throws him back again into the past, back into his grandmother's house.

For a long time Jeffrey ached for a BB gun. Although Granny has some safety concerns (*thank God she didn't say, "You'll shoot your eye out!"*), Jeffrey is convinced Santa Claus will give him a BB gun. Almost all of his classmates have lost their belief in Santa Claus. Jeffrey is a true believer, a defender of the faith. He wonders why some books about Santa set in the present fail to reveal Rudolph as one of the reindeer, but he figures that perhaps he only leads the sleigh team in emergencies. A major source of doubt is a photo he finds in the World Book Encyclopedia in the school library. He has always been curious about the North Pole, and he wonders if anyone has photographed Santa's workshop. The article on the North Pole does not mention Santa, a terrible omission. However, it mentions Robert Peary, "the first man to set foot on the North Pole." There is a photo of Peary and his guides and their huskies. An American flag stands upright in the ice. That is all there is - barren ice, bereft of any life but the exploratory team. No Santa. No workshop. No elves. No reindeer.

That scene strikes a blow against Jeffrey's faith but does not destroy it. Santa operates by magic. Magic does not follow the laws of nature. Magical things can disappear into their own world and reappear later. Santa would clearly not want to be discovered to reveal his secrets to Robert Peary and his team. He must have used magic to make his realm disappear until the American team was far away. Then Santa and his world would reappear.

Jeffrey has stopped talking to his classmates about Santa - they make fun of him and call him a little baby who still believes in Santa Claus. Jeffrey, however, remains content with his squelched doubts.

It is late September. One day after school, Granny is gone - she has left a note on the door saying that she is out shopping in Randallsville with Aunt Jenny. The door is unlocked and Jeffrey walks in, passing the upstairs door on his right and the antique piano on his left. He stops. Granddaddy died when Jeffrey was nine, only two years before, and although his room was rearranged, when Jeffrey is alone he enjoys coming inside, sitting on the floor, and remembering Granddaddy — the sounds of his record player, the squeak of his bed as he sat down and played his guitar, Jeffrey's favorite spot on the varnished dark wood floor under Granddaddy's bed where he lay to listen. Granddaddy's old cabinet is the only piece of furniture remaining in the room that had belonged to him. Jeffrey walks over, avoiding the mirror, and opens the small closet on the side. There stands a new Daisy BB gun, wrapped in its package, along with other Christmas gifts for which he has asked - a new chemistry set and a plastic model of the human heart. They still have *Sears* tags attached to them. How many times has Jeffrey perused the Wish Book, pointing out to Granny and to Aunt Jenny what he wanted for Christmas? Now he knows they are the ones who give him his gifts said to be *from Santa*. His own family told him a big lie.

Jeffrey's stomach sinks, and he has to lie down. He feels as he had felt when he was jumping on his neighbor's trampoline with R.J., two years younger than he but more agile. R.J. would land on his rear end and bounce right back up. Jeffrey decided to do the same, but for some strange reason failed to bounce. Instead, a wave of numbness flowed through his body, and he could not breathe. Uncle Lawton later explained that Jeffrey had the breath knocked out of him like those football players who stay on the ground a few moments and pop back up. That is how Jeffrey feels now, when what remains of his childhood wonder has flown away like maple seeds in a brisk breeze.

The cold, bare wood floor, no longer a comforting place after Granddaddy's death, chills Jeffrey. His rabbit-step heartbeats prance in his left ear. A rush of fear spreads from head to toe. He closes his eyes tightly, hands clutching his head, darkness filling the space matching the doubts racing through his mind. Doubt speaks, as if a whisper - What if Santa Claus isn't the only lie they're feeding you? What if God is a lie, along with those wild stories about Jesus healing and being raised from the dead? What if the universe does not need a God, as Jeffrey's Uncle Frank believes? Didn't Uncle Frank tell Jeffrey before his granddaddy died that without a God, Jeffrey would have to make it on his own? If growing out of belief in Santa Claus is part of growing up, maybe growing out of God is, too. No need to worry about unpardonable sins, no need to feel guilty about lusting after Granny's friend. Take it easy, eat, drink and be merry.

It is no use. Jeffrey stomach turns like a spool. When he dies, he'll still be six feet under, rotting in the earth, skin slipping away, muscle breaking down into fluid, maggots feasting until a hideous skeleton remains, its grin senseless as a slit in the throat of a slaughtered hog. With no God, death will be nothingness. At least Hell would be something, even if Jeffrey has blasphemed the Holy Ghost and is going there. He would at least be conscious and would not be annihilated. With no God, Jeffrey's death means no more Jeffrey. The gruesome rhyme children love to chant comes into Jeffrey's head:

The worms crawl in,
the worms crawl out;
the worms play pinochle
on your snout.

It no longer makes Jeffrey laugh.

Jeffrey imagines his heart slowing to a crawl, sixty beats per minute, fifty, forty, black spots before his eyes, heart rate thirty, twenty, blackness filling his field of vision, fifteen, ten, zero, the end, the eternal blackout. That will be far worse than Hell.

Since Jeffrey knows that Santa does not exist, how can he know God exists? He can no more see God than he could see Santa. *At least there would be no more guilt haunting my mind,* he thinks as he wrings tears from his eyes. He can do anything he wants. He can hold a girl down and listen to her frightened...

"Snap out of that!" Jeffrey says out loud. "You're sick, worthy only of Hell fire." He opens his eyes, sits up. He sees himself and realizes he is facing the mirror. Behind his mirror image two shapes approach, one skeletal and made of light, the other more solid and moving toward him. He tries to look away, but something fixes his gaze as if he is chained to the mirror with his eyes pried open. Something death-pale moves toward him, walking on two legs - but it is not human. The sickly creature, ribs sticking through thin skin, has lips as large as those painted on a clown. It opens its toothless mouth and smiles. Jeffrey wrenches himself away from the mirror and turns around. A thin, electronic-sounding voice says, "See you soon - in my house." The creature's mouth barely moves, as if someone sculpted a permanent grin into its skin and facial and jaw muscles.

Jeffrey wrenches himself away from the mirror, forces his feet to move, and runs outside. A rumble of thunder rolls in a darkening sky, and lightning flashes underneath a massive black cumulonimbus cloud. *Crap,* he thinks. *God, don't force me back inside, not now.* A flash strikes a bush on the fence line, parting it into pieces that scatter sparks into the darkness. A pile of leaves begins to burn, but rain pours along with quarter-inch hail and snuffs the fire. Jeffrey jumps back as a thunderclap slams his eardrums. He falls on the stone steps leading to the back door, gets up and opens the screen door. The wind slams it shut before he can close it, and he hooks the eye. He wants to turn on the TV to check for weather reports, but the lightning is too severe. He unplugs the TV as larger hail, sounding like golf balls striking, slams into the roof. Jeffrey looks outside, and in the distance a writhing, snakelike funnel connects cloud to ground. He runs to the basement door, opens it, steps onto the narrow stairwell, and turns on the light. He hooks the door and walks down dusty steps into dank dampness mixed with dirt and old, dead roots of forgotten trees.

The basement lies unfinished. Dry dirt makes up the walls and floor. Jeffrey turns left to a passage about six feet wide. To his right sits a large table, covered with dust and empty canning jars, most likely belonging to Mr. Benson's, the landlord's, mother, who once lived in the house. Underneath the table someone has built a storage area with built-in shelves. On each shelf sit jars of canned squash, green beans, and items Jeffrey cannot identify. Granny rarely cans, and what she does can she keeps in the kitchen cabinet.

Mr. Benson's mother died in 1948, so the jars were, at the very least, canned almost thirty years ago. Jeffrey wonders if the food has spoiled. The jars appear to be sealed. He picks up a jar of squash, tries to unscrew the top, but it has rusted. He gently knocks the lid against one of the plank edges. Eventually it loosens, and the lid creaks with a screech as he unscrews it. With the outer lid removed, he tries to break the seal. Jeffrey puts his fingernails under the seal and struggles to move it, but it does not budge. No matter how much he strikes the jar against a plank, the seal remains tight. Finally he tries breaking a small piece of the glass with a rock he found on the floor. When it breaks, all Hell breaks with it. The jar explodes in his hands. Instinctively his arms jerk away, and fragments litter the floor. He examines his hands for cuts, but there is only a small cut on his little finger that looks like a paper cut. It hurts like the dickens, and he puts the finger in his mouth, sucking it, but the pain throbs like a frog's swelling throat.

The stench arrives soon after. Even with a tight seal, the squash must have disintegrated and partly decayed over time. The scent of rot joins the odor of old vinegar, and Jeffrey grabs his stomach, runs to a corner, and throws up. Then he makes his way to the other side of the passage by the steps where the odor is less maddening. Outside, wind slams against the house, and Jeffrey fears the house will not be able to withstand the storm. He peeks through the tiny crawl space to a dusty window with faded, gray glass to check on the storm. Lightning flashes so brightly that the glass shines like a rectangular sun. As Jeffrey squeezes his eyes shut, a loud clap of thunder startles him, and he falls to the ground. All goes dark.

Jeffrey's ears ring for several minutes after he sits up, the basement black as night except for a faint light from the tiny window. He extends his arms, finds the first step on the stairs, climbs up two more and sits, lights flashing before his eyes. Outside, a roar like a freight train fills the air.

Jeffrey watches the weather enough on television to know that is not a train. The tornado has arrived. Jeffrey's heart sinks, and he cowers in the dark, praying the house will be spared, that Granny and Aunt Jenny are safe. The sound of hundreds of animals squeaking combines with the outside roar. Oh no – they are rats! They must be afraid of the storm, and the patter of small feet expands into a stampede, their screeches grating against Jeffrey's ears, which he covers with his hands. They must live in the crawl space. Hundreds of thumps follow as rats fall down to the dirt floor. Some land on the steps. Their shadowy shapes coalesce into a devil's dance, and a few rats chance to land on Jeffrey's lap. Sharp claws dig into his upper legs. He screams as razor teeth incise the side of his face. He tries to get up so he can run up the stairs, storm be damned, when a pale figure appears in front of him.

Has someone broken into the house, perhaps frightened by the storm? The figure floats closer, an inhuman hiss filling the dank air. Jeffrey prays that he is caught by a bad dream. He puts his hand over his chest, which feels solid, and his pounding heart makes it clear that he remains in the real world.

The creature floats above Jeffrey's head, sinks to the dirt floor and solidifies. A gray, sickly glow illuminates thick, toothless, pale swollen lips, an image of horror and disgust, the pupils of its eyes dark, dilated, and dead – and yet alive. Clawed hands emerge from reptilian arms. *It must be a demon.* Jeffrey is as sure of that as he is sure of the heat from the creature burning his arms. The demon turns its head slightly to the side, examining Jeffrey. Jeffrey forces himself to rationalize.

"I hit my head," Jeffrey says, looking away. "You're not real."

"You think I'm just your jostled brain, boy? Touch me. Then tell me I'm not real."

Jeffrey tries to formulate a theological defense against the horror. He never believed that demons could disturb people today, in line with his church's beliefs. The demon figure, therefore, must be an illusion. Jeffrey stretches out his right hand and grabs the demon on the shoulder. Jeffrey's hand involuntarily jerks back, and he screams, stumbles up the steps, coming close to falling back into those claws. The searing pain of heat travels from his hands to this brain, and he no longer cares about the storm. He reaches the top of the stairs and fumbles for the hook. He looks behind him to find the demon face has changed into a toothless skull. Its smile remains. Jeffrey screams, pulls the hook from the eye, steps out, and slams and hooks the door on the outside. He prays that thing did not make it through the door. Half-mad from fright and pain, he stumbles to the kitchen and runs into the refrigerator. He opens the main door, pulls open the freezer door, and reaches for the frost, which melts under his hand. That never happened before, not even when he burned his hand on a stove eye when he was six. The pain worsens, and Jeffrey wonders whether his hand will feel better if it explodes. His head clouds over, and his body crumbles to the floor.

Jeffrey wakes up, eyes fixed to the ceiling. The lights are on. Did he instinctively flick the light switch when he ran into the kitchen? However it happened, he is glad the power is on, and he finds the light comforting. His hand aches, but he is afraid to look at it, afraid that thing in the basement is real. He sits up, leans against the refrigerator. Jeffrey hears the screen door open and someone turning the door key. The front door squeaks open. He imagines a herd of demons, all sizes and shapes, invading the house. He squeezes his eyes shut to the point that they hurt, and he finds the pain in his eyes lessens the pain in his right hand - as if his body can fully attend to only one pain at a time. Footsteps approach, and Jeffrey opens his eyes to find Aunt Jenny standing over him.

"What in the world are you doing sitting down on the kitchen floor?" she asks. "You feel sick?" Jeffrey stands up but immediately realizes he has forgotten to hide his hand. Aunt Jenny starts, turns to Granny and says, "Mama, look at Jeffrey's right hand."

Granny walks over, looks at the burned hand. "Goodness gracious to Betsy," Granny says. "How'd you burn that hand so bad? You need to go t'mergency room."

Jeffrey raises his right hand and examines it. The bottom part is burned in a scale-like pattern. *Oh God, that thing must be real*. His own church has deceived him. Seems like lies are piling up after the Santa lie. At least if demons exist, there must be a God, and if there's a God, there's a chance Jeffrey will be conscious after death even if he is roasting in Hell. That thought gives him some comfort.

He has to think quickly - he imagines how Granny and Aunt Jenny will look if he says, "I went down to the basement because of the storm and met a demon who told me to touch him. I did and burned myself. The scales on the burn came from him." Then Jeffrey imagines Aunt Jenny making some phone calls, and an ambulance arriving with nice young men wearing white coats inside. He would be taken to Central State Hospital in Nashville where the crazy people live. Some of them are harmless, but others have killed people. One guy popped the eyeballs clean out of his mother with his fingers, cut them off with scissors, and squashed them with his feet. He told her, "Both your eyes offended you. I was takin' care of the cuttin' them out part."

Jeffrey rubs his eyes, imagining being locked up and watching the eye guy pass by. The eye guy is holding a spare key to Jeffrey's cell in his hand. No, Central State will not do, so he tells Granny and Aunt Jenny, "I was trying to cook some hot dogs. I was boiling water on the stove, but changed my mind about having hot dogs and poured the water out. I forgot to turn off the stove. When I walked back to turn it off, I slipped on the floor and my right hand touched the eye."

Granny puts her hands on her hips. "I told that Mr. Benson the floor gets too slick in the kitchen. I almost fell myself a couple times. Now Jeffrey's got himself hurt. I'll call Mr. Benson now."

"No," says Aunt Jenny. "I'll call him myself. He gives you a break on the rent, letting you have this house for under $100.00 a month. Jeffrey, you should have been more careful. You run too much in this house."

"I'm sorry," he says. "I know I'm too clumsy."

"I guess you learned a lesson. Let's get you to the hospital."

When they reach the emergency room, the receptionist takes one look at Jeffrey's hand and says he needs to go to the back right away. Aunt Jenny follows them. Soon a man who appears to be about 60 walks in. His name badge reads, "Dr. Helphall." He looks over Jeffrey's hand, starts, and says, "I'm going to dress these wounds. Do not bust the blisters. They will either burst on their own or go away in a couple of weeks. How did this happen?"

Jeffrey says, "I touched a demon on the shoulder and its scales burned me." Dr. Helphall's eyes widen. Aunt Jenny whispers, "What?" Then Dr. Helphall smiles broadly and laughs.

"Young man, you had me worried for a minute." He turns to Aunt Jenny. "Is he always such a joker?"

"I think that's the first time."

"Okay, Jeffrey, what really happened?"

"I slipped and my hand hit a hot stove eye."

"That's what I thought. Cooking on your own, were you?"

"Just trying to turn off the stove."

"It didn't work, did it?

Jeffrey laughs, but Aunt Jenny frowns.

"Be more careful, won't you, son. We'll get this fixed right up."

With the burn dressed, they go to the pharmacy to get a tube of burn ointment. When they are in the car, Aunt Jenny says, "Don't ever say anything about a demon again. I know you wanted to be funny, but not everybody understands that."

"I'm sorry. I couldn't resist."

Jeffrey begins to doubt what happened. Perhaps he touched the stove eye and the pain made him manufacture a story. When he gets home, he checks the basement. The evidence shows him that he has been there - his footprints remain along with the rat footprints, and his head still hurts from the bump. When he searches for odd footprints or any other sign that a demon has been in the basement, he finds nothing.

Is he going crazy? He knows that no one is too young to go crazy. He heard of a girl in another class who started screaming and pulling at her face with her fingers, saying "Get the bugs away!" Kenneth, a short, stocky boy known for saying bad words in class told Jeffrey and a group of other boys, "Yeah, she scratched her face off. Her eyeballs were hanging out her head."

"She couldn't do that," Jeffrey said. "She'd be dead."

"She was almost dead," Kenneth said. Jeffrey studied Kenneth's face, trying to see if he was like his Grandpa Conley telling a fish story, but he seemed sincere. "They took her to the hospital in Nashville. I hear she's in real bad shape."

"What made her go crazy?" Jeffrey asked, putting another hand under the stack of books he was holding.

"She didn't take no drugs. Billy Wilson knows her dad, and Billy says her mother went plumb crazy 'bout ten years ago."

As far as Jeffrey knows, his parents had never gone crazy, and he is certain that his grandparents were not crazy. That may not mean anything. Perhaps he is an odd exception, perhaps God is crazifying him so he will not be responsible for his sins and can still be saved. That would be good in a way. But if God is punishing him for his sins and is going to send him to Hell for the sins he committed before he went crazy, that would be a terrible thing, like going to Hell in this life and again in the next.

CHAPTER 6
THE ART OF TEMPTATION

The Antibeing folds its tentacles into the equivalent of a human crossing its arms. Tasty spite and the satisfaction of harming the human child Jeffrey swells Its head to three times its usual size. In Its true shape It is designed for haunting dreams, entering minds, wringing out their hope like water from a wash rag.

The Antibeing relishes the argument from analogy: if Santa Claus is a lie, then God must be a lie; Santa Claus is a lie; therefore God must be a lie. Valid? Yes. Sound? Who cares? Jeffrey buys into it. He has come so close to losing hope – but he's more resilient that It thought he would be. Still, Its pride is swelled even more than usual by Its success in the art of temptation, an art it has learned from studying the Enemy-manufactured *demons* and especially from studying human beings.

The art of temptation is easy. First, make a person believe a lie. Repeat the lie. Repeat it again. The Antibeing wonders how often the same lie must be told before a human believes it. It is not a high number, and that is disappointing since It loves to multiply lies. The fulfillment of defeating the Enemy and bettering His Messengers is exquisite, the triumph of a vulture enjoying gourmet road kill.

The revealing was precious – how that boy jumped, how quickly his blood pump thrust his life through his body, each fearful beat music to the Antibeing's ears. *Ahhh, the infliction of pain* – the Marquis de Sade could not come close to the pleasure It felt when Jeffrey's hands burned from Its touch. Soon It will feel infinitely more pleasure. It laughs with anticipation.

Zeke awakens, feeling a sense of relief. Jeffrey plans to be baptized. Yet he also senses the relief will only last for a short time. This demon – if that is what it is – is persistent beyond anything Zeke has experienced. Perhaps an exorcist has experienced more, but Zeke believes that an exorcist will not help with this particular creature. Jeffrey and the Good Lord, with what little help Zeke and Andy give him, will have to deal with the demon themselves.

What in God's name is it? There are enough things in heaven and earth already – Lord, there doesn't need to be any more. Zeke drifts back into an uneasy sleep.

He dreams of tentacles reaching out toward Jeffrey, then shifting and turning toward Zeke. Zeke runs, but a tentacle takes him and squeezes. He tries to breathe, tries to push the tentacle off his chest. He gasps out, "Deliver us from evil." The tentacle loosens, and the squid-like creature screeches like a thousand violins playing off key at once.

Zeke wakes up, breathing hard. He gets out of bed, walks into the store, reaches into an old-fashioned freezer, and pulls out an RC Cola. *It's going to be another long night.*

CHAPTER 7
THE BAPTISM

Luckily for Jeffrey, the demon stays away for a few months, though church in the evening can be Hellish as he struggles to stop blaspheming the Holy Ghost. Sunday mornings at church do not bother him. He supposes the reason is the daylight – this demon seems to come out only at night.

This is the day of Sunday dinner after church with Granny, Aunt Jenny and Uncle Lawton, with assorted great-aunts, great-uncles and cousins adding to the fun. There is nothing like meatloaf, lima beans, cucumber salad, deviled eggs, strong Southern iced tea, and for dessert, a choice - pecan pie, chocolate pie, Coca-Cola cake, lemon meringue pie - a heaven of food.

He is becoming more involved at church - his first job is collecting the small plastic cups used at the Lord's Supper and putting them back in their trays. After he finishes that task, Jeffrey surveys the small church library in a bookshelf covered by sliding glass. One day he found a book, Millar Burroughs' *The Dead Sea Scrolls*, and began to read. He did not understand a great deal, but he imagined joining a team of archeologists in the hot Judean desert, searching dry caves and finding a clay pot stuffed with a scroll.

Most of Jeffrey's wanderings in the world are by way of imagination. In that world he can be an archeologist - or an astronaut, sitting by the glowing control panel, sheltered from the blackness and vacuum of space, on his way to Mars. Maybe he will find life there. After Jeffrey saw the second *Planet of the Apes* movie, he took every free moment at school to draw complex ruined underground cities, tunnel after tunnel revealing remains of skyscrapers, columned libraries and banks, cars and trucks long broken and rusted. Mutants were chasing him, making him run for his life.

When Jeffrey turns twelve, worries about baptism fill his mind. On the one hand, he thinks he is damned no matter what, so why be baptized? On the other hand, the only way he can have any hope at all of escaping Hell is through baptism. As the summer passes into early fall, and the real life Hell of seventh grade begins, these worries burn him inside like a flame. The Harrell's Corner Church of Christ where he attends with Granny, Aunt Jenny and Uncle Lawton, like all Churches of Christ, end sermons with an invitation for anyone who wants to be baptized to come forward. Every Sunday Jeffrey fidgets during the invitation song, and on two Sundays he stretches his feet into the aisle, but he holds himself back. What finally does the trick in moving him forward is Cassie Smith.

Cassie is in her sixties and has attended Harrell's Corner for six years. She has never been baptized. Aunt Jenny is persistent in trying to get her to come forward or to go to Brother Noland privately to be baptized. Aunt Jenny and the other ladies on several occasions offer to baptize her if she feels uncomfortable with a man doing it. She tells them every time, "I will, but I want to wait so I don't have as much time to sin again before I die."

One Sunday she is missing from the service. She has missed before, but Granny told Aunt Jenny today that she has a funny feeling something is wrong. Uncle Lawton says he will drop by and check on Cassie after church. He drives down a long gravel driveway to her house. It is a small wood frame house with basement and attic that stands on about ten acres of farmland. The land has been fallow since Cassie's husband died thirteen years before.

Uncle Lawton pulls up near the door and tells Aunt Jenny, Granny and Jeffrey to stay inside. He knocks several times, but there is no answer. He turns the doorknob, and the door opens. Jeffrey tries to leave the car to follow, but Aunt Jenny says, "Don't! She could have something catching."

After ten minutes Uncle Lawton emerges from the house and signals to Aunt Jenny that they should stay inside the car. He walks over and says, "Miss Cassie is dead in the kitchen. Stone cold, holding a skillet filled with sausage."

"Oh, no," Aunt Jenny says, and she starts to cry. "Never baptized and dying without Christ." Then she turns to Jeffrey. "Don't you see, Jeffrey? Cassie Smith is in Hell being tortured by Satan because she waited too long and died without being baptized. If you wait too long, God might take you and then Satan would have your soul forever in eternal fire. Is that what you want? You need to get baptized as soon as possible."

"How about next Sunday morning service?" he asks.

"How about tonight's service?" Granny asks.

"No," said Jeffrey. "I want to think about it more and what it means before I do it."

"If that's what you want," Aunt Jenny says. "Pray nothing happens to you this week."

A sheriff's deputy's car and an ambulance pull up. The deputy talks to Uncle Lawton a long time. Then he asks Aunt Jenny to get out of the car and talks to her, then Granny. Ambulance attendants pull out a stretcher with the three hundred plus pound body on it. Everyone is back in the car by then and the deputy walks to Uncle Lawton's window.

"No sign of violence. Ambulance folks said it was most likely a heart attack. That woman looked like a heart attack waiting to happen with her weight and all. Thanks for coming by – I know her family will appreciate you finding her now rather than their finding a body in really bad shape a few days later."

Jeffrey figures he can live another week before getting baptized. He is fat, but not that fat. He imagines fat gathering around Cassie's heart, squeezing off its blood supply like a python. Jeffrey wonders if the fat is already gathering inside him, a ticking time bomb waiting for the final stroke. Will that happen this coming week, the week before he has planned to be baptized? In a way that would be God's justice, His way of punishing him for blaspheming the Holy Ghost. Then he would join Cassie Smith in Hell, and together they would feel demon whips on their bare, burning backs.

Who knows? Maybe God will be merciful and wash away his blasphemies against the Holy Ghost this one time. Maybe the unpardonable part only applies to people who are already Christians. When Jeffrey becomes a Christian, he will get another chance – but only one. If he blasphemes the Holy Ghost after he is baptized and has become a Christian, he will roast in Hell for sure. It is too risky to wait until he is old and at the point of death since death can strike at any time.

This week he waits...and waits...and waits. He presses his hand over his heart, feels for any skipped beat, avoids riding with relatives in a car and is careful not to run too fast outside lest his heart be overstrained. The week drains slowly like molasses through a filter, but finally Sunday arrives.

Jeffrey dresses nervously in his room upstairs, having to re-tie his shoes three times before he gets them right. He walks into Granny's room that used to also be Granddaddy's, smells the few remaining bits of talcum powder, still there three years after his death. He says, "Granddaddy, I'm getting baptized today. After that I will do my best to be good enough to join you in Heaven."

On the ride to church, his heart lurches at every bump in the road. A big rig takes a wide turn, and Uncle Lawton honks his horn as he hugs the road's shoulder to avoid getting hit. "You stupid fool!" Uncle Lawton says. Aunt Jenny turns red and said, "Don't you dare call anybody a fool. Jesus said that anybody who says 'Thou fool' is in danger of Hell fire."

"You'd have said worse if anything had happened to Jeffrey," Uncle Lawton says. Aunt Jenny's face stays red, but she does not reply. Jeffrey sighs with relief as they turn into the gravel parking lot at church. He pats his heart area and says to himself, "Keep on beating at least until I'm dunked and my sins are forgiven."

They reach the steps to the porch where Uncle Lawton greets Brother Noland and tells him that Jeffrey wants to be baptized. "Brother Miller," Brother Noland says to the Sunday school teacher standing nearby, "you can help him get dressed when the time comes. I'll turn on the heater in the baptistery. I'm glad you're doing this now, son. Too many people wait too long, and that's tragic."

Jeffrey barely pays attention to the sermon. His body shakes. The humming sound of the water heater used to heat the baptistery fills the air. Standing in front of a group of seventy people is not Jeffrey's cup of tea, and wearing that white baptismal gown in front of them will feel silly. Still, he knows what he must do, and when the invitation song, begins: *"All things are ready, come to the feast. Come for the table now is spread,"* he forces his right foot into the aisle, then his left, and walks to the front of the church. Brother Noland greets him, takes his hand, and tells him to stand beside him to confess Christ, then follow Brother Miller out the door to the Sunday school area after he announces the upcoming baptism to the congregation.

The song ends, and Brother Noland motions Jeffrey to stand up. His entire body shakes and he focuses on slowing his breathing. Brother Noland speaks.

"Jeffrey Conley has decided to make the good confession and be baptized into Christ for the remission of sins. He's grown up with us, and we're proud that he has decided to be added to the church. I'm going to ask him to make that good confession that we all make before we're baptized. Jeffrey, do you believe with all your heart that Jesus Christ is the Son of God?"

"I do," he says in a low, nervous voice.

"I know you do and that you will make every effort to make Jesus Christ the Lord of your life and to obey his will."

Brother Noland walks to the front and opens the door to the Sunday school section. Brother Miller stands beside Jeffrey and says, "Let's go back there and you can get dressed." They head back to one of the Sunday school rooms. "You'll need to take your clothes off and put this gown on. You'll have to take your drawers off, too. I'll close the door and help you tie the gown right once you slip it on. I'll be back in a few minutes."

Jeffrey was not aware that he would have to strip naked, but it makes sense. He will be immersed in water, and wet underwear is not comfortable – and he would not want people to think he had wet his pants. He takes off his clothes and puts on the gown. It is a kind of a wraparound with strips of cloth in the back to tie it off, so he is glad Brother Miller helps tie it correctly when he knocks and Jeffrey opens the door. Brother Noland joins them, wearing overall slicks that cover everything up to his chest area. His white dress shirt and tie are still visible. Brother Noland opens the baptistery door and walks down the concrete steps into the water. Jeffrey looks to his left and sees the large painting of a creek that is behind the baptistery close up. He imagines the baptistery as a creek, the painting of trees surrounding as a row of birches, the concrete steps as a rocky bank to cold water that chills feet heated by the summer sun. The fact that this is October does not matter – Jeffrey is in his own world, and it is a comfortable one – until he steps into the water.

The heater did not do a good job, or else the water is so cold that there was not enough time to heat the water to a comfortable level. When Jeffrey steps into the water, it soaks through the gown, chilling every bone in his body. He feels his privates shrivel. He is sincere about being baptized, but now he wants it to be over quickly. The only good thing is that if he freezes to death after he is baptized he will not have time to sin and will go to heaven – provided that he is right about baptism washing away the otherwise unpardonable sin.

Brother Noland gives him a folded piece of cloth and tells him to hold it over his mouth and nose when he is immersed in the water. He stands behind Jeffrey and says, "Jeffrey Conley, upon your confession of faith in Christ, I now baptize you in the name of the Father, and of the Son, and of the Holy Ghost. A-men." He immerses him totally in the water. It must have been only a second or two at most, but the cold must have distorted time. During Jeffrey's time beneath the water the demon appears, not with a sneer, but with its mouth twisting in unnatural ways, its body twitching like a newly-killed hog's. Then it disappears into the baptistery light as Brother Noland raises him out of the water. The curtains to the baptistery close, and Jeffrey looks around, though the chlorine continues to burn his eyes. He closes them again, rubs them with his hands. "You all right?" Brother Noland asks. Jeffrey nods and walks back up the steps where Brother Miller stands with a towel. He supposes someone will wipe the floor later. He returns to the Sunday school classroom, takes off the gown, dries himself, gets dressed, and steps back into the main auditorium. The congregation has been singing the song, "O Happy Day" during the wait.

The demon's writhing suggests to Jeffrey that his sins are forgiven, even his former blasphemies, and he now has a clean slate. He feels pure and gladly takes the Lord's Supper when the plates are passed. He breaks off a piece of unleavened bread that looks like a saltine cracker without the salt, then drinks the grape juice from the little cup when that is passed around. He pictures Christ's sufferings on the cross for his sins and the wailing of the demons who knew they had been defeated.

After church, most of the church members congratulate him – even his mean cousins, Billy and Dan Conwell, who years earlier had tried, without success, to disabuse him of belief in Santa Claus. When Jeffrey discovered the truth, they mocked him with "We told you, dumbass!" Today they smile as they greet him. "Glad you got in," Billy says.

"Was the water cold?" Dan asks.

"Cold as the springs on the creek."

"Wheeewww," Dan says. "They had it warmed up when I was baptized. Sorry you froze."

When Jeffrey gets home, he starts reading the Bible beginning with Genesis. The creation story has always fascinated him, and he wonders how it could fit into the science books he has read. The next day after school, he begins to read again when something strikes his heart, falls into his stomach, and sits like a cast iron pan. A dark beast in his mind spits out a thought: "The Holy Ghost is good, the devil is bad. Damn fool devil, but the Holy Ghost is good." *Not the mantra!* he thinks. The more he tries to stop it, the louder it shouts inside his head. It is only a matter of time before Jeffrey slips again and guarantees himself an eternity in Hell. How can he be so stupid? How can he take his baptism so lightly that he let the demon slip inside? Maybe he can avoid the worst for this day – but that is too much to hope for. "Damn fool devil, the Holy Ghost is good; Damn fool Holy Ghost."

Noooooo! Damned again! His stomach sways back and forth as sobs overwhelm him. He buries his head in his pillow. Hot breath touches his left ear, and Jeffrey hears a voice, a laughing hiss. "Got you for good this time Jeffrey. You're all mine, and I will soon share you with my old buddy Beelzebub." Jeffrey holds the pillow tightly against his chest in a fetal position, shuts his eyes, and prays for sleep that does not come.

After that day, the only escape from his personal Hell is via his imagination through books. In books he finds places to feel safe from bullies, safe from mockery, safe from demons - and safe from God. God's fiery glare searches for him like a great eye, the eye of the demon Sauron Jeffrey will later read about in *The Lord of the Rings*, lidless and unsleeping. Jeffrey knows he can only hide for a short time. Soon his mind returns to the real world, tries to steal what small moments of happiness remain before childhood flees for good and life turns into a nightmare adulthood.

CHAPTER 8
IT'S ONLY TEMPORARY

The Antibeing knows that Jeffrey's baptism is only a temporary setback to Its plans, and only a little time will pass before It re-captures the upper hand. What is so special about being dunked in water that keeps It from exercising its powers – at least until It can recover to tempt again? Odd – those magic tricks work well with the lesser beings, the Messengers who are the enemies of the Enemy. They should not work on the Antibeing, but somehow they can slow him down or drive him back. That will not last. *Maybe I have,* It thinks, *what humans call "the killer instinct" more than those pathetic demons. As soon as the boy lets his guard down a little, I'll jump in and nail him with his unpardonable sin. Whether the boy's error can be pardoned by The Enemy is not my concern. All that matters is that Jeffrey thinks his error cannot be forgiven. Once he sees no point in living, well, I have some suggestions on ways Jeffrey can commit suicide. Suicide. What a lovely word.*

Zeke awakens and quickly runs to a small bookcase on the other side of his bedroom. Between several Bibles, some business documents and old Sears catalogs he finds a black cardboard box. He opens it. Inside is a Bible, embossed with

Rheims-Douay Version on the spine in faded ink that he can barely read. Inside is a faded sheet of paper. He opens it up, finds it is in some foreign language – maybe Latin – and carefully folds it and puts it back inside the Bible. He has no idea how these things can defend poor Jeffrey from that being's attacks. All he knows for sure is that Jeffrey will stop by his store tomorrow.

CHAPTER 9
THE BIKE RIDE

The blasphemy against the Holy Ghost is not the only terror haunting the onset of Jeffrey's adolescence. Childhood is fading fast, and when R.J.'s thirteen-year-old cousin Sherry comes with him to visit and take a bike ride with Jeffrey, he has a chance to cross part of that bridge between childhood and adulthood. He hates the *in-betweenness.*

Let me be an adult or let me be a child, he prays to God, *not this puberty and adolescent nightmare world.*

God either does not hear, does not answer – or else He answers, "No."

It is a clear, warm Saturday morning when R.J. and Sherry arrive on their bikes. "Jeffrey, meet Sherry. Sherry, meet Jeffrey." Jeffrey reaches out to take her hand. His own hand is shaking so hard he is horrified that she might notice. Sherry climbs off her bike and lies down on her back in the shade of a lilac bush, her blond hair sparkling in dappled shadow and light. She rests her right hand over her heart, and much to Jeffrey's delight it moves fast with each heartbeat.

Unfortunately Jeffrey does not consider the fact that mamas are not the only people with eyes in the back of their heads. Sherry snaps her head around, stares him in the eye, and says, "What are you looking at?" Thankfully her tone of voice is playful, but a frog sticks in his throat as he struggles to respond. She smiles, and he says, his own heart hammering, “At you, pretty girl.”

His face is already red from the heat, but she blushes a darker shade and whispers, “Thank you.”

R.J. turns around and covers his eyes with his hands. He makes gagging sounds. “R.J., will you stop that!” Sherry says in a voice surprisingly loud. “Go look for hickory nuts. Some might be good enough to crack and eat.”

“Whatever you say,” R.J. says. “Have fun, Jeffrey.” His sarcasm is palpable, but Jeffrey will not let it ruin his time with Sherry. “Have you always lived around here?” he asks. Sherry lowers her head. “No. We lived outside of Randallsville for a while, then in a trailer court in Morhollow. Daddy and Mama fight all the time. He hits her.”

“Oh no,” he says. “Can’t your mama call the sheriff?”

“She’s scared, I guess. Daddy’s not always bad. Part of me wants him to leave forever, and another part of me wants him to stay.”

“I’m sorry,” he says, and Sherry starts to cry. Jeffrey lies beside her and holds her in his arms, feeling her heart pound. He struggles with his feelings, realizing that she only needs comfort now. At least that was what he is thinking when something like an electric shock moved from his lips to his heart to his spine and something warm and wet and soft touches his lips. His heart thuds against his chest like hail, and he joins the kiss, lost in a haze from which he never wants to emerge. “You’re the only person who’s really listened to me,” Sherry says, wiping her eyes.

“I have two ears,” Jeffrey says, immediately regretting putting it that way. He adds, “I’m happy to be here for you.”

“I’m happy you’re here,” and she gently shoves him onto his back and lays her head over his heart. Jeffrey thinks that if he dies there, all the pain in his life would be worth this moment.

His mood jumps even higher when Sherry whispers, “So loud. So strong.” She falls asleep, and that’s how R. J. finds them as he walks up holding the shirt he had taken off and used as a wrap to hold hickory nuts.

R.J. frowns. "Oh, gosh, how disgusting," he says.

Jeffrey raises his head and replies, "Oh how heavenly." R.J. makes barfing noises, so Jeffrey decides to change the subject. He asks, "You think those hickory nuts are any good?"

"Oh, these? Yeah." R.J. cracks a couple and eats them. "They are very good. Look, I've saved some for you." Jeffrey picks out a few pieces and eats a couple. They are stronger than black walnut, but they taste fine.

"Gamey nuts," Jeffrey says. R.J. laughs.

Sherry sits up and says, "Was I sleeping?"

Jeffrey smiles and says, "You fell asleep for a few minutes. Wait until you're totally awake to ride again. Here, have some hickory nuts." He hands her some nuts and she takes a bite.

"Gamey nuts," Sherry says, and R.J. and Jeffrey laugh. Sherry stretches, and Jeffrey is pleased with the sight of her breasts pressed against her tee shirt. She smiles at Jeffrey, and he blushes. "I'm awake now," she says. Then she looks him in the eye and adds, breathlessly, "More awake than I've been in my whole life." More heat climbs to Jeffrey's face - and other places. Sherry says, "You're blushing. How sweet."

R.J. puts his hands on his hips. "Stop the mushy stuff and let's get on the road."

They mount their bikes after taking a sip from their water bottles. It is a few miles to the country store where they hope to buy some Cokes, so they only take a few sips. They start to ride, with the sun now higher in the sky and the heat beating the tops of their heads. Thank goodness the breeze from riding offers blessed relief. This is hill country, and they do not have gears on our bikes. *Reaching the tops of the higher hills*, Jeffrey thinks, *is like pushing through molasses.* It reminds him of the molasses truck in Boston he once read about that busted open, and several people drowned in molasses. The humid air thickens, and Jeffrey finds it hard to breathe. He squashes the image of the people's breath cut off out of his mind and looks at Sherry.

The heat and humidity is worth the downhill run, with their hair blowing behind their backs (except for Jeffrey, the nerd with a regular haircut that is way too short for the 1970s - but at least it keeps his head cooler). They ride on another seven miles before reaching the country store, a rickety wood building that has seen better days.

Slivers of old, gray wood stick out like knives. A wood door stands between two windows, pale with the accumulation of dust. A cardboard sign with the pale, red letters, OPEN, written in an uneven hand, hangs on a rusty nail in the door.

"This place is creepy," Sherry says, and she snuggles next to Jeffrey as he pushes the door, which opens with a long creak. "That sounds like a creak in a horror movie," R.J. says. "I don't know about going in there."

"Are you chicken," Jeffrey asks.

"Hey, watch what you call me," R. J. says, balling his hands into fists.

Sherry walks between them and says, "Both of you, be nice. I'll go in myself." She walks inside, with Jeffrey following and R.J. bringing up the rear. Inside, Sherry takes Jeffrey by the arm. Once they get used to the dim light inside, they notice merchandise sitting on dusty shelves. Some items are new - cans of Campbell's soup, smaller containers of Vienna sausage and potted meat, a row of potato chip packets and fried pork skins. Other merchandise has been on the shelves for years - cans of motor oil, hammers, wrenches and other tools, a shelf of old, outdated medications including castor oil, cod liver oil and Dr. Morton's Patent Potion to Cure Ague, Headaches, Colds, and Female Trouble. Jeffrey pulls R.J. over and said, "Look at this - *female trouble*."

"I know what that is," R.J. says.

Sherry untangles her arm from Jeffrey's and meets his eyes. "You are disgusting. If God had made you a woman you'd know why I'm mad."

His head drops and so does his stomach. "I'm sorry," he says. Sherry walks away with her arms crossed.

R.J. says, "Girls. They're like that you know. Change how they feel in a second. She'll be kissin' you 'gain before long. You'd have to do something really, really stupid to piss her off for good."

"I mess everything up," Jeffrey says, his eyes getting wet.

R.J. pats him on the back. "She gets over things all the time. She's a fast firecracker, not a slow sparkler."

Jeffrey manages a laugh. "What should I do now?"

"Look around the store some more. Where's the owner anyway?"

"Turn 'round," a high-pitched voice says. It reminds Jeffrey of the mad scientist voice on cartoons saying, *"Fools! I'll destroy them all!"*

Jeffrey pops up like a jack-in-the-box. The group turns around in unison, as if their combined strengths can deal with whatever face was behind the voice. A bent-over, white-haired man in overalls and holding a cane stands in front of them. Prunes look smooth compared to him. He appears as if all his blood has been sucked dry by a vampire, forming pits on his skin. Stubble stands like tacks on his face, and Jeffrey has the feeling that if he touches it, the old man's skin will stick his hand like one of Granny's sewing needles.

Sherry walks up to the man and says, "Hello, sir."

"Call me Zeke. Short for Ezekiel. Good morning, Jeffrey, Robert James and Sherry."

Sherry grabs Jeffrey's arm. R.J. stands frozen. "How...how'd you know our names," Jeffrey asks.

"Some'n the Good Lord gave me when I's born, I reckon. Gift of predictin.' Readin' minds. Knowin' things. 'Spose I could'a become one of those fortune tellers and made a whole lot of money. Heck, I'd make myself more money sellin' moonshine than runnin' this store. I get a few cust'mers here and there - mostly boys and girls like you ridin' around or somebody passin' through on the way to somewhere else. Guess I scar't people -

should'a kept m'mouth shut. Hell, if I know somebody'd better get to t'doctor or die I'm gonna tell him."

R.J.'s voice quavers. "You mean you can tell when a person will die?"

"Sometimes," Zeke says. "Depends. Can't read that 'bout you or Jeffrey."

"That's a relief," Jeffrey says. "What about Sherry?"

Jeffrey feels Sherry's heart pound as she draws him tighter. He feels her warmth despite her shivering. Then he is disgusted with himself for thinking that fear makes the feeling of her pounding heart better somehow.

"I can read Sherry - at least I know a range. Ninety to ninety-five."

"Oh God," she says.

"That's great news, ain't it?" R.J. asks. "Not many folks make it into their nineties."

"Now when I get to be ninety I'll be scared and keep asking myself, *Is this the day?*

"That's a long way away," Zeke says. "You don't know how you'll be thinking then."

Zeke smiles, revealing a pair of half-rotted teeth. He looks them one by one in the eye, his stare reminding Jeffrey of a mischievous cat before the cat unrolls the toilet paper.

"Sherry's got a pretty good heart. Ain't that right, Jeffrey?"

Jeffrey turns red, praying that R.J. and Sherry will think Zeke was using *heart* as a metaphor. His breath leaves him, and he struggles to breathe enough air back into empty lungs to regain his lost voice. Finally he says in a voice barely above a whisper, "She sure does. She has a wonderful heart."

"She's not as sweet as you think," R.J. says. "You ought to know that from a few minutes ago." Sherry shakes her fist at R.J., but Jeffrey sighs tension away, recovering the rest of his breath, knowing his secret is safe - for the moment.

Zeke steps closer to Jeffrey, says in a low voice, "Let me talk to you privately."

Zeke tells Sherry and R.J. to look around the store some more while he talks with Jeffrey. They go out a screen door at the back of the store. In the back yard stands a large hickory tree and two oaks. Zeke pulls up two wood chairs from under a tarp by the store and sets them down under one of the oaks, and he and Jeffrey take their seats. Acorns and acorn fragments litter the ground. Scattered hickory nuts, wrapped in their green cloaks, lie amidst the acorns.

"I'm not sure what I'm reading when it comes to you," says Zeke. "But it scares me, and it's rare that anything I read 'bout somebody's scary. Now I'm not sayin' you're bad, but there's somethin' bad after you. May be somethin' inside you, may not be. Can't tell for sure. Have a feelin' it's outside of you. Somethin's tryin' to suck your soul dry as a bone, to dry up what should be the best time of yer life. Ain't no use dwellin' on bad things. You heard what the Good Lord said? *Sufficient unto the day is the evil thereof*. Why don't you take every day you see something that looks evil and clear it out of your mind. It's like seein' a bunch of spider webs, like those that get into yer hair when you walk in the woods in the morning. Nasty, sticky, but won't hurt you unless you get careless and some black widow's bitin' yer back. And don't worry about the Good Lord frying you. Lord knows He's got enough on me to fry my ass like a bass on a skillet, but He ain't got nothin' on you that bad. Yer hear?"

Jeffrey laughs at the image of Zeke's ass on a skillet, but he answers, "Yes, sir," and feels a reprieve, a palpable sense of relief that flows through his body like a surge of energy. The day seems brighter, and Jeffrey is ready to get back on the road. "Thank you, Zeke," he says. "We're gonna buy some RC Colas and get on the road."

They go back inside. The store no longer feels creepy to Jeffrey, but more like an old familiar house that one can leave but longs to return to see again. "Boys and girl, come over here to the freezer," Zeke says. The group joins him around an old-fashioned cola machine, one of those where you have to slide a bottle down to the right slot and pull it out. Jeffrey had seen one of those when he was in first grade. Granddaddy took him to a country store on Hill Top in Morhollow. Mr. McAdoo, the owner, would pull the cola out after Granddaddy had put a dime in the machine. It looked like it would hurt, having to pull the bottle out by its sharp-edged top. Today Zeke does it like a pro and pulls out three RC Colas. Jeffrey, R.J. and Sherry start to gather some change to pay for them, but Zeke motions them to stop. "Nope. Won't take it. Have a good ride."

"Thank you," the group intones.

"Don't mention it." Zeke's snaggle-toothed mouth opens wide into a smile. "Next time, though, I'll charge for 'em. Oh, Jeffrey, come here - got somethin' for ya. Got this old Bible from some feller in Nashville a few weeks ago. He said I'd know who needed it when the time comes. Figure that time's come."

R.J. mutters to himself, "Jeffrey gets all the attention."

"Heard that," Zeke says. "You don't want to be in Jeffrey's shoes, now. His mind's a scorpion twistin' in a whirlwind." Zeke hands Jeffrey the Bible. "Take this, boy - it may come in handy."

"Thank you so much," Jeffrey says. Sherry and R.J. thank him again and all three step outside, hearing the screen door slam as they mount their bikes.

"What kind of Bible did Zeke give you," Sherry asks. He opens the Bible. It is old, but is not the King James Version with which he is familiar. It is a "Rheims-Douay Version." Jeffrey has read enough to know that is a Roman Catholic translation.

"It's a Catholic Bible," he says.

"Oh, Lord," R.J. says. "Pretty soon you'll be worshippin' the Virgin Mary and kissin' rings and all that shit."

Jeffrey laughs. "I don't think so - I'm still in the Church of Christ."

"That's even better," Sherry says sarcastically. "You think everybody but you folks is going to Hell."

"I don't want to talk about that now," Jeffrey says. "Hey, what's this?" He pulls out a folded piece of paper from inside the Bible. On it is written something that he is sure is in Latin.

He has been fascinated as a child by the Roman Empire and has read enough Latin names and phrases to recognize the language when he sees it. He understands a few words, but he cannot translate what someone scribbled in all caps on the page. It reads:

HUMILITER MAJESTATI GLORIAE TUAE SUPLICAMUS, UT AB OMNI IN FERNALIUM SPIRTUUM POTESTATE, LAQUEO DECEPTIONE ET NEQUITIA NOS POTENTER LIBERARE, ET IN COLUMES CUSTODIRE DIGNERIS. PER CHRISTUM DOMINUM NOSTRUM. A-MEN.

At the bottom a message is scribbled in the center of the page, unlined and written in bold in larger caps. It ends with seven exclamation points.

DESPERATIO ACCIT EXTERMINANDEM!!!!!!!

R.J. looks at it and laughs. “Hey, the guy must have had bugs. He was desperate for an exterminator.” Sherry giggles, and Jeffrey chuckles.

“I think the message is more profound,” Jeffrey says.

“Ooooohhhh,” R.J. says. “A secret message, only for Jeffrey. Only the great Jeffrey can figure out what it says.”

“Cut it out, R.J.,” Sherry says. “You heard Zeke. Jeffrey has a lot of things bothering him and this might help him. You want to have lots of things bothering you, maybe things worse than bugs?”

“I’m just kiddin’.” R.J. pats Jeffrey on the shoulder. “Anyway, it’s cool. How you gonna figure that message out?”

“I guess I’ll go to the public library and find a Latin dictionary,” Jeffrey says. “I don’t know the language, so I’ll have to do the best I can.”

“Ain’t no Latin teachers ‘round no more,” R.J. says. “My mom said they used to have one at the high school, but she retired a long time ago.”

"If I could find her..." Jeffrey says, and R.J. interrupts.

"Reckon you could, if you went to Greenlawn. Mama says the lady died 'bout ten years ago. Wanna dig her up?"

Jeffrey hits R.J. on the side of the arm. "No, I don't want to dig her up. Somebody has to know Latin around here."

"What about the Catholic Church," Sherry asks. "St. Rose of Lima? Maybe the priest knows Latin."

"Maybe not that well," Jeffrey says. "I have some first cousins who are Roman Catholic and they say they don't use Latin anymore. Everything's in English now."

"Hey, let's get to ridin' our bikes again or else it will be dark when we get back. Lots of places to see today." They take off and go the same route R.J. and Jeffrey had taken with Jeffrey's granddaddy years before, turning right onto a road filled with hills. Rugged limestone outcroppings strut from plowed earth, too large for any farmer to move. They stop to examine one, walk to where it is in a field of newly cut hay, and find a small cave.

"Let's go in," R.J. says.

Sherry steps back and says, "I'm scared to go into that dark place. We don't have flashlights."

R.J. peers inside the cave and says, "Sunlight carries quite a ways back in here. I think we'll be okay if we don't go too far."

Jeffrey takes Sherry's hand and steps inside first. The cave is dry and has a high ceiling. Jeffrey thought all caves had stalactites and stalagmites, and he is disappointed not to see any. He walks further back. The gray floor darkens, then grows damp and sticky. Suddenly Sherry slips and falls. Jeffrey tries to lift her with his hand but she falls against him, and he crumbles to the floor. They slide down slick limestone on a downhill slope, moving so fast that Jeffrey feels like those kids on the waterslide ads on TV must have felt, except that they were not scared out of ten years of their lives.

He catches his breath enough to ask, "Are you okay?"

"I think so," Sherry says. "I can touch the ceiling. It's only a foot above my head."

Jeffrey raises his hands, touches cold, damp rock, hoping no bats, cave rats, or cave crickets are slinking around. Something strikes his nose, then something else. "Close your eyes," he says. "Cave crickets won't hurt you, but they'll fly anywhere and crawl anywhere."

Sherry cries out. "They're so many!" Jeffrey swings his hands blindly, hitting the ceiling so hard the pain stings from his fingertips to his toes. There seems to be an endless supply of crickets, and he focuses on suspending his usual mouth-breathing to breathe through his nose. If one of those bugs crawls into his nose, it will be summarily executed. Eventually all the crickets fly away or lie dead on the damp floor.

"Do you have room to scoot off me?" Jeffrey asks.

"Let me try." The weight on his body lessens. He stretches out his right arm - there is plenty of room that direction. "I think the only barrier is this back wall," Sherry says.

"Can we walk blindly in this dark, back the way we came?" Jeffrey asks.

"Maybe we can crawl."

"Better than being skeletized down here."

"Cut out the morbid stuff. That could really happen."

"I'm sorry. Let's keep talking so we know we're still beside each other."

They keep talking and move on, Jeffrey guesses about fifty feet, when a distant light appears. "Look - that's the opening up there," Jeffrey says. Follow the light." The light grows as they move slowly up the slope. Jeffrey thinks getting to the entrance will be an easy task. Without warning, a green light encircles him.

"Why did you stop," Sherry asks. "Need to rest?"

"Don't you see it?" Jeffrey asks.

"The light? It's straight ahead, like you said."

"No, there's a green light around me."

"I can't see it. Are you sure you're okay? You may have hit your head without knowing it."

Jeffrey feels a flush of anger but stifles it and rubs his head and neck, searching for any bumps or sore spots.

"I can't find any head wounds," he says. "I could be dehydrated. I wonder if that can cause hallucinations? Oh, sh..."

His voice sticks in its box. The green circle has widened into a path. A door appears and opens. Something floats through the door and rises from the cave floor. It hisses, and Jeffrey thinks of Gollum from *The Lord of the Rings*. The being he sees, however, is no corrupted hobbit. The toothless circular smiling mouth speaks, and Jeffrey shivers, hides his eyes. Jeffrey's body levitates, rising from the cave floor. He opens his eyes. He now floats upright - but a demon stands in front of him, its hot breath burning Jeffrey's face.

"A...a..." Jeffrey's voice sputters.

Sherry asks, "What's wrong?"

"De...de...mon," he says.

"A demon? I don't see anything. You're hallucinating. Nothing that you're seeing is real."

"The cave is real. You are real, and I hear your voice."

"Hussshhhh," hisses the demon. "You're little sweetheart is wrong." The demon's lips barely move as it speaks. Its mouth remains an always-open hole bordered by unnaturally wide lips and an ever-present smile. If sarcasm and spite could be grafted onto a smile, they are welded onto the demon's face.

"I have come to check on you," it says. "My future prey. Oh, don't look so worried. Not today. When the time is right you will join me in the flames. There I will torture you again and again, laughing all the way. Ho ho ho! It's so convenient when you young Christians blaspheme the enemy's Spirit. The Enemy must be a cruel God indeed to set up an unpardonable sin, then tempt young teenagers to fall. Oh yes, they fall, and hard. You will, too – more fuel for the fire, a new back for my whip."

Jeffrey tries to control himself to keep from getting sick in front of Sherry - she might not feel the results but by God she would smell them. The word *forever* bounces in his mind like a super ball on polished blacktop. Hopelessness overwhelms him.

He considers sliding to the back wall, waiting for death and Hell to take him. Then he squeezes Sherry's hand and knows he cannot fail her.

"Who are you talking to," Sherry asks. "Let's go. Let's get out of here and get you some water."

The demon fades and said, "Remember me, Jeffrey. See you soon!"

As Sherry starts talking about the myriad complexities of her girlfriends' relationships among themselves and with guys, a topic as exciting to Jeffrey as watching paint dry, he debates whether he is going crazy like Mrs. Cheever, his first grade teacher. *After she retired, she wore socks on her ears. She thinks she is a bunny rabbit*. Her family had the state take her and place her in a mental institution. Granny had known her in the past and stopped to visit, dragging Jeffrey and Aunt Jenny along. When Mrs. Cheever saw him, she screamed and said, "Get that dog out of here. He's come for dinner and I'm it." Now Jeffrey imagines being a beagle and eating Mrs. Cheever. He laughs, and Sherry looks at him with big eyes.

"What are you laughing at? You sound like a madman on a TV show."

Jeffrey laughs louder, and coughs out words. "Just a...funny joke someone told me."

"Would you care to share it? I could use a laugh."

Jeffrey giggles. "Crap, I forgot it."

Sherry puts her hand on his forehead, and Jeffrey winces. She says, "I'll be glad when you get some water so you can be yourself again."

They struggle up the hill on the slick mud surface. R.J., still searching with his flashlight, stops the light when it strikes Jeffrey's face. "Hold on," R.J. says. "I'll pull you up."

He pulls Sherry up and then Jeffrey. They run down the dry pathway away from the cave and stop to rest under a shade tree, a large oak with yellowing leaves. Jeffrey swears that the leaves were totally green when they walked into the cave, but he stays quiet. No need for Sherry and R.J. to be confirmed in their view that he is temporarily insane.

"I can use an RC now," he says.

"You have some water first," Sherry says. "I'll get your thermos." She walks to his bike, locates the triple-lined plastic sack tied to it, and pulls out a thermos. She unscrews the top, pours in some water, and gives the top to Jeffrey. He drinks fast, and Sherry takes the cup in her hand and moves it away from his mouth. He tries to jerk it back, but she says, "Don't drink too fast. I'll give you another cupful when you finish this one."

The water is so good that Jeffrey imagines it as Jesus' living water. He supposes that sulfur water would taste good to him now. R.J. and Sherry drink some water, and Sherry gets the RCs out. As Jeffrey drinks he savors the cola's flavor, this small moment in life with two friends, one with whom he is falling in love, and the memory of the demon in the cave grows distant. Maybe Sherry is right, that what he saw is because of a head bump combined with dehydration. After all, his traumatic experience during the tornado is bound to haunt him.

The rest of the ride is uneventful. When they reach Jeffrey's house, R.J. and Sherry are about to leave when Sherry pulls Jeffrey behind the house out of Granny's sight and kisses him on the lips. They hold the kiss for a few seconds. Something warm and wet enters his mouth, and it feels good. Then she jumps on her bike, waves goodbye and she and R.J. ride home. Earlier, they agreed to take another bike ride, this time to Limestone Springs, an old resort near Perry Lake. Jeffrey approaches the door, where Granny holds it open for him. When he looks at her there is a broad smile on her face. His heart lurches when he thinks it might be a knowing smile.

CHAPTER 10
FRUSTRATION AND SATISFACTION

D*amn*, the Antibeing thinks, lowering itself to crude human speech. It is unable to read what is written on that sheet of paper Zeke gave to Jeffrey. Normally that would be no problem – with Its heightened awareness It could read anything via oversensitive sense organs or through what humans would label as ESP. Yet Zeke – damnable Zeke – blocks It. Has Zeke made a deal with the Enemy? It considers this possibility, and ponders an alliance with the inferior beings called demons to assault the Enemy. It decides to hold off on that plan until It gains more strength.

The Antibeing doubts that document can do It any permanent harm, but it might be used in some magical ritual to delay Its plans. Delaying Its pleasure is not a nice thing to do to the Antibeing. It must deal with Zeke, sooner rather than later. Trying to control a human's mind to make him kill Zeke will not work quickly enough. No, this is something that Its Holiness – the Antibeing laughs at the image of It wearing a miter and having to figure out which tentacle will hold the crozier - will have to do Itself.

Andy sits in an old-fashioned wood chair in Zeke's store. Zeke sits across from him near a Franklin stove. Andy drinks a bottle of Nehi Grape, while Zeke drinks an RC Cola. Dust fills the floor and floats around them, visible in the morning sunlight streaming through the side windows.

"Zeke, you want me to come over one day and help you clean this place? I can help after our little talk today if you'd like."

"Nah, no use anyway. So few folks come by that it ain't worth the trouble."

"Somebody came by yesterday."

"Just as I dreamed. I knew somehow the old Bible I picked up at Duncan's Books on Church Street in Nashville would help Jeffrey. Old Man Duncan told me he thought somebody would need it one day. He never said anything like that before, but damn if I didn't take that Bible right quick. Old Man Duncan didn't charge me, though I kept offerin.' "Book's been blessed," he said. "Can't sell anything that's been blessed." Zeke raises the bottle of RC and takes a long drink. "That sheet inside the Bible is also part of the help – maybe the key. Hell if I understand how it's gonna work."

Andy takes a swig of his Nehi. "Did you copy or write down what was on the sheet of paper?"

Zeke chokes and says through his coughing, "Oh crap. I didn't. Old brain's startin' to rot."

Andy sighs. "I could come by his house to copy it myself."

"I have a feeling," says Zeke, "that Jeffrey is meant to figure this out himself, even if it's a razor wire that divides him between life and suicide."

"Let's hope and pray he can find the key to beatin' that thing - else we'll be busting Hell wide open with two deaths on our heads."

Zeke shakes his head. "Naw. If, God forbid, Jeffrey does himself in, I don't think either suicide would be on us. Some things we ain't able to control. Maybe we tried too hard last time. Sometimes the best help is to stay away."

"Wish my arthritis would stay away," Andy says in a deadpan voice.

Zeke wheezes out a laugh. “Thanks – I sure as heck needed that. How’s that garden of yours?”

CHAPTER 11
UNCLE IRWIN

A week after the bike ride, the blessed kiss, the stranger with the strange Bible and the adventure in the cave, Jeffrey trudges along the fence line behind the garage. He parts honeysuckle vines with his hands and examines the ground, searching for skulls – another part of his death obsession. He has a gathered a collection that he hides in his desk drawer - dog, cat, birds of all kinds. He even found a fish skull in a dried creek bed. Granny walked outside one day and found him spraying a cat skull with clear-coat. "Something wrong with you, keeping junk like that," Granny had said, and she crushed the skull with her feet.

Today he does not find a skull, and his body fills with tension which he wants to release. He squeezes through a thick tangle of honeysuckle hugging the back wall of the garage. For a moment his chest feels tight and he grows claustrophobic, imagining the vines as demon claws ripping into his back. He emerges into sunlight and runs in circles around the back yard. His heart beats harder, faster. He likes that feeling of life, and takes off his shirt, stops running, and presses his right hand over his heart. *Something so powerful will never stop. Zeke says Sherry will live into her nineties.* The thought that she will die at all makes him sad. He will, however, live longer than that. He will never be a skeleton in the ground to be found by some curious boy in the far future. His chest and groin grow warm. He runs inside the house, into his room, and locks the door.

Jeffrey opens his desk drawer and pulls out a stethoscope. He finally found a cheap one when Aunt Jenny and Uncle Lawton took him to a flea market in Randallsville. He saved five dollars from his allowance money, and the stethoscope was only three. After he got home, he listened to his own heart. *So strong*, he thought. He wanted to listen to Granny's heart because she was old, and her heart might sound different than his. But when he asked Granny, she reddened and said, "You want to be a doctor or something?"

His body shook all over. "I only want to hear your life."

"What's that? That's crazy talk. First the skulls, now this. No, you ain't gonna listen to my heart. And don't go botherin' your aunt and uncle, either."

Jeffrey pushes the memory away as he grabs the stethoscope and listens to his own pounding heart. He throws it back in the drawer and runs outside when the gravel drive crackles with the sound of an approaching vehicle. He sits on one of the concrete steps by the front door. Around a sharp curve of the gravel drive comes Uncle Lawton's old Plymouth, originally white but now gray with a coating of limestone dust mixed with red clay soil. The car stops. Granny steps out, then her brother, Jeffrey's Great-Uncle Irwin. Uncle Lawton steps out of the car and opens the trunk. Uncle Irwin gasps for air, clutching the top of the car for support. Uncle Lawton pulls out the walker from the trunk. Uncle Irwin grabs the handles and snails toward the front door, his face a faint shade of blue. He wears a yellow dress shirt with the first three buttons undone. His chest is big around, like a barrel. He stops, wheezes and coughs.

Jeffrey's heart lurches. He fears that Uncle Irwin will drop dead in the driveway.

Granny had told Jeffrey that Uncle Irwin would be staying in the guest room downstairs because he is sick and needs someone to watch him. Plus, he cannot climb the stairs. Jeffrey is glad to keep his old bedroom during Uncle Irwin's visit.

Jeffrey stands up and says *Hello* to Uncle Irwin, who grunts a greeting.

"He's got emphysema. Makes it hard for him to breathe," Granny says. "He can't talk too good right now. But he appreciates you talking to him."

Uncle Lawton helps Uncle Irwin up the steps. The walker clangs as it hits the first step and Uncle Irwin stops and takes fast breaths interrupted by coughing. Uncle Lawton lifts Uncle Irwin's walker to the second step as Uncle Irwin tries to hold on to the walker and lift his feet. Jeffrey tries to help, and he places his shoulder under Uncle Irwin's right arm. More wheezing and coughing follow. Uncle Irwin makes it to the second step as Uncle Lawton eases the walker inside the door while Granny stands to the side, holding open the screen door with her hand. Finally, Uncle Irwin disappears inside.

Jeffrey sighs and walks to the pear tree near the gliders. Before he died Granddaddy had told him that his parents had planted it shortly before they were killed. It has not rained much this summer, and a few dead leaves, brown and blighted, float to the ground.

Jeffrey goes back inside the house. Uncle Irwin is slowly making his way to a lounge chair at the back of the living room. He coughs some more, and Granny brings him a coffee can to spit in. Jeffrey retches when he sees black mucus come out of Uncle Irwin's mouth but wills himself not to throw up.

That evening, Aunt Jenny visits and watches TV with Granny. Uncle Irwin still sits in the same chair, smoking a cigarette and wheezing. Jeffrey hates the odor. Why does Uncle Irwin smoke since it makes his cough worse? *Sometimes*, Jeffrey thinks, *for people who are supposed to be smart, adults can be dumber than dirt.*

They watch an old movie with a scene about mine workers. In one scene an explosion occurs near the mine's entrance, and miners from outside pull an injured men out. The first miner they pull out is an old man, his shirt blown off by the blast. His chest is hairy and looks larger than normal. Jeffrey figures that his lungs are supposed to be bad because of coal dust. He glances at Uncle Irwin, then returns his gaze to the movie. A doctor takes his stethoscope, places it over the old man's heart, and listens. After a few seconds, the doctor says, "He's dead."

Jeffrey's stomach churns again. He imagines his great-uncle's heart struggling to contract as the oxygen-starved muscle strains to force blood out with each beat. He imagines the heart slowing, stopping, and Uncle Irwin lying in bed, pale and dead.

Uncle Irwin is dying. His heart must be interesting to hear. Jeffrey wants to hear how a heart sounds when it is straining for air. He shivers at the delightful thought that he can gain secret knowledge of what dying sounds like. He will listen to Uncle Irwin's heart. Uncle Irwin, though, would think it is weird if Jeffrey asks him directly, and if Granny or Aunt Jenny found out, they might send him to Central State with the nice men in white coats. Jeffrey must find a way to listen to Uncle Irwin's heart in secret.

Night arrives, and the wood stairs creak as Jeffrey climbs them to his bedroom. The planks of the top floor are even louder. He pulls out his stethoscope from the desk drawer and slips it under his shirt, a button-up blue shirt tucked loosely into his jeans. Uncle Irwin had gone to bed first, at nine. Granny went to bed after the ten o'clock news. After planning out how he is going to pull off listening to Uncle Irwin's heart, Jeffrey walks downstairs, kisses Granny goodnight. She steps inside her bedroom and closes the door.

Jeffrey climbs upstairs and waits a few minutes. He creeps down the steps to the third step from the door at the bottom. There he waits. Finally, he figures enough time has passed for both Granny and Uncle Irwin to be asleep. To be safe, he cranes his neck and listens a few more minutes, then cracks the door. Silence. He opens the door enough to squeeze through, lowers himself to the floor onto his hands and knees, and slowly pushes the door to. He crawls on the cold, slick floor. The house creaks and groans. Jeffrey prays that no one wakes up.

His stomach knots when he realizes a problem with his plan. The guest room where Uncle Irwin is staying has a hook and eye latch - on the inside. He could walk through the downstairs bathroom, but to do that he would have to go through Granny's bedroom, and she would wake up for sure. Jeffrey's heartbeat slams his body. He will not give up. There is a gap in the door through which he might be able to unhook the latch if he can find an object thin enough to thread the gap. But this raises another problem - how to close the door behind him and hook it again.

He slithers to the coffee table in the living room and takes a large family Bible, cradling it in his right arm. Then he crawls to the table next to Uncle Irwin's door and finds a pair of scissors in the top drawer. He sets the Bible on the floor, slips the scissors through the crack and pushes against the hook. It snaps out with a loud pop. Jeffrey starts, listens for any movement from Granny's room. There is none, and Jeffrey holds the door ajar with his hand and listens for any stirring inside.

Uncle Irwin takes a breath. It begins with a drawn out wheeze that grows higher pitched. Then it pauses. *His lungs must be made of Styrofoam*, Jeffrey thinks, and he wonders how Uncle Irwin can breathe at all. After a long pause, the air hisses out of Uncle Irwin's nose and mouth with a whistling sound. Then Uncle Irwin does not take a second breath. Jeffrey's hair stands up on end as the seconds pass. Finally, a gasp, a hiss, another breath.

Jeffrey picks up the Bible, slides it slowly to the other side of the door, stopping it just far enough to let him slip in. He returns the scissors to the drawer, pushes it shut, then half-crawls, half-slides into the room. The planked floor creaks as he inches toward Uncle Irwin's bed. His knees ache, and he wants to stretch his legs, but squelches the thought. Whatsoever he does he must do quickly, he thinks, and remembers that is a reference to Judas the Betrayer of Christ. He feels sick, but curiosity drives him forward like a whip drives a racehorse.

Jeffrey reaches the side of the bed and fetches the stethoscope from under his shirt. Moonlight illuminates the sheets that cover Uncle Irwin. Jeffrey tries to slow his breathing as he pulls down the sheet, exposing Uncle Irwin's chest. Jeffrey places the stethoscope earpieces in his ears. Then he guides the diaphragm until it hovers above the right side of Uncle Irwin's left nipple. He lowers it, inch by inch, and lets it go as it softly lands over Uncle Irwin's heart. Jeffrey is afraid it will get caught in the chest hair, but it lies flat and snug on a bare spot.

Jeffrey hears muffled beats, as if from inside a full barrel. The heart stops and skips a beat every few seconds. Jeffrey's eyes widen. Now he knows what dying sounds like. The chill of discovering secrets returns along with hardness in his groin.

Jeffrey's stomach turns at the shame of being aroused by dying, but he feels driven to keep listening - so he does. He does not count the passing time but holds his breath. The heartbeat grows louder, faster, and there are more skipped beats. Suddenly Uncle Irwin sits up, and the stethoscope falls on the bed. His head turns in slow motion toward Jeffrey. Uncle Irwin's pale skin glows in moonlight streaming through the still-open blinds, his face gaunt like a grinning skull's. Jeffrey snatches the stethoscope, but it falls to the floor with a *clang!* Jeffrey freezes, his gaze fixed on Uncle Irwin's cavernous eyes, feeling as trapped as the mad soul in Poe's *The Tell-Tale Heart.* Uncle Irwin's low voice groans, "What are...you...doin'...in here...boy?" Jeffrey's own heart skips a beat when he realizes that Uncle Irwin's words came in the same irregular rhythm as his heartbeat. Then Jeffrey notices that Uncle Irwin's eyes stare past him. Uncle Irwin falls back on the bed and begins to snore and wheeze at the same time. Either Uncle Irwin has fallen back asleep right away, or he has been talking in his sleep. Whatever happened, Jeffrey decides to get out fast.

Jeffrey grabs the stethoscope from the floor and wraps it around his neck. He places his hands and knees down on the cool wood, trying to keep the stethoscope from hitting the floor. He opens the door and slides the Bible away. It is then that he realizes how hard it will be to get the door latched again.

Jeffrey sets the Bible and stethoscope down, holds the door open with his right hand, and takes the scissors from the table drawer with his left. He lifts the hook with the scissors, and pushes the door closed as far as he can while still having room to work, trying to drop the hook into the hole. The hook drops with a soft click but misses the hole. Jeffrey's heartbeat feels like firecrackers exploding in his chest. Granny stirs in her room, and the bathroom light comes on. Jeffrey holds his breath as he tries to drop the hook into the hole again. This time, the hook catches, only a little, but enough to hold. There is the sound of a toilet flushing followed by water running in the bathroom sink. Then Granny's footsteps echo, sounding as if they are approaching Uncle Irwin's room. Jeffrey stays silent as a stalking cat, crawls faster and reaches the door to the stairs. Granny's footsteps sound out from her bedroom. *Please, please,* Jeffrey thinks, *don't go to the kitchen for a snack*. The creak of a bed tells Jeffrey the coast is clear. He opens the door, carefully climbs the stairs, and reaches his bed, focusing on calming his frayed nerves and racing heart.

Jeffrey awakens at 9 a.m. to a thrill of guilt and delight that he got away with his plan. He stoops to avoid hitting his head on the low ceiling and listens for signs of life downstairs. Dishes clang and the odor of bacon wafts up from the kitchen. Granny calls out, "Jeffrey, get up. Remember Aunt Jenny and Uncle Lawton are taking you to the swimming pool today."

Jeffrey forgot all about the planned trip to the swimming pool at Cedars of Lebanon State Park. Although he never learned how to swim, he enjoys cooling off in the cold water. He dons his swimming trunks, races downstairs to the bathroom and to breakfast, where he gulps down sausage biscuits and drinks two glasses of milk. Uncle Irwin sits at the table, mutters "G'mornin,'" and eats breakfast. Jeffrey glances at Uncle Irwin out of the corner of his eye. Uncle Irwin's color is pinker than before, and when he leaves the table, he walks without using his walker.

"Going to set outside and smoke," Uncle Irwin says.

"You sure look better today," Granny says.

"Feeling better. Reckon I'll be ready for a nap at noon, though."

"You get your rest."

There is a knock at the door, and Uncle Irwin and Aunt Jenny come in. "Towels and suntan lotion are in the car. You ready to go?"

"Absolutely!" Jeffrey says, and runs to the car, sliding into the back seat. Granny follows the group out the door.

Aunt Jenny says, "Glad Irwin's looking good today. He told me he was real tired last night and hadn't slept too good. Well, we'll get going. See you later, Mama. It's already mid-morning."

When they arrive at the pool, Jeffrey climbs down the ladder into the cool water, letting it leech the heat from his body. When he gets up his courage, he holds his nose and ducks under the surface, his eyes shut tight. A hollow, thumping sound surrounds him, as if coming from an empty drum.

It sounds like something dying, he thinks. *God, it's my heart.*

A sudden thought pushes Jeffrey toward panic. *If I drowned,* he thinks, *how long would it take my heart to stop?*

He feels himself sink, and his arms and legs try to move the water so he can rise to the surface, but it feels like he is pushing through Jello. The world begins to blacken, and lights flash in front of his eyes. Then all turns blue, and he walks on the bottom of the pool. *Why am I here,* he asks himself. *This is the shallow end.*

Ahead is Uncle Irwin and Granddaddy and *O God that can't be them!* standing side by side in front of him. Uncle Irwin steps forward. He is naked. His chest becomes transparent and his heart beat sounds out one, two, three beats. Then it stops.

Uncle Irwin remains standing. His skin fills with holes and sloughs off in the water. His eyes turn into jelly and melt into the blue of the pool. The rest of his flesh falls off and disappears, leaving a skeleton whose bones collapse, floating to the bottom of the pool where they turn into a shiny, black scum on the floor. Granddaddy now stands in the spot where Uncle Irwin had been. But Granddaddy's been dead for years. Suddenly sunlight shines in Jeffrey's eyes as his head pops to the surface of the pool. He gasps for air... *just like Uncle Irwin.* He stifles a sob and stands still for a few moments, taking deep breaths, the surrounding water shimmering in slow motion. Then he wipes hair away from his eyes, closing them tightly, waiting for the chlorinated water to drip off his face before opening them again. Had this been a dream or had he seen two ghosts? He climbs up the steps out of the pool and walks over to his aunt and uncle, stretches his arms, and yawns.

"Looks like the pool wore you out," Aunt Jenny says. "You ready to go?"

"Yes, ma'am," Jeffrey says, and he sighs with relief when Uncle Lawton says, "Too darned hot out here anyway. Get yourself washed off in the shower and we'll leave."

When they get home, the house seems empty at first until they find Granny in the kitchen chopping squash. "Let me check on Irwin," she says. She walks into her bedroom, through the bathroom, and into Uncle Irwin's bedroom. Granny says, "Irwin?" and there is a sound as if she is shaking the bed. A minute or two later, Granny emerges and says, "He's gone." She cries and steps back into Uncle Irwin's room. She reaches the bed, and Jeffrey creeps inside, standing behind her. The nipples on Uncle Irwin's barrel chest are as pale as the rest of the skin. Jeffrey has never seen anyone so white. He thinks of the color of zombies he has seen in movies.

Jeffrey stares at the chest. It seems to move, and he jerks back, but then he figures it is a trick of the eyes. He considers running upstairs, retrieving his stethoscope, and sneaking into the room before someone removes the body. That plan comes to naught when Uncle Lawton and Aunt Jenny step into the room and Uncle Lawton says, "Get out of here, Jeffrey. You don't need to see this." Jeffrey runs out of the room and into the front yard.

A half-hour later, an ambulance pulls around the drive, tires crackling loose gravel before it stops. Two men in white coats emerge. "Heard you had a man who died," one of them says. He staggers some and his voice is slurred.

"He's in the bedroom back here," Aunt Jenny, who is standing at the door, says.

The men slide a stretcher out of the ambulance and lift it over the concrete steps through the front door. Jeffrey follows them inside. A few minutes later, the bedroom door opens and the men leave with the body on the stretcher covered with a sheet. Uncle Irwin's feet stick straight up like dead people's feet in old Dr. Kildare movies. Jeffrey follows them outside and watches them leave.

"Don't go too far," Uncle Lawton says. "We gotta to take care of things in town."

Jeffrey paces around the yard, the memory of what he did last night pricking his heart. He wonders if he hastened Uncle Irwin's death. Even though Uncle Irwin had emphysema and his death was just a matter of time, maybe Jeffrey had caused him to have a nightmare that had strained his heart too much, causing it to stop.

That night, Jeffrey takes a flashlight and stethoscope and sneaks into the guest room. He lies on the bare mattress and on the same spot where Uncle Irwin's body had lain. He places the stethoscope on his own chest and hears the drumming of his heart.

He closes his eyes. A loud voice booms out in the darkness - Uncle Irwin's voice. It says "I died in this bed!" Jeffrey snaps fully awake and opens his eyes. He hears a heart racing way too fast and starts when he realizes it is his own. His heart skips a beat. Jeffrey hears the pause, amplified by the pulse in his ear, like Uncle Irwin's, like that voice saying, "What are you doing in here?" *Maybe I am dying*, Jeffrey thinks. *I will rot into a skeleton like Uncle Irwin.*

Jeffrey takes the earpieces out and places the stethoscope on the TV table Uncle Irwin had used. He shuts his eyes and seals them with his hands. When he does that, he sees Granny standing in a swimming pool on the oily scum that was once Uncle Irwin. He thinks, *Got to see if Granny is okay*.

He takes the stethoscope, stepping through the bathroom into Granny's bedroom. He passes by his granddaddy's white dresser where he used to keep Old Spice shaving lotion and talcum powder when he was alive. Creeping carefully past Granny's bed, he trips on a slick spot on the varnished wood floor, but softly lands beside Granny bed.

Jeffrey takes the stethoscope and places the earpieces into his ears. He taps the end of the stethoscope with his fingers. The sound is fine. He places the end piece on the left side of Granny's chest.

One, two, three beats ring out. A pause. One, two, three seconds. Jeffrey twitches into a panic. Finally the heart starts again, strong and regular. Jeffrey silently thanks God and leaves the room.

CHAPTER 12
THE CHALLENGE

Jeffrey marks his place in the journal, then pages ahead, trying to find an entry on the Latin phrase on the sheet from the Bible Zeke gave him. Nothing. How had he forgotten to check the meaning of those words? Had he somehow lost the sheet? Did he find the meaning and later forget it? Or was some providential force for good or evil blocking him from translating a potential key to his freedom from the obsession with the unpardonable sin? He knows the key is in the Latin, a language he now can translate, but how that fits with all the events in the journal - that must wait until he reads it in its entirety. He needs to read the scene in which Jeffrey, if that's what happened, translates the Latin and finds its meaning for him.

The more Jeffrey reads from the journal, the more he will understand the interconnectedness of all his obsessions. Physical life and death, eternal life vs. eternal death - both fascinations are on the same continuum. Each subset - the obsession with the heart, with the blasphemy against the Holy Spirit, with death in general - feed on one another, cannibals eating cannibals but somehow holding together and gaining mass. What is most frightening about the entries following the Uncle Irwin entry is that Jeffrey placed his own life at risk to fulfill his obsession, as Jeffrey discovers by reading the next entry, from a week after Uncle Irwin died.

Jeffrey's obsession with life, death and the heart takes a new turn when he decides to challenge his heart. "Challenge his heart" are the words his best friend Karen would tell him many years later. She had understood that was exactly what he was trying to do when, in his twelfth year, he takes a plastic bag from a drawer in Granny's kitchen.

Jeffrey has no intention of dying from his *experiments* - he has confidence that his heart can take any challenges he offers. He begins with the challenge of holding his breath as long as he can. He takes off his shirt, puts the stethoscope on his chest, takes a breath so deep it hurts and holds it until his chest burns, until he feels like passing out, all the time listening to the changes in his heart rate and rhythm. When he begins each breath hold, his heart beats more slowly and with more force. Then the rate increases, though only by about ten to fifteen beats per minute. The force of his heartbeats continually increase until he can see his chest and abdomen bounce with each beat. Each time Jeffrey does this exercise, he feels a warmth in his groin like the warmth he had felt wrapping his legs around the maple branch. Finally, as his abdomen begins to convulse, Jeffrey release the breath, listening to the heartbeat grow louder than ever before calming down to a slower than normal rate. It takes a minute or two before the rate returns to normal. His heart has easily passed this challenge. It is a strong heart. Now Jeffrey has to give it a more stringent test.

Normally Jeffrey can only hold his breath one minute, at most a minute and a half. Now he reasons that if he gets more oxygen into his body, he will be able to hold his breath longer. If he breathes fast for five minutes, he will most likely be able to hold his breath for two or more minutes and hear how his heart reacts.

He tries this for the first time one night after he has been in bed for a half-hour and knows Granny is asleep. Jeffrey takes the stethoscope from under the covers where he has hidden it. He flicks on the switch to the lamp beside the bed and unbuttons his pajama top. He can already see his chest and abdomen jump with each heartbeat, so he takes slow deep breaths to slow down his heart - the less energy used, the longer he will be able to hold his breath. He sets his watch in a position where he can keep an eye on the second hand, puts on the stethoscope, and listens. Once his heart slows he begins to breathe, at first taking fast, deep breaths, then shifting to fast, shallow breaths after his arms and face turn numb. His heart rate increases and its rate varies a bit more, but he anticipated that might happen. He starts to feel lightheaded after two minutes but he makes it to three. Then he takes the deepest breath he can and holds. One minute passes. The tingling in his arms lessens but is still present. Two minutes. The tingling is gone, but Jeffrey starts to feel the urge to breathe. His lungs burn, and his head feels as if it is expanding. At 2:40 he lets the breath out, gasping precious air into his lungs. His heart beat hard but strong throughout the experiment - it passed another test. Jeffrey feels driven to go further, to further explore his limits.

A major part of his obsession is sexual – he is aroused by the sound of his own heart and how it reacts under stress. When in the throes of the obsession he does not consider how odd his actions would appear if someone knew about them. His obsession is like a man kissing a woman other than his wife who becomes so turned on that at a certain point he simply has to keep going, the force of passion trumping reason.

Passions overthrow Jeffrey's reason when he takes a plastic bag, hides it in his pants, hides the stethoscope under his arm, and sneaks out to the back yard after supper one summer afternoon. Supper is at four, so there is plenty of daylight left. Jeffrey crosses the gravel drive, locates an opening in the line of bushes surrounding the drive, and crawls back to his hiding place between the driveway and the field. In this *room* in the bushes with a comfortable, grass surface, Jeffrey has tied some vines together to form a makeshift roof. No one can see him from the house, from the yard or from the field. He sits down, feeling his heart race and a warm, good feeling spread from his abdomen to his private parts.

Jeffrey takes off his shirt and stares at his sweating chest jumping hard from his pounding heart. For this experiment, it does not matter if his heart slows down before the test. He lies down, struggles to get up his courage. Finally he seals the plastic bag around his head and places the stethoscope over his heart. He begins to breathe. Immediately his heart speeds up and pounds harder. His head becomes hot as the drive for oxygen and the higher carbon dioxide level in the bag forces him to breathe faster. His heart pounds harder and faster than he has ever experienced. His entire body shakes with each beat. His groin is hot. He starts to feel faint. He pulls the bag off his head, gasps in fresh air which lends a powerful feeling of relief to his body. How far can he push his heart? It passes every test easily.

It is invulnerable.

Looking back, the insanity of his act is obvious. If he had passed out before taking the bag off his head he would have been found dead - Lord, by whom? Granny? Probably not - she would not have had the strength to look through the bushes when the odor of decay arrived. Aunt Jenny? Uncle Lawton? Another relative? A police officer? If the dead are aware of the living he would not have been able to hide from the embarrassment and the shame his family would feel at his dying that way. The journal shows that he repeated the bag experiment and combined it with other experiments. Jeffrey points to his head and says, “Something is missing here,” laughs, and returns to reading the journal.

✦✦✦

The hiding place is not the only spot for experiments. The field, eighteen acres of open expanse, leaves plenty of room for Jeffrey to run and not be noticed. He runs with the stethoscope in his hands, runs until nausea forces him to stop. Then he listens to his heartbeat. After that he tries to run with the same intensity, holding his breath immediately afterwards, and listening to his heart during the short hold. When that fails to satisfy his craving, he tries something that is the closest Jeffrey will come to accidently discovering whether he had really committed the unpardonable sin. He runs until his strength is out, crawls under a bush, puts the bag over his head, and listens to his heart. As he breathes into the sealed bag, his heart begins to skip beats. Then it starts to slow down, and Jeffrey feels faint. Black dots flash in front of his eyes. His heart sounds are muffled. In the distance a shape floats toward him. The air thickens and he feels as if he is immersed in a tank of hot water. The shape grows closer. The closer it gets, the slower his muffled heart sounds come. He tries to get up when the thin, skeletal face of Mirror Man appears, its bony hands reaching out with hooked fingers to claw away his soul from his body. Jeffrey reaches out to fight it, but its gaping skull mouth comes closer, sucking air and life from him. Jeffrey sweeps his hand to strike it, and then all turns black.

When he wakes up he is in the same spot breathing fresh air. The sound of a strong, regular heartbeat fills his ears. He looks to his left, finds the plastic bag, wet with condensation inside, lying on the ground. He checks the time - only ten minutes passed since he began his jog through the field. He tries to reconstruct what happened. He must have come close to passing out. When he saw the skeletal figure and swung at its face, that action pulled the bag off his head. Jeffrey knows he pushed himself too far, and as the closeness of his death sinks in, fear fills him like some viscous liquid - not the kind of fear that makes one's heart pound in an adrenaline rush, but the kind of fear that kicks a person in the gut and leaves him walking around the rest of the day with the breath knocked out of him. There is no warm feeling in the groin - just a nausea that hangs around all evening. Jeffrey vows that he will never try the bag again. He does not feel that his heart failed him, but that he came too close to cutting its oxygen off totally, something that would eventually stop the strongest heart. He knows his obsession has grown to the point that he must back away, even if he does not have the strength to go cold turkey. Holding his breath in whatever variation, Jeffrey thinks, is fine as long as he has access to air when he releases the hold.

What also concerns Jeffrey is the nature of that skeletal creature that approached him. Somehow he knows that if it had reached him, merged with him, that he would have died. The creature must be Death – Death dwelling in a mirror, escaping from time to time to drain a soul from a living body, leaving behind a stinking, rotting soup of noxious chemicals dripping down dead bones. Jeffrey does not believe the death creature to be only a figment of his imagination. Jeffrey flirts with Death, is fascinated with his habits, his forms, and now he finds he has been all too ready to go out on a date with him - an eternal date.

Jeffrey slams the journal shut without marking his place. What he has read is more than enough to sicken him. Having Death pursue him like a stalking lover, inviting him to an eternal feast – with Jeffrey as the meal – must be a message from God to stop reading. Jeffrey takes a bathroom break, heats up some milk to help him sleep, and returns to the room, shutting the door behind him. The journal lies on the bed, wide open to the same place he left off reading before leaving. Jeffrey stifles a cry and tries to open the door. It will not budge. He debates calling for help. He pictures Aunt Jenny running with her bad legs and falling just as she reaches the door when it swings open. He decides God has given him a sign to stay in the room and continue to read the journal.

Jeffrey knows there is no guarantee that he is correct that God is the one who wants him to read the journal After all, it would be like a death demon to have a keenly sharpened sense of humor, sharper than its bony claws. Either way, if Jeffrey must finish reading the journal, he will do it. He starts to read and finds a strange passage interspersed between the entries, one that throws him back into the past.

You, readers of this journal, had better take care yourselves. Death is stalking you. Maybe he hides in the mirrors of your house. Perhaps you men will see him as you shave, when he licks the blood you spill when you cut your face, and you will fall into death while shaving like Calvin Coolidge. Women, he may find you as you brush your hair, a shadowy shape floating from the mirror to your head, his skeletal fingers brushing your hair into broken streaks and bloody roots. He takes your spent heartbeats and feeds on them, waiting with rotted breath to feast on the final one. The harvest indeed is plentiful, the laborer One - but sufficient - and Death will have his harvest.

Jeffrey puts his pen down on his desk upstairs and rests his head in his hands. His eyes burn. *Why the Hell did I write that*, he asks himself. Then a terrible idea invades his mind, one he immediately regrets, yet one that drives him to act in an obsessive way. The idea is that it would be good to get Sherry in on his experiments. Not the bag, of course - that is over and done with, never to be revived. Yet listening to her heart with the stethoscope - surely that is not a bad thing. It is only what the doctor does every visit. For him this would add a different *dimension* to the experience. Sherry seemed to like letting him put his head on her chest, and she made a comment about listening to his heart that was positive. Once he convinces her to let him steth her, then convincing her to hold her breath should be an easy matter. Exercise combined with breathholding will surely follow.

At first the plan works perfectly. Sherry rides over on her bicycle one day when Jeffrey is home by himself. Granny is out shopping with Aunt Jenny. He asks her, "Wanna see my room?"

"Sure," she says, and they walk upstairs. He left his stethoscope lying plainly on his bed. She looks that direction, walks to the bed, sits down, and picks up the stethoscope.

"Oh, neat. Where did you get this?"

"Bought it at a flea market for four bucks."

"Seems pretty cheap. Does this work?"

"Try it."

She places the earpieces in her ears and puts the diaphragm over her heart.

"Wow. Cool. Umm...slower than I thought it'd be. Let me listen to yours. Pull up your shirt."

Jeffrey feels he is in heaven, but it is heaven haunted by a hint of fear. *What is there to fear,* he thinks. *Pulling up my shirt will do no harm, and Sherry will hear better.*

Sherry listens for what must be at least five minutes. Then she says, "Take a deep breath. Let it out." She repeats as she shifts the stethoscope to different positions. She is playing doctor! Any lingering fears die.

"Your heart is strong and healthy," she says. "Now check mine."

Heaven suddenly gets a lot better. Then she stuns him. "I'll pull up my shirt." Jeffrey begins to vibrate like a June bug vibrates when he picks it up and holds it in his fingers. It is good that Sherry keeps her bra on or Jeffrey would be one dead teenager.

Jeffrey says, "Do you want to put this where you want it."

"No – you place it."

He places the diaphragm just to the left of her breast bone, under her bra and over her heart, and listens to the regular rhythm, his groin so filled with warmth that he thinks he will catch on fire and burn alive. The curves of her small breasts drive his thirteen year-old hormone-filled body mad. After a few minutes of listening he says, "I'll be right back."

Sherry laughs and says, “All this playing doctor has made you want to give the doctors a sample?”

Jeffrey laughs and twitches his finger back and forth in a “You’re naughty” sign. Then he rushes down the stairs and to the bathroom, locks the doors, and drops his drawers. The built up tension explodes, and he uses half a roll of toilet paper to clean up, flushing a couple of times to destroy the evidence and hide the odor. The scent remains strong after the last flush, so he takes the deodorizer sitting on top of the toilet and sprays down the bathroom. When that is done he flies back upstairs. He checks his watch - only three minutes have passed. That is good. Despite her naughty comment, Sherry will not suspect that he could climax that quickly.

When he leaves the bathroom, something is different. He is no longer interested in stething Sherry. What is happening? How could those powerful feelings that were formerly present disappear into pleasant tiredness? Are the feelings he had for Sherry part of his body but not part of his mind? He cannot be sure, because he still aches to go upstairs and talk to Sherry, to get to know her better as a girl and not just as a girl with a physical heart. Maybe that is a good thing.

When he returns Sherry lies flat on the bed, her top still pulled up. “How you are feeling?” Jeffrey asks.

“Feeling good to be out of the house and to be close to you. Mama and Daddy had a terrible fight last night. They threw things, and this morning both of them had bruises on their faces. The only thing that makes me feel better is knowing that my Mama got in some good hits. He had a black eye, too.”

“Good for her,” Jeffrey says. “Have they always been that way?”

“As long as I can remember. I’ve heard they were good to one another the first two years they were married. Then my Daddy got laid off and started drinking. My Moma gets giggly when she drinks – she is so funny! - but Daddy gets mean. If only they would get along like other married folks. I hear you lost your parents when you were a baby?”

"Yeah. Two years old. Hit by a drunk driver in a semi. I don't remember them. Sometimes I think I do - bits and pieces - Daddy rolling a ball toward me, for instance. Maybe it's not a real memory. When Granddaddy died I was nine. That was terrible. We used to walk to that thicket of woods at the end of the field – you know, where the woods stick out over the fence line?"

"Yeah. You and R.J. have been there."

"Yep. There are vines there you can swing on."

"Can you take me? Maybe later today?

"I'd love to."

The feelings Jeffrey had earlier creep up on him like a stranger sneaking up behind him. This time they arise from caring about Sherry, from talking to her. Somehow those feelings seem less dirty, although they are still focused on her heart. Jeffrey wonders if, when he is married, whether he will be able to do what Uncle Lawton said he would have to do. Maybe he would be able to do it if he listens to his wife's heart at the same time. Will that heart be Sherry's?

Jeffrey asks her, "Do you want to try something?"

"Ooooohhh, what did you have in mind?"

Jeffrey is beginning to feel uncomfortable at her sophistication - she seems to know more than he - or she has watched too much TV. He wonders whether she had a boyfriend before he came along.

"Can I listen to your heartbeat while you hold your breath?"

She smiled. "Getting kin-KEE?"

Heat rises in his face. "Uh, it's okay."

"Just kidding. Go ahead."

She holds her breath and Jeffrey listens. Her heart rate varies more than his. He supposes that girls' hearts are different. Girls are different, period.

His groin grows hot again. He wants to *up the ante*, a term he learned from his Great-Uncle Rick when he talked about unions and factories. Boring stuff to Jeffrey, but Uncle Rick would get into bad arguments with another great uncle, Frank.

Uncle Rick called Uncle Frank a *scab lover*. Jeffrey could never figure out how someone could love scabs. They are ugly and he likes to pull them off.

"You can hold your breath longer if you breathe fast for a few minutes."

Sherry looks at him funny. "Could that be dangerous?"

"Oh no. I wouldn't ever ask you to hurt yourself. I lo...I care for you a lot."

She sighs. "What is your record for holding your breath?

"Three minutes and ten seconds."

"Did you breathe fast before breaking your old record?"

"Yes, for four minutes."

"Okay, I'll breath fast and hold my breath if you break your old record."

"I can try. Could you listen to my heart while I do that?"

Sherry sighs again. She says in a low voice, "Okay, sure." Jeffrey takes off his shirt. She frowns at him and puts the diaphragm over his heart. He begins to breathe fast. A minute passes. Sherry starts to hum to herself. He wants her to stop humming but he has to concentrate on what he is doing. Two minutes pass, then three. After four minutes her humming grows louder. Finally at the five minute mark he takes a deeper breath and begins to hold it. Sherry stops humming and looks at her watch.

"One minute," she says. Jeffrey feels tingly, but fine.

"Two minutes." His lungs start to feel full, but he feels better at two minutes than any other time when he held his breath.

"2:30." His stomach starts to convulse.

"Three minutes." Jeffrey focuses all his strength on keeping his mouth closed. He squeezes his nose shut. His stomach convulses until it looks like a flying carpet rolling in the air.

"3:15." *Thank God. Broke the record*. Jeffrey lets the air out, gasps for a few seconds, and looks at Sherry.

"That looked like it hurt," she says. "Your heart was beating funny, changing its rate, and even skipped a couple beats."

"It's no big deal. Anyway, you promised."

"So I did." Jeffrey heard the sarcasm in her voice. He knows it is best to apologize and stop, but the burning in his groin is too much for him.

He places the diaphragm of the stethoscope on her chest and listens. Her heart rate is high. He looks at his watch, times it at 120. *Nervous,* he thinks. She starts to breathe fast. Her heart races faster and harder, and the faster it goes, the hotter his groin becomes. She breathes fast for three minutes and then holds her breath, but only for a minute and a half. *Her heart is racing*, Jeffrey thinks, *from excitement*.

Later in life, Jeffrey would wish he had read that study on emotions by Schlacter and Singer that noted a high heart rate is consistent with lots of emotions besides nervousness and excitement. Anger is on their list. He would not have had the opportunity to read that article then, but, Lord, the value of hindsight.

Sherry's face is red, and tears streak her eyes. "It felt like pins and needles were pricking my entire body. Then my lungs burned and my heart felt like it would stop beating. I'm going home now."

"No, you're fine," Jeffrey says, his head forming – so he would later think - into the shape of a jackass. "Your heart won't stop – it beat real strong the whole time. I bet you could exercise and hold your breath. Now that would be real exciting."

"Oh God, you're a freak! Why did I ever meet you? You're trying to murder me. I never want to see you again."

Jeffrey runs down the stairs, crying and yelling, "I'm sorry, I'm sorry, I'm sorry." Sherry runs out the door, jumps on her bike, and speeds away. Jeffrey collapses to the cold, slick floor, repeating "I'm sorry" like a monk repeating a mantra. He hears the screech of gravel in the driveway. He stands up, walks to the kitchen to grab some paper towels, and wipes the tears off the floor. He runs upstairs to his room, where he cries on his bed until, exhausted, his eyes close in sleep.

The phone ringing downstairs wakes Jeffrey up. He checks the clock by his bed. An hour has passed. He walks downstairs to the door and listens to Granny talking to...*oh no*.

"Yes, Martha. He's here. You say he did what to Sherry? I don't understand. Made her feel sick? Of course I'll tell him. Of course we'll have a talk. And I'll keep an eye on him, too. Don't worry. I'm so sorry about this. Glad you don't blame me. Oh, Jeffrey couldn't afford anything like that unless Lawton and Jenny could pay, but they barely get by themselves. I'll have Jenny talk to him, too. He trusts her. Thank you, Martha. Bye."

Jeffrey tries to stay quiet as he rushes upstairs to sit at his desk. He pretends to read. Granny's footsteps come fast and hard, just like Sherry's angry heart. He does not want to think about what this must be doing to Granny's heart, old as she is.

"Jeff-REY! Oh, there you are." She sits on the bed. "Turn around, face me. Mrs. Toombs called."

"What about?"

"You know what it was about."

Jeffrey lowers his head. "I reckon so."

"You reckon. Here's some reckoning for you. Mrs. Toombs has banned you from going to her house, even to see R.J. She's also banned Sherry and R.J. from visiting you. Now I don't right understand everything she said. Sounds like you're plumb crazy, but I don't believe that. I believe you did something you shouldn't have done, didn't you?"

"She seemed to go along, but then..."

"I'm going to take that stetho whatever you call it away. Now."

"No!" Jeffrey says, and he runs to his desk drawer, takes the stethoscope, cracks the window, and throws it into the lilac bush. It disappears into the bush and he shuts the window. Granny does not see him, and it takes her ten seconds to get to where he is.

"Where is it?"

He remains silent.

"Okay, you're going to stay in your room until supper. You're not allowed to leave the house for a week. I'm gonna have Lawton talk to you about this. Maybe Frank and Rick. That's man stuff, and you ain't ready to be a man yet. Lordy, Lordy, I thought I raised you better than that. And you goin' to church and helpin' pick up the Lord's Supper trays. Jenny and I were proud of you - we were just talkin' 'bout that today. Now I don't know what to think."

Jeffrey starts to cry. "Please don't tell Aunt Jenny."

"I'm going to tell Lawton, at least. I'm sure he'll tell Jenny, or he might ask you to tell her. At least he'll give you a choice. Why not tell Aunt Jenny yourself? She might understand better than I could what Mrs. Toombs said. Do that and I'll keep quiet. She's coming over tomorrow to clean the house."

"I'll talk to her," Jeffrey says in a low voice.

"You promise me that?"

"I promise."

CHAPTER 13
WORRIES

Zeke wakes up, his stomach turning so much he does not fix his usual breakfast of bacon and eggs. Jeffrey is in trouble. Somehow he has gotten himself into a mess over that girl he is so crazy about. How Jeffrey managed this Zeke cannot read, but he knows that there is another force pushing Jeffrey toward the wrong choices – and he knows what that force is. That face on the demon reminds him of something, something that may give a clue to its fragmented personality. He senses a being more powerful than a traditional demon, but just as devious and filled with spite and pride. It hides its true face, not like an actor per se - *O Christ, like a clown* - something that hides its real face behind a mask. Zeke is sure that what lies beneath the mask is far more hideous. He concentrates on an image of Jeffrey in his mind, trying to send a message, praying Jeffrey will receive it.

The Antibeing laughs with a hiss that sounds like a snicker. *You sick boy*, It thinks, sarcasm dripping from its spiteful mind, *I'm so proud of you*. The Antibeing has never had such success with any creature so soon – even the Suggoths of his own universe were more difficult to destroy than this human boy. Its last human victim did not have a fetish, but he worried so much about the unpardonable sin that he was an easy target – and a delicious meal.

Jeffrey, on the other hand, is sumptuously vulnerable on so many fronts. This has been the most fun It has had in the billions of earth-years It has lived. When the Antibeing defeats Jeffrey, which is inevitable, It will gain sufficient strength to remain in this universe indefinitely. What joy it will be to drain the souls of every human. Suicide will become the chief cause of death. The Antibeing will gain power until It rules this universe. The Antibeing – with Its allies, the pathetic Messengers called demons and their lord who calls himself the Day Star helping him to the Enemy's door, It will confront and defeat the Enemy, blanking him out of existence. Then It will destroy the Day Star and his servants, and Lord Azathoth will be God of Gods, raining chaos across all universes, with the Antibeing Azathoth's high priest. The Antibeing is the real thing. *Like Coca-Cola,* It thinks, and hisses out a hateful laugh.

CHAPTER 14
UNCLE FRANK'S ADVICE

Jeffrey shuts the journal and cries, embarrassed that at age fifty he is still upset over a girl he lost over thirty-five years before, a girl whom he barely knew at the time but whom he loved as much as a thirteen-year-old boy could love a girl. He understands now why he could not let go, why he kept pushing Sherry on the breath holding until she thought he was psycho. Asperger's Syndrome. Psychiatrists may not use that name any more, but Jeffrey prefers it because it is not as severe as full-fledged autism. He was not diagnosed until he was forty.

Asperger's Syndrome, now called High Functioning Autism Spectrum Disorder, is a milder condition on the autistic spectrum in which a person has poor social skills, has difficulty looking people in the eye, is clumsy, sometimes walks on one's toes, and who tends to be obsessed with specific interests. Jeffrey has all those traits. Over the years his social skills improved, but at a party he is still the odd person out. He walks on his toes. He is a super-klutz who would trip on a speck of dust if it touched his shoes. He is obsessed with death and with the heart, and still has a fetish that he struggles to control – for instance, to stop bringing the heart into every conversation. His wife, Lisa, understands, *thank God,* but to expect Sherry, a thirteen-year-old girl from rural Tennessee to think of him as any more than a loon is unfair.

However, the rejection not only broke his heart, it led him to focus on his weirdness to the point of making his obsession far worse. Even though he had never considered harming someone, whenever some weird crime or murder was in the news, he was sure that somehow he had walked in his sleep and done the deed, even when someone was caught red-handed in the act. Jeffrey did his best to keep his fetish underground, but as he got older, and his desire to talk to women grew, the situation got worse. Not only did he have to overcome his initial shyness, he had to overcome awkward situations regarding the heart.

Once in his sophomore year in high school, a beautiful girl in his biology class saw a beef heart in a jar and asked, "What is that?" Jeffrey was so afraid of the fetish that he was a smart ass and said, "It's a heart. What do you think it is?" Today he thinks a better way to deal with the situation would have been to say, "It's a cow's heart. Your own heart looks similar, but is smaller, about the size of your fist." Perhaps something interesting might have happened. Probably not – but fantasy is the Asperger's individual's refuge from a world that seems to be like another planet.

In his thirteenth year the situation at home turns out better than he imagines. He never tells Aunt Jenny the truth about Sherry. Instead he tells her he starting kissing Sherry, and he put his hand inside her bra. She thinks that talking to Uncle Frank might help him more than talking to Uncle Lawton. "Uncle Frank's got some funny ideas, but he respects women and he's good to Aunt Lucy. He was in the Army and lived in Detroit a long time before coming down here. I think he could give you some advice on how to better treat a young lady. Why don't you take your bike down there and see Frank and Lucy?"

Jeffrey has no problem visiting Uncle Frank and Aunt Lucy. Uncle Frank is cool, with his pickup truck and hunting dogs – all beagles – and a basketball goal stands in his front yard. If Aunt

Jenny knew Uncle Frank is an atheist she would never permit Jeffrey to visit. Jeffrey rides down Bramble Lane on a sunny day with the last dewdrops evaporating from the hay in the fields lining the road. Bramble Road was paved a year ago, and Jeffrey enjoys a smooth ride. The whir of wind of the wheels calms him. His hair jostles in the breeze, and he passes a herd of cattle lying lazy on the ground under the shade of oaks. He flies by a boarded up house on the right with brown weeds higher than his head lining the front yard. To the left is Trash Hill, a trash pile in the field at his grandparents' which has been there as long as he remembers. A 1940s-era black car tops the hill. Jeffrey thinks it looks like a car from a gangster movie, like those old movies in which Edward G. Robinson is the bad guy who always gets killed at the end.

Jeffrey is not allowed to get inside the car, though he sneaked in many time over the years, pretending to drive. *Only three years now,* he thinks, *before I will be able to drive a car. For now a bike will do.*

Jeffrey whirls around a curve past a grove of hardwoods, past a field where Uncle Frank hunts doves, past the house where Buddy, a boy Jeffrey used to play with, once lived. The people who live there now keep to themselves. Today there is yelling coming from inside the house. Uncle Frank says that yelling is the extent of that family's intellectual abilities.

When Jeffrey sees the basketball goal mounted on a wood post, he know he is at the right house. Uncle Frank is in the yard holding a local brand cola, and he smiles as he greets Jeffrey and passes him the cola. "Have a pop," he says. Even Aunt Lucy calls Cokes "pop" and she is from Tennessee – Jeffrey's granddaddy's sister. "Thank you," Jeffrey says, and he opens it and takes a swig, enjoying the cold liquid wetting his dust-dry mouth and quenching his thirst. Uncle Frank is tanned and shirtless and his beer belly sticks out. He can drink as many beers as he wants and still seem sober.

"Your granny said we needed to have a little talk. Finish your pop, and we'll take a walk in the field." Uncle Frank points to a grove of oaks surrounding a sinkhole. "We'll sit on those rocks lining that sinkhole."

Jeffrey finishes his Coke, and they climb the barbed wire fence at its lowest point and walk toward the sinkhole. "There are good blackberries out here that haven't quite stopped producing. Later this week you can help me pick some. Your granny can make blackberry pie."

"That would be great," Jeffrey says, trying to stifle the dread of telling Uncle Frank what really happened with Sherry.

They reach the sinkhole and sit down on some flat limestone. Uncle Frank says, "Tell your story. Take your time." Jeffrey tells Uncle Frank the entire story of the fetish, even the bag part, and what happened with Sherry. Jeffrey was afraid Uncle Frank would tell him to get the Hell off his land, but instead he said, "Hell, boy, I lived in Detroit for twenty-five years. You'd be surprised to know what turns people on. Only problem with your turn-on is that bag, and you tell me you'll never do that again. Make sure you stick to that. Neighbors in Detroit had a boy about your age. They found his body in his room, a rope around his neck. No, it wasn't a suicide. He was turned on by cutting off the oxygen to his brain. He thought he had a way to get out of the bind he got himself in. It didn't work. Damn, what a way to go. Family covered it up pretty good, but the father told me a few years later what really happened. Don't you be that boy."

"I won't."

"The problem you had with Sherry is that you didn't know when to let go. You kept pushing and pushing until she did something she wasn't comfortable with. You should have backed off then. Way off. Hell, she may have come back to see you. Who knows? Now she's a lost cause. Put her behind you. Hell of a lot more fish in the sea. Next time you want to tell a woman about that heartbeat stuff you let her fall in love with you first. Head over heels. So much so she'd trust you if you told her to chop your, er, hand off. Even if she's totally in love be careful not to push her too far."

"So Sherry didn't love me."

"You're both too young. Real love comes later. Now you said there was something else you wanted to tell me, something you said I would never believe. Try me."

Jeffrey tells Uncle Frank about the demon appearances and the skeletal figure. Uncle Frank whistles loudly.

"Whoo—ee, that's a tale. Don't get me wrong. I believe you had the experience of seeing something that looked to you like Death and something else that looked to you like a demon. Seems to me it's what you expect to see. Remember that talk I had with you years ago after your Grandpa died?"

"Yes, sir."

"I told you then that you needed to grow up, to take responsibility, to realize that no magical being in the sky would be able to take care of your grandma. I know you want your grandpa to be in Heaven, but we have to man up and face life as it is. The problem now is that fundamentalist religion has messed with your mind. Those preachers scare you to death about going to Hell and before long you're seeing death and demons everywhere."

"There's also Zeke," Jeffrey says.

Uncle Frank starts. "O Hell. Zeke. Yeah, I know him. Most country people around here have known about old Zeke for years. Some people belong in a category of their own." Uncle Frank is quiet a moment, gazes out over the field, then turns to Jeffrey again. "Science will eventually explain everything – no need for a God or demons or angels. When it comes to telling the future, who knows what time really is? It might be scientifically possible for somebody with a special gene to tell the future."

"Do you think Zeke can?"

"Yes. Surprised that an atheist would believe that? But I've seen him tell the future, and I won't deny what happens in front of my face. He's not one hundred percent accurate, but maybe ninety or ninety-five percent. If I were him I'd be making big money, but he has no desire to do that. I don't know why.

Maybe Old Zeke found out that someone he cared about was going to die soon and figured his ability was too dangerous to use. But if he thinks someone needs to know when he will die, Zeke will tell him. Maybe to keep that person brave, maybe to make him stay on course with what he's doing in life."

"Has he told you when you're going to die?"

"Me? Hell, no. Don't you worry about that. But Zeke's for real. He told you some things?"

"Yes, and he gave me a Catholic Bible. It had a sheet of Latin inside, but I lost it. I've been trying to find it but can't."

"Look, I don't believe the Bible and some Latin Catholic gobble-de-goop. But I know Zeke wouldn't have given you that sheet of paper if he didn't know it would do you some good one day. That means most likely you will find it – eventually, when the time is right. If I were you, I'd start looking now. Determinism – fate – may be real but your deciding to look for that sheet of paper may be part of your fate."

"I'll look again."

"You do that, and remember what I said. Take it easy on pushing your *interest* with the ladies, and lay off believing in superstition. Give it a try at least."

"I'll think about it."

They walk back to the house where Jeffrey greets Great-Aunt Lucy. She gives him another *pop*, which he guzzles down before he takes the bike, waves goodbye and rides home. The day is hotter, and the sun and the humidity causes sweat to pour off Jeffrey's body even with the breeze from the bike ride. Still, he feels a weight has been lifted off his head, despite what happened with Sherry. The fact that Uncle Frank does not consider him crazy is a relief, and that may keep Jeffrey from literally going crazy this year.

Despite their history, R.J. sneaks by sometimes when Jeffrey is on Trash Hill. He and Jeffrey like to sit inside the black car and pretend to go on trips to Florida or California. Late in the day that Jeffrey visited Uncle Frank, they repeat the ritual. This time they are driving to the Vegas Strip at night. R.J. checks his watch, and says, “Darn it, I’m late. Gotta get home before Mama catches me over here,” he said. “She thinks I’m over at another kid’s house. He’s even weirder than you - oops, sorry. That didn’t sound right.”

Jeffrey swallows hard, but R.J. remaining his friend after the incident with Sherry is a big relief to Jeffrey, so he says, “That’s okay. You come over here any time you can get away. Don’t think I’m crazy weird.”

“Nope,” R.J. says, and pulls his bike out of the brush and rides down Bramble Lane, taking a circuitous route to sneak back home. Jeffrey glances at the full moon in the sky, watches the ghost glow that will soon overcome the reds and oranges of the sinking sun. He gets back inside the car on Trash Hill and watches the remains of the sunset through the windshield. Something strikes the side of the car.

Jeffrey’s heart lurches, and he is afraid it really will stop. A hiss and rattle fills the still air inside the car, and he turns his head slightly to the left. Into a hole of the back left window formed by broken glass a large snake slithers into the car. It crawls slowly, and Jeffrey figures he has plenty of time to escape. He turns the latch. The door fails to budge. *Not now, O God,* Jeffrey thinks. The snake flops to the floor by the back seat, and its rattle echoes loudly in the enclosed space. Jeffrey tries to roll down the window. The handle will not move. Jeffrey’s heart pounds so fast he hopes its vibrations will scare away the snake. He strikes the glass on the driver’s side window, but it will not break. It is as if the glass has hardened to keep him inside while the rattlesnake bites him and he dies a painful death. Jeffrey starts to scream, but his voice evaporates – his mouth moves, air escapes his lungs, but no sound comes out. Everything moves in slow motion – his arms, his feet, his mouth. Even his heart seems to slow to a crawl.

The snake’s head emerges between Jeffrey’s legs and rises straight up like a charmed cobra. The serpent stares at him with un-snake eyes, a demon head and leering lips. It hisses its speech, its mouth not shifting from the horror-smile. “You had so much fun the other day," it says. "I had even more fun, getting you to put that bag over your head. Poor Jeffrey. Sherry didn't want you. The bitch. Don't you think so? Too bad you didn't use the bag on her – with her tied down, her little heart slowing, crawling to a stop. Wouldn't revenge be sweet? You could take her bra off and listen to her dying heart. I bet you'd get a hard-on, too. I bet you'd come hard, too, boy."

Jeffrey's arms involuntarily jerk as adrenalin surges through his body. "Snake from Hell," he says with a squeaky voice. "I would never harm Sherry. It doesn't matter what happened or if she hates me. You can't make me hurt anybody either."

"Oh, I have more power than you think." The demon-snake laughs, a series of hisses that sound like the wheezing laugh Jeffrey heard, *Oh God, from Great Uncle Irwin*.

"Fuck you!" Jeffrey says. "Go back to Hell from where you came."

"I can keep the first part of your request," the snake says with another laugh, and it begins to slither behind Jeffrey. Jeffrey grabs the head, twists it hard. He thinks he might be able to break the snake's neck and send the demon back to Hell, but the demon head splits from the body and falls to the ground, still alive, its thick lips muttering "Until later, Jeffrey. Remember, I'll honor your request – except my going back to Hell." Jeffrey looks down, but the snake and its demon head have disappeared.

Jeffrey opens the door easily and runs at full speed through the field to the fence, opens and hooks it back, and he stops only when the screen door slams shut when he gets inside. Granny is wiping off the bar in the kitchen.

"Goodness gracious to Betsy, where have you been? I was thinkin' 'bout callin' the law to find you."

"I was playing in the field."

"Playing. None of the Toombs there?"

"No, ma'am."

"Good. Last thing I need is trouble with them folks. I made you some cheese crackers and milk."

"Thank you, ma'am," Jeffrey says, and eats, happy that he had the strength to fight back against a demon. He no longer doubts it is a real demon, no matter what Uncle Frank says. *He lets his atheism cloud everything so that he sees the world only one way*. Jeffrey cannot worry about Uncle Frank – he knows he must figure out a way to get rid of that demon. He does not understand why it wants him above all the other boys and girls in the world. If he can learn more about demons, maybe he can find a way to rid himself of this pest.

Jeffrey is sure that demon tempted him into tricking himself into blaspheming the Holy Ghost. Could the demon have exaggerated Jeffrey's fetish, making it stronger, so that he felt more driven to push Sherry too far?

The demon must be part of the explanation for the strength of Jeffrey's heartbeat fetish. Even if Jeffrey's personality created the fetish, and even if it could explain how strong it got, only a demon could explain how Jeffrey drove away his first and only girlfriend when he should have seen with his own eyes that she was getting irritated.

There is one problem – his church. He attends the Church of Christ, and that church does not believe in demon possession. It teaches that demon possession ended after Jesus' apostles died. That means if Jeffrey tries to get rid of the demon or asks someone to do it for him, he will be going against his church, and that will break Aunt Jenny's heart. She is convinced that the Church of Christ has the whole truth. How can he disappoint her – along with Uncle Lawton, Granny and other relatives who are church members? He knows he has to choose. Either he can continue to suffer with that oval, spiteful smile and sneering voice remaining all his life, and Lord knows doing what to him – or he can betray those he loves the most. He figures, in the end, that since he is going to Hell anyway, there is no need to be totally miserable in this life. He will try to force the demon to leave.

The next day Jeffrey lies on his bed praying for strength to speak to the demon. He sits up, and says out loud, though softly enough to avoid Granny's ears downstairs, "Demon. Come here." A minute passes, then two. He begins to wonder whether the demon will come at all.

Jeffrey gets up, looks down at a trunk used for storage, its top covered with faded varnish that maintains a shadow of its former shine. Another shadow appears in the shine. It draws closer. Demon-lips grin an upward oval, a living leer. A voice, ancient, cold, filled with hate, hisses from the mouth. "What you do want, boy? I am busy in Washington, D.C., my favorite place. I am getting much accomplished there."

"You know I'm going to Hell for blaspheming the Holy Ghost. The other stuff with the heartbeat will add to my punishment but nothing more. Why don't you bother someone who hasn't fallen yet?"

A cackling laugh reverberates throughout the room, and Jeffrey hopes Granny hears something and goes upstairs. Jeffrey feels he is a fool to face the demon alone. The demon must read Jeffrey's mind since it says, "Only you can hear me, boy. I *bother you,* as you put it, because I can. I enjoy hurting you, all you sick twisted little boys with shit for brains."

"I don't have an abnormal brain," Jeffrey says, swinging his head to face the leering lips.

"Well, you'll just have to wait a few years to discover that, won't you?" the demon says, its smile widening.

"What do you mean?"

"What do you mean?" the demon replies.

"Get new material," Jeffrey says. "You're as interesting as dried cow shit."

Laughter spews from the still lips. "You're crazier than two old sows full of bourbon fighting over a boar." More laughter. "I'll arrange things so you end up in Central State. Then I'll have my way with you, boy, if you know what I mean." He spread out the *oy* of *boy* over five seconds.

"I am not crazy," Jeffrey says. You are spiteful."

"Of course I'm spiteful, boy. I'm a demon. What the Hell do you expect? By the way, some of my friends have taken great pleasure laying a lash to your granddaddy's ass."

"No!" Jeffrey says and lunges for the demon. He lands hard on the trunk, knocking the breath out of him. Something touches his ear, and he screams. The pain of the burn sears his nerves into knots of throbbing agony. The demon, now back in snake–form, though as large as a Burmese python, crawls over him. It feels to Jeffrey as if a living stove, loaded with hot coals, has become flexible like a snake and crawled onto his body. The leering lips draw near to his face, the demon's sulfuric breath gags Jeffrey.

Then its face changes. The shape of the head elongates, turns white, then gray, as the hideous skull of Death appears. The skull speaks, its teeth clacking as the jaws lock together with each word.

"Did you think we were different, Boy? You conjured us up with your obsession with death. Death and Hell, you know, go together – what is it The Enemy said about *the second death*? You still have hope, but you realize that's unreasonable. If you know you're damned, you should despair."

"I have something so say to you, Demon."

"What's that?" the skull asks.

"Our Father, who art in Heaven, Ha..."

The skull screams and melts away. Jeffrey sits back on the bed, trying not to despair, but suddenly he blurts out, "Damned fool Holy Ghost." He pulls himself to the bed and cries, not a cry of grief, but a near silent cry, like a whispered laugh, a cry that arrives only when the last hope is gone and all that remains is death – and eternal night.

CHAPTER 15
GOOD OL' UNCLE FRANK

G*ood ol' Uncle Frank. What a pathetic creature,* the Antibeing thinks. The Antibeing could reveal Itself in its true form, tentacles and all, and Uncle Frank would think he is dreaming. *The miserable fool. It will be fun to torture him one day, but now is not the time. He is way too useful. The poor bastard means well. If only he knew how tightly Jeffrey binds faith and hope – without the first, he cannot have the second.* The Antibeing laughs, the sound like a death gurgle under water. *You've been such a help to me, Uncle Frank. Maybe I can wait to take your soul until after you're dead. Ah, the dreams I will send you then. You will wish you were in Hell.*

Yeah, Jeffrey, you're right. All that remains is death – and Hell. It's a good thing that I can appear in more than one way. Mirrors are easy to manipulate. Even if I can't get through to your pathetic world, Jeffrey, I can make you see me. You have a gift, and I want to squash it, to squash you, boy, until your brain melts. All in good time, boy, when I have broken your spirit. By the way, I've decided Zeke is a liability to me. I will send him pain beyond belief before he falls into the abyss of death.

In your case, boy, I have no need to appear as a demon all the time. You fear annihilation more than Hell. That's soooooo good. I'll let you think, boy, that your journey toward annihilation is inevitable. If you're not annihilated, I'm sorry,

Jeffrey, that I misinformed you. I'll leave it up to the Enemy punish you and feed on your pain before I destroy you both and send you to nothingness.

CHAPTER 16
THE REPRIEVE

Jeffrey is not in the mood for supper but eats anyway. The strong iced tea revives him. He puts his hands on the slick, 1960s-style three-section dining table. He has always liked that feeling since he was a small child. *At least one thing that has not changed in a chaotic world*. The old black wall phone, another symbol of sameness, rings, and Jeffrey offers to answer, longing to hold one more item that keeps the blessed past in memory.

A deep, rich voice answers. "Jeffrey, that you? Good. This is Brother Noland, from church."

"Yes, Brother Noland. I love your sermons on the Kings and Chronicles."

"So your aunt tells me. Thank you very much. She'd called earlier, saying you were interested in getting more involved in learning about the Bible. She told me that might keep your mind off some things that were bothering you. Anything you want to talk about?"

"No, sir."

"Okay, Brother John Doty of the Farris Road Church lives close to you. Now we both go to the Randallsville School of Bible and Preaching that meets at the East Main Street Church. It meets Monday and Tuesday nights from six to nine. You'll learn a lot of useful things, but it will be hard for you to keep up with those classes when school starts. Are you interested?"

Although Jeffrey is saturated with demon-fueled horror related to religion, Jeffrey wants any distraction from despair. He says, "Sure."

"Great. Can you make it next Monday night?"

"That will be fine."

"Great. Brother Doty is a good man. His wife usually comes with him. I'll tell him to pick you up around 5:30, okay?"

"Okay."

"Good. I'll talk to you later."

Jeffrey hates to meet new people. Going to the same school system is nice because he sees enough of the same people year by year to soften the blow of the students he does not know. At church, he encounters the same folks most of the time, and even if Aunt Jenny and Uncle Lawton take him to a gospel meeting, they, at least, are there, and there are usually several visitors from his own church. The service is also similar to the service at his church. The preaching school - that is a big change - a strange place, new people. The unknown.

Monday evening arrives and Brother Doty's Chevy Impala crackles its way down the drive. He greets Jeffrey, introduces him to his wife, Anne, and invites Jeffrey to sit in the comfortable back seat. There Jeffrey closes his eyes and listens to the gravel crackle as the car starts to move.

Brother Doty interrupts the mantra of car sounds. "Heard you were baptized last October," Brother Doty says.

"Yes, sir, by Brother Noland."

"Good, good. He's a fine preacher. At the preaching school, we're an easygoing bunch. I've heard you're shy, but you seem to fit in well with older people. Brother Noland calls you *The Little Professor.*"

Jeffrey lowers his head and averts his eyes. "Lots of people say things like that. Kids on the school bus call me *Scientist.*"

"Do you like science?" Anne asks.

"Yes, ma'am. Especially astronomy. I'm fascinated by stars and planets."

She laughs. "Maybe you'll be making great discoveries one day and be on the news."

"Oh, I don't know," Jeffrey says, and he feels heat rise to his face.

They reach Broad Street in Randallsville and turn on East Main. A brick building sits on the corner, and Brother Doty pulls in a parking space by the basement door. Brother Doty tells Jeffrey that the building had stood since before the Civil War and soldiers from both sides had attended there. Jeffrey imagines people climbing the steps in their nineteenth century clothing, and soldiers, some walking with crutches, joining the group. Buildings are like time tunnels, and Jeffrey likes to imagine them in different times and spaces.

Classes take place in the basement. As soon as Brother Doty opens the door and lets Jeffrey in, the scent of fresh-made coffee fills the air. Jeffrey hates the taste of coffee, but he loves the aroma. Brother Doty shows him the room where cookies stacked on paper plates are on a table next to the coffee pot, and Jeffrey takes a few to eat. Men of all ages are there, some wearing old business suits and ties, others dressed in jeans and pullover shirts. Jeffrey is glad because he does not feel out of place in his jeans. On a table inside the main classroom are Church of Christ journals, and Jeffrey takes some, thumbing through them. Most of them have articles condemning what they label *liberalism*. Jeffrey hopes he is not a liberal for believing that a demon is after him.

Brother Doty introduces him to two elderly men who run the school, Brother Luck and Brother Charles. Brother Luck's skin hugs his skull like old leather, and Brother Charles reminds Jeffrey of his granddaddy. Jeffrey thinks they must be wise, their skin like parchment on which are written the truths of the Bible.

Jeffrey enjoys the lessons about the Bible since they include a lot of history. He has learned about Egyptians, Assyrians,

Babylonians, Syrians and how they treated ancient Israel and Judah, and likes to imagine himself back in those times, walking the rocky paths of Palestine.

After an hour the class takes a break, and Jeffrey eats more cookies. The next class begins, and as soon as Brother Luck begins talking Jeffrey's stomach falls to the floor.

"Tonight we're in Matthew chapter 12. The Pharisees had accused Jesus of casting out demons by Beelzebub, the prince of the demons. He replies by pointing out how absurd it is to think that a demon would cast out a demon - only God could do that. Of course we know that demons do not possess people today. They only work indirectly on someone's mind.

"Now we reach the passage for tonight, about the unpardonable sin, the blasphemy against the Holy Spirit."

Jeffrey fidgets in his seat and his heart starts to race. He looks up at the schoolhouse lights and tries to concentrate on their yellow color, to find a hiding place in that warm yellow glow to avoid that passage in the Gospel of Matthew that condemns him to Hell. Brother Luck's voice will intone Jeffrey's doom like the voice of a somber judge.

"I know a lot of young people who think they have blasphemed the Holy Ghost. They read about speaking a word against the Holy Ghost and how they then speak a word against the Holy Ghost - and they think they're going to Hell. We've all been children and probably remember being told not to think something - the first thing you know you think the forbidden thought. If that's going to damn us, we're all in a lot of trouble."

The first hint of hope Jeffrey has heard in months of despair enters the room like a sliver of sunlight in a dark cave. Jeffrey cranes his neck. If his ears could shift forward like a cat's he would try it. Brother Luck continues.

"To understand this passage, look at the context. The Pharisees had accused Jesus of casting out demons by Beelzebub. That meant their hearts were so hardened that they would never accept Jesus as the Son of God no matter how many miracles he did. Blasphemy against the Holy Ghost is a final, irrevocable rejection of Christ. So if you've ever wondered if you've blasphemed the Holy Ghost, the very fact that you wonder about it is the best and surest evidence that you haven't committed the unpardonable sin."

Jeffrey stifles a cry that is a mixture of relief and joy. Although he might go to Hell anyway, at least there is now a chance he can avoid it. He hopes this will be the end of his worries about the unpardonable sin. If only...yet that moment is what he will one day call *the Platonic Form of Relief*, as if the very weight of Hell has been lifted off his soul.

Jeffrey talks to Brother Charles during the break before the last class. The Matthew passage is about demons, and Jeffrey knows Brother Luck's opinion, so he asks Brother Charles whether he thinks demons can appear to people today.

"Personally I don't think so. But I'm not as strong as Brother Luck on this view. While I don't think possession is possible, a demon might appear to somebody to torment him and try to make him despair. No person is easier to tempt than a man who's given up. Now I wouldn't preach this, and don't you go repeating it. You seem mature for your age. That's good. Is there a reason you're asking?"

"No, sir, just curious."

"Curiosity can be good, but it can do harm as well. Remember what it did to the cat. Keep that in mind and you'll be fine."

In his Aunt Jenny's house in present day Randallsville, Jeffrey pauses – he wonders what he meant when he wrote, "If only..." How could he have returned to despair over the unpardonable sin after finding it does not apply to him? What changed his mind?

The next entries are from the following year, from seventh grade. Jeffrey remembers that painful part of his life like a moving picture - not only the continuing struggles about sex and his fetish, but also his nerdiness that made him a target for bullying. The worst bullying was from a distant cousin, Ron, and from his friend, Alex.

Every seventh grade class has its Hell-raisers, and Ron and Alex fit the bill in Jeffrey's class. They steal items from classmates, they smoke cigarettes, both the usual kind and the *funny* kind, and they bully students they consider to be weak. Jeffrey fits the bill perfectly - he must have an *I'M A WEAK WIMPY NERD, PLEASE BULLY ME* message tattooed on his butt. Ron and Alex are happy to oblige his request.

Jeffrey sits in gym class the first day before the students leave for the locker room to change. Coach Simmons is explaining his policies - *Guys have to buy a jock strap*. Jeffrey does not know what it is - students laugh at him when he asks - and when he learns what it is he feels gross. He has to wear something like a bra around what? A sharp pain pricks Jeffrey's left earlobe, and he feels the sting of a finger flicking it. He turns around, and Alex says, "Hey, who you lookin' at? Turn back around or I'll kick your ass."

Jeffrey turns around, but soon another sharp pain pricks his right ear. He spins around and asks, "Why are you picking on me? Pick on somebody your own size."

Ron says, "Hell, no, we won't stop. We figure it's our job to pick on queer-looking little wimps like you."

Thankfully the bell rings and Jeffrey works his way through the throng of students. He keeps looking behind him, trying to keep away from Ron and Alex. He brushes against Rachel Miller, a student in his homeroom who is the most beautiful woman at Thomas Frame Junior High School. Tall, slender, blond, she has proportionate breasts, full lips and blue, piercing eyes. Jeffrey is in the middle of a long distance relationship with her - in his mind. The mistake he makes is telling his friends at school he is in love with her.

One day Jeffrey sees her talking to another girl before math class one morning. He wants to impress Rachel in some way, to talk to her, but does not know what to do. His mind and body feel dissociated, as if an alien force is moving him. He stands, walks up to the girls and bumps both of them - hard. Maria, the girl standing by Rachel, puts her hands on her hips and says, "Jeffrey! Will you control your emotions?" Rachel looks him straight in the eye and says, "Stay away from me, you creep." Jeffrey stands still, eyes wide open, unable to breathe. Rachel, red-faced, gets into Jeffrey's face. "You heard what I said, creep. Get away from me or I'll tell the teacher all about your stalking."

Jeffrey starts to breathe, his breaths coming fast as he comes to himself and slinks back to his desk, the heat of his face matching only the position of his stomach. The class laughs. "Jeffrey got told off by a girl." "Rachel hates you, Jeffrey," different class members say, and soon there is a mantra as the same class members repeat, "Jeffrey is a creep." Jeffrey is crying, and he runs out the classroom into the bathroom and throws up. When he comes out into the hall, Mr. Henry, the principal, says, "You're white as a sheet. Are you feeling sick?"

Jeffrey nods, and Mr. Henry takes him to the office and calls Jeffrey's Granny. "You grandmother said your aunt will come pick you up." Jeffrey nods, struggling not to cry, not to have to explain what he has done. When Aunt Jenny arrives, she wants to take Jeffrey to the doctor, but he convinces her he is better off resting at home. Once he is home, he gets into his bed upstairs, hides under the covers, and cries so hard his head and eyes ache. Finally, his tear ducts are dry, and he senses the mercy of sleep arriving.

Later, Jeffrey finds out at school that Rachel has told all her friends that he is a creep. Any normal person would back off, and Jeffrey knows this. Yet the force driving him to obsess leads him, or he allows it to lead him, to keep telling people he loves Rachel. "I'm stupid as Hell," he says out loud, imagining his brain shrinking to pea size in his head, and he feels sick again.

One day Jeffrey decides to look for Rachel's house, not to talk with Rachel, but to gaze at her house. He does not know exactly where she lives, but knows the general area she mentions to her friends in class. One day he tells Granny he is going for a bike ride down Bramble Lane. He guesses that Granny will understand his delay in coming back as a stay at Uncle Frank's and Aunt Lucy's – as long as she does not phone them. He rides all the way down to an old, closed airbase and explores some of the subdivisions in the area, searching for Rachel outside on one of the lawns. Nothing comes of that trip other than getting in trouble with Granny - she phoned Uncle Frank and Aunt Lucy - and Aunt Jenny gives him a good lecture. At least Jeffrey has enough sense not to tell anyone where he went and what he was doing.

Ron and Alex have fun with Jeffrey's crush on a girl with whom Jeffrey never speaks. "Guess she likes you a lot since you never talk to her," Alex says with his perpetually sarcastic voice.

"Yeah," Ron said. "Like she would have anything to do with a nerd like you. Especially since you ran into her – for real –in class. What a fool!" Alex flicks Jeffrey's ear. Jeffrey swings at him, but Ron pulls Jeffrey up by the flaps of his face. "Fatboy. Hey, look at that fat face. You ever try anything like that again, nerd, and we'll send your ass to the hospital." Since Jeffrey believes that his ass is better off outside the hospital, he decides to avoid a fight with Ron and Alex and keep away from them as much as humanly possible.

That turns out to be impossible. His tormenters show up in Jeffrey's classes since they are in his homeroom, gym, and geography class. His ear is red at the end of almost every school day unless both Ron and Alex cut class. *Thank God they do that often*. Jeffrey's hatred grows to the point that he wishes them dead.

One night after the reprieve of Christmas break, after another day of torture, Jeffrey lies in bed banging his fists on the pillow, pretending that it is Ron's and Alex's heads. The air turns chilly, and he is afraid to turn around. He creeps under the covers, shuts his eyes until he calms down, then opens them after something cylindrical and reptilian crawls over his body. He stays still, his heart banging his throat so hard he wonders if his carotids will explode. He prays this is a dream. Something forces his eyelids apart, a snake whose head is a death's head. It speaks. "Not your turn yet, boy. I'll soon put your mind at ease about one, er, *inconvenience* you suffer. Not for your sake boy, but for the soul that I'm claiming for an old buddy of mine. Beelzebub's soft compared to me, but he will love feasting on this boy. Pot's been simmering a long time."

Jeffrey shuts his eyes again and feels the pressure on his body ease. When he opens his eyes nothing is there. He glances at the clock. *Midnight. Great - first a demon and now the witching hour.* A train whistle blows at the Farris Road crossing. A scream, human, not demonic, fills the air with a nightmare sound. Granny stirs downstairs. She yells, "What in tarnation was that? Jeffrey, you hear that noise?"

"Yes, ma'am," he says. "Somebody screamed. Sounded like it was way off but still loud."

Sirens wail and flashing lights blink as ambulances and police cars fly by the house. "Goodness gracious," Granny yells. "Reckon some car got hit by a train up there at the crossing? Guess we'll hear 'bout it in the news tomorrow morning on the radio. Try to sleep."

"Yes, ma'am," Jeffrey says, but he cannot sleep. Around 4 a.m. he finally drifts off, but at 6:15 Granny calls him down to breakfast so he will be ready in time to meet Bus 40 at 7:15. Still groggy, Jeffrey dresses, shaves off peach fuzz, pours alcohol on his face, which stings but still feels good in a way, and splashes on Old Spice, the odor reminding him of Granddaddy. Downstairs, Granny cooks sausage, and Jeffrey has sausage biscuits with tomatoes for breakfast. The radio is on to the Randallsville station, and the news begins.

"The top story tonight is a tragedy. A teenager, a passenger in a car with an alleged drunk driver, died last night when the car was struck by a train at the Farris Road Crossing near the

New Randallsville Highway. Fourteen-year-old Alex Roddy was pronounced dead at the scene shortly after the accident at midnight."

Jeffrey jumps up from his chair. Granny starts and says, "Heavens to Betsy, what on earth's wrong with you?"

"I knew him. He was in homeroom and two of my classes."

"I'm sorry," Granny says, putting her hand on his shoulder. "He a friend of yours?"

"More of an" - Jeffrey pauses, then completes the sentence - "acquaintance."

Alex dead. That is what the demon meant. That is why it wore its death's-head face. What is worst is that Jeffrey is glad Alex is dead and even gladder that the demon said that Beelzebub would torture Alex in Hell. Jeffrey forms a mental image of Alex in flames, two demons behind him, one to flick the left ear, the other the right. When Jeffrey leaves to walk to the bus stop near Bramble Road, he laughs the entire way, thrilling at each new image of torture he imagines for Alex.

The more Jeffrey thinks about it, though, the more frightening the situation becomes. The demon accurately predicted Alex's death. Could it have caused Alex's death, too? Alex's passing seems to be due to his friend's stupidity, which Alex shared and of which there was never a shortage. Either way, the demon has more power than Jeffrey realized. If the demon is not real, but is somehow a projection out of Jeffrey, then that means that Jeffrey knew when Alex would die. If that is true, then Jeffrey has the power to kill. Waves of chill creep up and down his body. He feels cornered by God and Fate and Demons and himself - with no way out.

CHAPTER 17
THE DEMON

Fifty-year old Jeffrey feels a chill. There is a draft in the guest bedroom, and he takes a quilt and wraps it around him. He stoops, retrieves his bottle of George Dickel, and pours some into his water glass. He takes one big swallow, then sips the rest. *What kind of power did that demon have? What if the demon is still a part of me? If the demon was self-created, how evil was I as a child - and how evil am I now?* Jeffrey wonders if finding out is worth the nightmare of reading the rest of the journal. If he does have a power of his own, he should know so that he doesn't harm others – and God must have some reason for his reading the journal. Perhaps Jeffrey buried something that he should have dealt with as a child, some spiritual syphilis that he had suppressed that has been eating at his soul over the years and is now about to enjoy the last morsel. Jeffrey cannot let that happen. He reads on.

Alex's death ends Jeffrey's torment from bullies. He supposes his cousin, who genuinely grieved his best friend's passing, was driven to rethink his life. That makes school more bearable. At home the demon, or that bad part of him, leaves him alone. There is enough of a child left in him to enjoy swinging under the maple, his body flying over the gravel drive, his feet high above the bushes on the other side. The air flow exhilarates him. The scent of honeysuckle and wild rose mixes with the odor of grass and trees, and Jeffrey feels as if his former world has not changed, that Granddaddy still lives, his garden full of watermelons ready for harvest. When he stops, as he has to stop due to hunger or the call of nature or having to do his homework, the illusion disappears and he remains caught in the pubescent present. At least his other relatives are still living, something that lends familiarity to Sunday dinners. Jeffrey realizes that life is only a loan and that *Change* and *Decay* are the names of God's games this side of eternity.

Jeffrey walks along the gravel drive near the bushes bordering the field, sniffs the orange day lilies, and picks passion fruit off vines creasing the ground near the bushes. He tears open the pod and files slick fruit off the seeds with his teeth. He enjoys the tangy flavor. Reprieves like this are a blessing. At the back of his mind a dark thought remains that reprieves are called by that name because they are brief.

Jeffrey enjoys listening to religious programs on the radio at night, especially programs that include Southern Gospel music. Although the Church of Christ does not use instrumental music – they sing *a capella* – Jeffrey still enjoys the four-part harmony of quartets such as the Chuck Wagon Gang, The Blackwood Brothers, The Cathedrals, the Kingsmen and the Speer Family. Whenever gospel music is on the radio, even as part of a preaching program, Jeffrey listens. He enjoys the sermons, too – especially the Hellfire and brimstone sermons. As an ultra-orthodox member of the Church of Christ, he relishes the thrill of condemning others to Hell, either because he does not want to feel lonely when he goes there or, more likely, to make himself feel better. The Reverend Eaton Sandwich's show airs on Tuesday nights at eight, and Jeffrey tunes to an AM station from north Alabama to listen. This night Sandwich begins to preach on Matthew 12, but Jeffrey is not worried since he knows that he has not really committed the unpardonable sin. Sandwich reads the passage about the blasphemy against the

Holy Ghost. Then he says, "You know, I've heard a lot of curse words in his life. I've heard people curse God in about any way possible. But I have never in my lifetime heard anybody curse the Holy Ghost. No matter how much a person hates God, he would never blaspheme the Holy Ghost. Someone bad enough to do that deserves to go to Hell. According to the Lord Jesus, he will go to Hell, no matter what else good he does in his life. He could be a preacher, love his wife and kids, give to the poor – but if he curses the Holy Ghost one time in his life - he will be damned forever in the eternal fires of Hell."

Jeffrey turns off the radio and lies down in silence. His room is dark and without the glow of the radio dial and with a new moon outside it is near pitch black. God once surrounded Abraham with *the horror of a great darkness*. This darkness in Jeffrey's room is palpable. Black fingers of night fondle his body, freezing it cold as ice. The floor grows colder. Jeffrey sits up to turn on the light, but footprints sound out – not Granny's or any relative's, for they would have flicked the light switch at the bottom of the stairs. Nothing – that is, nothing human – can walk in that darkness. Two eyes appear, bloodshot, pupils dilated and rolled upward toward the ceiling. A foul odor fills the room, something rotten, like two day old road kill. A hand grabs his arm. It is wet and oily, more ooze than solid. The wet oily stuff has such a stench of rot that Jeffrey throws up on the floor. That adds to the odor, and he cannot stop retching. The hand releases his arm, two hands clamp the sides of his face, and a tongue, also filled with the stench of decay, licks them. Jeffrey's heart pounds, then slows so much he feels faint. He is about to collapse to the floor, but those hideous hands hold him up. He finds enough strength to open his desk drawer and pull out a mini-flashlight. He turns it on and shines it on the face of the thing that grabbed him.

Shaggy blond hair. Face half decayed, mouth unnaturally large due to decay of the flesh surrounding the teeth. Shirt off, revealing a chest and abdomen filled with rot, filth and worms. The creature takes one hand away, reaches inside its chest, and pulls out a pale, gray, dead heart. The creature speaks – in Jeffrey's voice – and says, "I am your future. Your near future. Here is your heart. I've always wanted to see my own heart. Now I have the chance – as you – you will be me, sharing these precious moments."

The face, though rotted, is recognizable. Jeffrey's face. The body proportions, the chest, the length of the limbs, the voice – his. His dead heart, still and stinking, resting in his hand.

"Do you want to drop your drawers," the Jeffrey-thing says. "We could have a little pleasure watching our heart. We know it turns us on big time."

Jeffrey's fear and adrenaline excrete in screams. Pure terror cries out, perhaps the voice that would have come out of Munch's screaming women in the painting if she had been real. Granny cries out. *No, God, please,* Jeffrey thinks. *I don't want to scare her to death*.

Dogs bark in the neighborhood. Jeffrey keeps screaming. Granny does not come upstairs, and he fears she is dead of a heart attack or stroke caused by fright. He does not know how much time passes before flashing lights shine through the window, illuminating a room empty except for Jeffrey and a pool of vomit on the floor.

There is a knock on the door downstairs. "Sheriff's Department," a voice says. There is the sound of a door opening and footsteps - then, thank God, Granny's voice. "I'm so glad you got here. Heard a terrible scream. Don't know where it came from. Seemed to come from everywhere."

"Yes, ma'am, we received several calls from neighbors. Some of them thought the sound came from upstairs here."

"From Jeffrey's room? Lordy, I hope not!"

Jeffrey yells out, "I'm okay. I have no idea where those screams came from."

"How long you been up?" Granny calls out. Before answering Jeffrey finishes changing into his jeans and pullover shirt, and he runs downstairs, hoping that no one can smell the puke on his breath. He opens the stairs door and walks in. The deputy shakes his hand.

"I got up when I saw the lights and heard the siren," Jeffrey says. "Granny, I tried to call out to you when I heard the scream, but it was too loud."

Jeffrey hates to lie, but the sheriff's office would cart him down to Central State in a cage had he told the truth.

"Okay, ma'am, thank you for your call. We'll keep checking this out."

"Hope you find an answer," Jeffrey says.

The deputy thanks them and drives off.

"Goodness gracious, what a night. I thought the devil himself had got into somebody's house."

"I sure hope not!" Jeffrey says.

He climbs upstairs, tries not to be sick as he cleans up the puke with toilet paper and flushes it down a little at a time, hoping Granny will not hear the constant flushing. Once the floor is clean, Jeffrey washes his mouth out and brushes his teeth, leaving the bathroom light on as well as the lamp by his bed. He does not know how much longer he can take this... Haunting? Possession? Something worse? - but if he stops dealing with it on his own, he will have to tell Aunt Jenny he needs help. She cannot afford what Uncle Frank calls *a shrink*. Jeffrey knows a little bit about psychology from school or he would have taken Uncle Frank literally. Having his head shrunk would not be as bad as seeing his own rotten body and dead heart next to his bed. Jeffrey has no desire to harm himself, for dying leaves only two alternatives. If his religion is false and God does not exist, he will be annihilated, and he would rather stay with his rotted demonic body forever and remain conscious rather than blank out into nothingness. The other alternative is Hell. Jeffrey's only realistic option is to take care of himself so he can live as long as possible before he dies. If he goes to Hell he will have to make the best of it and take comfort that he still exists and is conscious.

He tries not to think about the other alternative – but how is annihilation an alternative? Annihilation is not-Jeffrey, the negation of Jeffrey, blackness that he would not even know is black because he would not be there to experience it. As Alex would have said, "That really sucks." He wonders whether Alex has been annihilated. While Jeffrey hopes Alex is in Hell, he does not desire that anyone, including Alex, to disappear for eternity. Turning into nothing is worse than not having lived at all.

Whatever Jeffrey saw earlier by his bed has to be the fruit of the sermon he heard on the radio. That preacher gave some legitimacy to the idea that using curse words in reference to the Holy Ghost was blasphemy against the Holy Ghost. Brother Luck had made it seem like no preacher believed that a sin like Jeffrey's is unpardonable, mind trick or no mind trick. From believing that he is damned to believing he has some hope, Jeffrey has now moved to being agnostic regarding hope. Somehow that is worse than knowing hope is absent. Not knowing whether he is certainly damned decays into a renewed despair, and once more Jeffrey imagines his resurrected body seared by roaring flames and his mind tormented by beings with no mercy, God and Jesus having abandoned him for good.

Jeffrey remembers the old Laurel and Hardy re-runs. He laughs, and realizes the laugh is on him - what a fine mess Jeffrey has gotten himself into. A surge of anger fills his face with heat, and he wants to strike *The Reverend* Sandwich. Jeffrey was doing okay until the good *Reverend* destroyed the peace he had made with himself. Jeffrey considers asking Aunt Jenny to take him to the mental hospital – but if *One Flew over the Coo Coo's Nest* is accurate, if Jeffrey were sent to Central State, the equivalent of Nurse Ratchet would torture him – and so would the demon. There would be no heroic figure coming around to save Jeffrey's ass.

Religion itself is not all bad, Jeffrey thinks, *but The Rev. Sandwich's religion is pure evil - using fear to torture people as he did in his sermons was sadistic.* Yet a wave of shame spreads from his face to his toes, choking him into a sob. He is the same way – he is a future Rev. Sandwich. He imagines people roasting in Hell, having their backs whipped by demons – and enjoys it like a sadistic freak. *Freak?* Sherry is right. Jeffrey realizes that while there may be times that people need the Hell scared out of them, too much fear makes demons fly. How many other children suffer as he does, how many boys reaching puberty and not understanding what is going on come to knowledge of sin – and curse the Holy Ghost? Jeffrey knows he is at that age when bodily changes bring emotional turmoil so powerful that some adolescents resort to suicide. How many teenagers listening to The Rev. Sandwich lack Jeffrey's fear of death? How many of them commit suicide because of despair, believing that they have committed the unpardonable sin? How many have their own demons haunt them by their bedside, tormenting them, driving them to go to the storage shed, retrieve a rope and tie it to a tree.

Hope keeps people going, and people like The Rev. Sandwich sell despair. Jeffrey ponders, *Who is more likely to be separated from God in eternity: some poor child convicted of despair by The Rev. Sandwich or The Rev. Sandwich himself? Who are the demons who torment The Rev. Sandwich?*

CHAPTER 18
THE POSSESSION

Ah, the Reverend *Sandwich*, the Antibeing thinks. *What a pitiful fool, what a weak mind. I usually work alone, except when I call on ol' Beelzebub from time to time. To nail Mr. Sandwich, I enlisted the help of one of the lesser entities humans call* demons *– an average demon, not a commander like Beelzebub or the Day Star. The demon's name doesn't matter. I needed the* Reverend *Sandwich to be on my side, and for that to happen required my having complete control over his mind. Unfortunately, this dimension gives me trouble, but demons, while weak compared to me and compared to the Enemy, work in this dimension with ease. I offered to increase the pain of another demon who double-crossed this particular demon, and he agreed to help me. Revenge is a dish best served - hot! – at least in Hell. I had Sandwich by the soul in less than an hour of earth time. I coached the demon on the radio sermon the* Reverend *Sandwich would deliver and made sure the timing was right for Jeffrey to hear the broadcast. Sandwich went along, thinking the whole time that his take on the unpardonable sin was his brilliant idea.*

Bingo! Agony and despair for Jeffrey, more pleasure for me. How I dined on the despair returning to that pitiful boy! Such nourishment – how does Jeffrey's Holy Book put it? I've found -

strength in my loins. *I don't really have loins – but you get the point. Soon I shall stay in this dimension - permanently. Soon, like my ancestors, I shall have power to alter this universe as I wish. It has been millions of years since the Enemy drove us out of this third planet. This will not happen again. When the human child Jeffrey falls, we shall rise from the bowels of the deep.*

CHAPTER 19
THE URN

At the start of seventh grade Alex says that Jeffrey's geography teacher, Mrs. Rogers, looks like she has been dead thirty years. Jeffrey must admit he has never seen a face so turned inside-out. Her white hair is no surprise, but deep-lined wrinkles surround the sides of her mouth like mini Grand Canyons. Her forehead is furrowed as if lost in constant worry. Her hands, covered with black spots, are stretched and skeletal, with fingernails so long they would not only put a person's eye out, but slice into the brain and kill him. She has a unique ability – she can draw a perfect circle on the chalkboard with one swoop of her arm. Jeffrey tried that himself once, but he twisted the joint between his humorous and his scapula so badly that he ached for days. His *half-arc* attempt to draw a circle was barely curved enough to avoid being a straight line.

Mrs. Rogers presents detailed descriptions of Paris, London, Amsterdam and Tokyo. Her pronunciation of "Rotterdam" sounds obscene to Jeffrey, and he stifles a laugh whenever she says it. Laughing or talking in her class does not bode well for the guilty student. Ten licks by Mr. Hurley, the principal, is enough to discourage any return of laughter. He has a perfect arc, too, when he swings his thick wood paddle. Thank goodness Jeffrey never experienced the paddle - even Alex had come into the room in tears after Mr. Hurley wore him out.

In March the students turn in their class notebooks for a grade. Jeffrey has written on notebook paper and placed the paper into a folder. Unfortunately for Jeffrey, Mrs. Rogers said earlier in the school year that class notes should be in a spiral notebook. She gives Jeffrey a *D* on the assignment. He feels foolish for being the only student to turn in the wrong kind of notebook, but he is angry that Mrs. Rogers thinks it matters. He asks her if he can rewrite the notes in a spiral notebook and turn it in again. She says that he can and that she will re-grade the notebook only if he turns it in the following day. He thanks her and starts to walk away - then he notices an urn in her open drawer. He pretends not to see and leaves the classroom to catch the school bus. He knows what an urn is, though his own family members do not believe in cremation – not as much for religious reasons as much as that they believe a body lying in state makes it easier to say goodbye. Surely Mrs. Rogers does not keep human ashes in an urn in her desk drawer. Maybe she lost a beloved dog or cat and those were the ashes in the urn. Maybe the ashes are from students who misbehave in her classes.

Jeffrey spends all night re-writing his notes, turns the paper in on time, and gets an A-. He forgot about the urn until a week later when he hears two young teachers gossiping in the hallway after the bell rang for the end of the school day. They are giggling. One of them says, "You know Mrs. Rogers, the geography teacher?"

"You mean the one who looks like a corpse?"

"That's the one. She has a corpse in her drawer."

"Noooooo..."

"Oh yes, her husband Wayne's ashes. He died five years ago and she's kept his ashes in her drawer ever since."

"How weird. Does Mr. Hurley know?"

"Apparently so. He told Wynette Ryn, his secretary, that he wasn't going to stop an old woman from mourning her late husband in her own way."

"That's something else."

"Yep, it sure is," Jeffrey mutters to himself, furious that two teachers are so cruel to a colleague. He decides to call Aunt Jenny and say he missed the school bus. He walks toward Mrs. Rogers' office, figuring that she is probably mean at times because she is still upset about losing her husband Wayne.

Jeffrey steps inside Mrs. Rogers' office. She holds the urn, rubbing it and talking to it. She stops abruptly, tries to put the urn away when Jeffrey says, "I'm sorry you lost your husband. I know that's difficult."

Mrs. Rogers slams the drawer shut and turns red, an effect that makes her wrinkled face look like a lighted Halloween witch's. "How dare you come in here just to get a look inside that urn. Enough students have done that already. I'm going to Mr. Hurley's office now." She stands up and starts to walk toward the classroom door.

Jeffrey starts to cry. "No, ma'am, please listen. I heard these two mean young teachers making fun of you and I didn't think it was funny and I wanted to say I'm sorry for your loss. I know it's not like losing a husband, but my granddaddy died four years ago and I still cry about that."

Mrs. Rogers relaxes, sits down, pulls Jeffrey near her face, and strokes his hair. "It's all right. I didn't understand. I thought you were like all those other students. I'm sorry about making you re-do the notebook. That was too hard. Lord knows I wish there were more students like you who really care."

She takes off the top of the urn and said, "This is all I have of Wayne. I guess your granddaddy was buried."

"Yes, ma'am, in Greenlawn."

"I wanted to have something to touch, some real part of Wayne to stay with me. I'm old and don't have much time left in this world. The way I look I know a man won't want me, and I wouldn't want a man anyway. I'll see Wayne whole again in Heaven. Until then, this is the best I can do."

"I wish it were different for you," Jeffrey said.

"Me, too, young man. As for those young whippersnapping bitches – you heard me – that's all they are, prissy-pants who think they know everything, picking on an old woman who's trying to hold on to all she has left of her husband – they'll pay in Hell one day. I'm glad you didn't laugh with them, and that says a lot for you. Life is too fragile. You're young – you'd better take what comes or you'll lose it all and end up looking like me."

Mrs. Rogers stands up and searches the bookshelves lining the classroom.

"Ah, yes. Here's my extra copy. You can have this. It's a book called *Meditations* by Marcus Aurelius. He was a Roman emperor who was a philosopher. Imagine that. I know one thing for sure – we'll never have a president who is a philosopher. I think you'll like this book."

"Thank you so much. I'm glad you're able to hold onto Wayne in a real way."

"Real? No – these ashes are just remains of a shell. But it helps me. God bless you, and I'll see you in class tomorrow. Now wipe those tears off and get home!"

Jeffrey wipes his eyes and replies like a private speaking to a drill sergeant. "Yes, ma'am!" She laughs and waves him out the door.

Jeffrey goes to the office phone and calls Aunt Jenny, asking her to pick him up. He also asks if she would stop by Greenlawn so he could see Granddaddy's grave. She says, "It's good that you missed the bus, now that you reminded me – I've been meaning to put fresh flowers on that grave for a while." She picks him up, stops at Bessie's Flower Shop in Morhollow to buy a bouquet, and drives on the New Randallsville Highway to Greenlawn Cemetery. They enter the cemetery, turning left toward the section where Granddaddy is buried. Jeffrey admires the statues of Jesus and of Mary, Jesus' mother.

Looking at her statue makes him wonder if Jesus is really as eager as preachers say He is to fry people in Hell. Surely He is at least as kind as his mother.

Aunt Jenny rides to the end of the road, circles around, and stops near Granddaddy's grave. They step out of the car and walk on soft, fresh-cut grass to the grave. Jeffrey reads the marker for what must be the thousandth time:

DAVID ("BUD") WILSON
JULY 23, 1901
AUGUST 25, 1968

Aunt Jenny pulls the old spent flowers out from the urn, puts them into a disposal bag, and replaces them with a multicolored spray — red, blue, yellow - brightening the grave on this cloudy, gray day. Jeffrey prays that God will have mercy on Granddaddy and forgive him his sins. Sometimes Granddaddy had been mean to Granny, and Jeffrey hopes he repented before he died.

How little of us remains, he thinks. *What small shells we leave behind. A body minus a soul that even in a sealed casket will mold, the casket leaking air soon to make sure decay does its destructive deeds. There is Wayne Rogers' dust, the rust of death that wind will blow away into an open sky if Mrs. Rogers opens the urn outside.* Aunt Jenny and Jeffrey stand by the grave until clouds darken and it starts to sprinkle. Jeffrey and Aunt Jenny leave to make the best of their fates while still alive, each beat of their hearts hastening their inevitable end.

I was not a normal child, Jeffrey thinks as he closes the journal and opens his briefcase. Among the papers inside lies a small black book with a worn cover. He opens it to the title page: *Marcus Aurelius, MEDITATIONS*. He begins to read, focusing on passages he underlined over thirty years ago. One of the passages fits well the day that Mrs. Rogers gave him the book, the day he saw one man's ashes and another's grave: "Whatever this is that I am, it is a little flesh and breath, and the ruling part." All three. Flesh and breath are as essential as the soul. Without flesh and breath, all is lost. *What, then, are Wayne Rogers and David "Bud" Wilson? Where are they? Their flesh remains without breath and without the ruling part. God promises to re-make flesh and breath and join them to the ruling part.* Even so, there remains that issue that haunts Jeffrey, a person's eternal fate in Heaven or in Hell. Wayne Rogers and Bud Wilson lie beyond Jeffrey's power. Does Jeffrey have the power to change his fate, or was it sealed by his sins as a child? *If God throws out fifty or sixty or seventy years of someone's life due to a slippage of words directed to the wrong person of the Trinity, does not that make God a real sonofabitch, an evil and arbitrary being?* Jeffrey re-opens the journal and finds those same thoughts expressed by his thirteen-year-old self after his return from the graveyard.

Why did Granddaddy die in his sixties of a heart attack when God knew I needed him, Jeffrey wonders. *Why did God allow me to blaspheme the Holy Ghost and to wallow in the misery of fearing Hellfire? Worst of all, why would God give a demon, His own creation, leeway to rebel against God and torment God's own creatures, including me, a thirteen-year-old boy? Finally, if God is so evil, why do I waste my time going to church?* None of the teachers in the preaching school answer his questions, and they lose patience when his questions include doubts about God's goodness. That tells Jeffrey that they are actually afraid that he is right in questioning God.

How can he get out of going to church without hurting Granny, Aunt Jenny and his other relatives who go to church? Uncle Frank would be proud of his independence, but Aunt Jenny's heart would be broken, and the thought of that causes his own heart to feel queasy. He arrives at a compromise – he will miss church at least once a month due to sickness – later he will worry about creating more excuses. He would be lying, but at least he would not be lying to himself by going to a church to worship a God he cannot stand.

The first Sunday he plans to miss, he sneaks outside early and runs around the field. He tries to run hard enough to make himself sick, to make his face red, to keep his heart pounding for at least an hour after he runs. His hot face should suffice to fake a fever. He circles the field, soft soil due to recent rains forcing him to work harder. His stomach hurts, his chest aches and his legs are in agony after his second lap around the eighteen-acre field. His heartbeat is fully automatic rifle fire. He runs back to the house without stopping, keeping as quiet as he can before trodding with aching legs up the stairs. The stairs worsen his leg pain, and he grimaces to keep from crying out. He makes it to bed, covers himself up, heart-bullets shooting from his chest and striking the covers.

When Aunt Jenny arrives, Granny calls him to breakfast. He yells out that he is sick. Aunt Jenny walks upstairs, takes one look at him, and says, “You need to go to the doctor.”

Jeffrey’s mind stops a moment, and he opens his mouth without speaking. He did not plan on a doctor’s visit. He did not think he had done a thorough job of looking sick. Instead, he made himself look like Hell. After a moment he replies. “It’s just a fever.”

“I can see your heartbeat move the covers – that’s way too fast.”

By now Jeffrey is starting to panic. He has to calm down to lower his heart rate. He needs to stall Aunt Jenny so she would not call the doctor. “It was faster before, but it’s slowing down.”

A strange feeling comes over him, one he knows and likes and hates it at the same time. Jeffrey throws off his covers, pulls up his shirt, and says, “Listen to my heart.” She leans over and puts her ear over his chest.

Now the real battle begins within Jeffrey. Aunt Jenny’s blond hair tickles Jeffrey’s nipples, and he feels a hardness in his groin. His heart pounds harder, and he takes a deep breath to calm himself. He can see under Aunt Jenny's shirt as she leans over, the curves of her breast under her bra, the edge of her light pink areola. The hardness in his groin aches, and he thinks of her heart beating between her breasts. He almost comes, and he barely holds back. He forces his concentration on the best day of his life, when he and Granddaddy walked to The Thicket between the field and the larger forest beyond. There they had a picnic, and Jeffrey swung on vines growing between trees. Afterwards he lay on a bed of oak leaves, mesmerized by dappled shadows dancing in the breeze. He fell asleep under oak and birch, a denouement to a day in heaven.

Aunt Jenny raises her head. "You heart is slowing down quite a bit, but you have a fever. I'll get the thermometer and take your temperature.

Lucky for him, the thermometer is in the downstairs bathroom. Jeffrey runs to the bathroom and in less than a minute he releases has lack of self-control, drinks two glasses of water, and wets down his face and upper body. He dries himself and returns to bed, feeling mellow as a sunning seal. When Aunt Jenny returns she takes his temperature. "100.5. Not bad, but you need to stay home from church. Anything you need?"

"No, ma'am," Jeffrey says, relieved but guilty.

"I'll buy you some cranberry juice anyway."

After Aunt Jenny, Uncle Lawton and Granny leave for church, a wave a nausea overcomes Jeffrey as he realizes that he has not only lusted after his own aunt, but satisfied his lust with his hand. Disgust fills his stomach with nausea, and he relives the results of his guilt in the bathroom. His head hurts, and he cries until his eyes dry up and ache. He goes to the bathroom, and pours water over his eyes, and returns to bed.

Trying to shift his mind away from his sexual sins, Jeffrey takes the *Dixon New Annotated Bible, King James Version* that Aunt Jenny and Uncle Lawton had given to him off his desk and reads the chronology of the Old Testament at the back. It says that creation happened in 4004 B.C. and the Great Flood took place about 2400 B.C. Jeffrey knows from books about ancient

Egypt and Mesopotamia that their civilizations date to at least 3000 B.C. Since nothing could survive a great flood intact, especially clay tablets in Mesopotamia, how could the Bible be right? He begins to search through dates in the Bible and add them – how old Adam was when his son Seth was born, how old Seth was when his son was born, how long the Bible said the Israelites were in Egypt, and so forth. He calculates the dates of creation and the great flood, and the dates are about fifty years later than the chronology in the back of the Bible.

The Bible must be wrong. If the Bible is wrong, everything it says about God must be wrong, including the passage on the unpardonable sin. Everything about Jesus is wrong. Maybe Jesus never existed. Maybe there is no God. Maybe Jeffrey will be annihilated when he dies. His body jerks with hard chills, and he wraps himself in sheets and blanket. He closes the Bible and falls into fitful sleep.

Jeffrey dreams he is walking outside in the back yard by the coal pile. Near the coal pile are bookshelves filled with books on religion, science and archeology. He takes one of the books and begins to read as he wanders around the bookcases. As he rounds a corner a face glares at him with a sarcastic grin, unnatural lips turned upward in an oval smile. The head is on a snake's body. "Do you like my books?" it says. "Now you know the Bible is wrong." The voice changes from a hiss to a folksy Tennessee accent. "Follow your Uncle Frank's advice, Son. You'll be better off. A lot happier, too." Jeffrey wakes up in a daze, not knowing what to think or feel.

CHAPTER 20
THE INCREASE OF SIN

Within the shadow of Its existence, the Antibeing wriggles Its tentacles, Its version of a belly laugh. It croaks out loud in a voice sounding as if it comes from under water, *Incest! Incest! I never dreamed* – at this It chortles again – *I would be this successful with Jeffrey. That boy thought about doing his own aunt. Soon he'll feel so guilty that I'll suggest a fitting way for him to kill himself. There are so many. A fetish-related one would be exquisite. He could put a bag over his head and refuse to take it off while he listens to his heart's final beats. He could shoot himself with a handgun in the side and listen to his heartbeat as it slows toward a standstill. So delicious. I'd try to get him to make a pass at his aunt, but that's too much work. I need a break. I think I'll join the dancing throng around Azathoth. Dissonance is joy!*

Zeke takes the phone book out of the desk under the counter and phones Jeffrey's granny. She answers, and he asks for Jeffrey. She hands him the receiver.

"Hi, Jeffrey, it's Zeke."

"Hi. I'm so glad to talk to you. I'm a mess but I'm too ashamed to tell anyone. I hope you didn't see."

"I didn't see, no, not that way, but I got the general drift. You're not a bad boy. You're a good boy with normal, human screw-ups like me, like Andy, like your granny, like your aunt. You don't know what all was in her mind either. You have to put up with yourself. I've put up with myself all these years, Lord knows why. I reckon you do the best you can and rely on the grace of God. 'Course we never really do our best. Somethin' out there is takin' care of us or else the whole darn world would be gone by now. Don't know if that helps much, but that's 'bout all the wisdom I have today."

"Thanks. That helped a lot. Really. I was having terrible thoughts about my life being worthless and that maybe the world would be better off without me. Now I don't feel that way."

Zeke turns away from the phone, takes a deep breath. "Good for you! Remember - you're a human being, not God. Perfection is a pipe dream this side of Heaven."

"I'll remember."

CHAPTER 21
THE GIRLFRIEND

At Aunt Jenny's house, Jeffrey folds his arms and hugs himself hard until he feels pain. His face is hot with shame. *Dear God*. He is in a bedroom in a house with the same aunt he masturbated to when he was thirteen. He hopes she never suspected. He balls his fists, furious at his lack of control, frustrated that he can do nothing to change the past.

His dream about the demon concerned another kind of guilt, he thinks - his guilty conscience for questioning the truth of the Bible. Books have power – he has been in the academic world enough to understand the power of ideas expressed in words. Hitler's *Mein Kampf* had the power to help cause mass murder. Other books have the power to build or destroy faith.

Yet life trumps books, Jeffrey thinks. *Parents, spouses, heart disease, cancer, deaths of loved ones, broken relationships, a boy's first experience with love – these add to and take away from faith*. Jeffrey begins to read the journal once more, moving ahead in time to the eighth grade. He remembers and dreads facing again a heartbreak far worse than the end of his relationship with Sherry, an agony that cut to his heart, pulled out the faith that was inside, and let it bleed out. Her name was Kathy Smithson.

Kathy is in Jeffrey's homeroom and in four of his six classes in eighth grade. She has dark auburn hair that hangs over her shoulders, combed straight, a slender build, glass-fragile, as if she would break if anyone touched her, and pale skin. Jeffrey first sees her in homeroom. Bud Hill, a student who has been in Jeffrey's classes off and on since first grade, says, "Look at that weird girl. She's as pale as a body in a coffin. Think she's some kind of vampire? I bet she's your type. You like skeletons."

Jeffrey peers to the other side of the room. Kathy wears a blue dress, and her face looks skull thin. Jeffrey says, "I like skeletons, but I don't want a girl to look like a skeleton. It's a wonder she's alive."

"Maybe she ain't," Bud says, and he laughs again.

It is the fall of 1972. In the wider world President Nixon is on the path to a landslide win in November over George McGovern. Watergate is still considered a botched burglary, nothing more. At school, the older kids who picked on the weak in seventh grade have either failed another grade or dropped out of school. A group of nerds, including Jeffrey, have formed a circle of friends - math nerds, science nerds, chess nerds. Jeffrey has not learned chess, but he is interested in learning, and puts that on his list of future tasks.

When homeroom period begins and students take their seats, Kathy sits at the desk next to Jeffrey on the right. She turns to Jeffrey. He blushes, and his heart starts to pound. She smiles and says, "Hi, I'm Kathy Smithson."

Jeffrey swallows hard. A girl is speaking to him out of the blue? That's a first. He answers, unable to keep his voice from shaking, "I'm Jeffrey Conley. Good to meet you."

"I just moved here from McNairy County," she said. "Daddy got a job in Nashville at St. Thomas Hospital."

"Is he a doctor?"

"No, he does boring work in the business office. Doctors are more interesting."

"I agree. I've thought about being one."

She gazes at him with brown eyes that grow wider. "Really?"

His heart glows warm and skips a beat. He gasps, gains control, and says, "That's what I want to be. I want to be a cardiologist. I want to fix sick hearts."

Jeffrey blushes at the lie, and the warmth spreads throughout his body, and he hears the pulse pounding in his ears. A nervous frog sits in his throat and refuses to move.

"That's cool," she says. "I'd like to be one, too. I'm fascinated by the heart."

After that, it takes a few more seconds for Jeffrey to drive the frog in his throat away far enough for him to croak, "What made you interested in the heart?"

"Because my heart's sick. Well, not the muscle but the aortic valve. It leaks. The doctors say I was born with it, but they didn't want to do surgery until I am old enough. The doctors say it's time, and I'm having surgery over Christmas Break."

"On your heart?"

She laughs. "Where else, silly? That's where the aortic valve is."

"I know that," Jeffrey says. "I'm not thinking straight. Do you have a murmur?"

"I murmur all the time. It's a bad habit."

Jeffrey pauses until the pun sinks in. Then he giggles and dips he head because his voice sounds like he has been sucking on a lemon.

"Yes," Kathy says. "I have a heart murmur. It's loud. You really want to be a cardiologist?"

"Well, I'm not totally sure I want to be a medical doctor. But if I become one I'll be a cardiologist, too."

Kathy laughs again, and her voice is like the tinkles of wind chimes in a light breeze. Her eyes are turning into gemstones. "Are you saying that now because that's what I want to be?"

"No. I'm really interested in the heart. I have a stethoscope. I listen to my heart all the time."

"We have that in common. Your heart's okay, right?"

"Yeah."

"Good. In school I wasn't allowed to run and play with the other kids, and I can't take PE as an activity class. I have to take a boring class where we read about games and take tests."

"I'm sorry," Jeffrey says.

"It's okay. Where do you live?"

"Corner of Bramble Road and the Old Randallsville Highway."

"Wow, I live down Jenson Road off Bramble Road. You turn just past the guy with all the beagles."

"My Uncle Frank."

"Really? He's nice. He waves at me and my mom and dad when we drive by. My dad introduced himself one day, and they're planning to go rabbit hunting together this winter."

"Cool. Do you ride the school bus?"

"No, Mom takes me to and from school."

Jeffrey groans, then glances at Kathy, but she does not seem to notice. What should he say next? He has to talk to Kathy alone outside of school. If he visits her house, her parents will probably keep their eyes on him and he will never get a chance to talk to her alone – or to ask if he can listen to her murmur. An idea pops into his head. A brilliant idea, he thinks.

"Would you like to come and visit my Uncle Frank and Aunt Lucy?" Jeffrey asks. "We could go outside and talk, and your parents could talk to them inside."

She smiles. "Maybe. I'll ask my mom and dad."

It is amazing how a girl can restore a boy's faith in God. Jeffrey prays all week that Kathy's parents will say "Yes." Granny is not a problem. Jeffrey has her permission to visit Uncle Frank and Aunt Lucy as long as he tells her when. She probably could not care less whether a girl is visiting as long as Aunt Lucy and Uncle Frank are in the general area. Kathy's parents might be overprotective. Jeffrey would not blame them if they were – if Jeffrey was her father, he would want to protect her, too, especially when a surgeon is going to slice into her heart in a few months. Jeffrey worries about that, but that is months away – a long time. In the meantime he has an opportunity to enjoy some heavenly moments.

Uh oh – he is getting ahead of himself again. Kathy and he had one nice conversation. That does not mean they are boyfriend and girlfriend or even good friends. He has to be careful – and he can never ask her to do anything to stress her heart, not even a breath hold. He wants to listen, but this time not only for that warm feeling he gets in his groin. He wants to listen to her heartbeat so he can feel close to her. Shit, now he is really jumping the gun. "One step at a time, please," he whispers to himself, and then he repeats it like a mantra.

Jeffrey gives Kathy his number the next day at school, and Granny gives him a funny look when she calls, "Jeffrey, it's for you. Some gal."

Jeffrey blushes, takes the phone. "Hello."

"Jeffrey, this is Kathy. Mom and Dad said it would be nice to come visit your great-aunt and uncle. They know you'll be there and they don't seem to mind. They're going Saturday at two. Is that okay?"

"That's great!" Jeffrey says, and he holds his hand to his mouth, embarrassed at the loudness of his voice. He repeats a new mantra: "Don't scare her away."

"What?" Kathy asks.

"Talking to myself – a bad habit. I look forward to seeing you."

"Me too. See you then," Kathy says.

Jeffrey sets the receiver in its socket and jumps in the air, jerks his arm over his head and says, "All righhhttt!" That gets Granny's attention.

"Thinking 'bout courtin,' are you?" she asks. Jeffrey cannot understand why old people call a boy meeting a girl *courtin'*. At school and on TV he has heard of *dating*, and he read some books on dating from the church library that warned against *petting*, and *necking*. Necking was just kissing, and Jeffrey cannot see the harm in that. Petting - touching a girl's breast – and other places – Jeffrey sees how that can get someone in trouble. The idea of doing to a girl what Uncle Lawton has described no longer seems gross, and Jeffrey knows that petting leads to that act. He is not ready for that – not until he is married.

Saturday creeps up slower than Christmas comes for a six-year-old child. Jeffrey talks to Kathy at school every day, and he learns a great deal about her past – problems with crooked people in town, gunfights, drugs – and all that in a rural area. Jeffrey had no idea country people could be so mean.

Jeffrey tells her about his parents' accident and his granddaddy's death. She lets him cry on her shoulder afterwards, and he heard a hint of her heartbeat that increased his appetite for the full experience. Every day Kathy grows more beautiful, her eyes richer in color, her breasts more proportionate and firm, her hair glimmering in sunlight. Jeffrey desires to look into her brown eyes forever, sink deep into their wells and never surface. He is falling in love – no, not falling - he is already in love with her. He reads that boys fall in love quicker than girls, and Jeffrey hopes Kathy will eventually return his feelings.

On Friday afternoon before math class she tells him of her fear of dying in surgery. "I know the doctor says it's safe, and so do Mom and Dad, but how safe?" Jeffrey checks in the school library and in the Randallsville Public Library for statistics, but reaches a dead end. One day he tells Aunt Jenny, "I need to go to the university library."

Aunt Jenny frowns. "That's clear on the other side of Randallsville. Why do you want to go there? Don't the libraries here have enough books for you to read? I swear, all those books will make you crazy as Hell itself."

Jeffrey's stomach cramps. He will have to lie. Another sin. A necessary evil. "I'm going to do a report for school on the history of the Church of Christ and I can't find the books I need in the other libraries."

Aunt Jenny's expression changes from a frown to a smile. "That's okay, then. You picked a good topic. Get washed up, and we'll leave in ten minutes."

At the library, Jeffrey looks through some books on the Church of Christ and pretends to take notes. Then, keeping an eye on Aunt Jenny, he finds the medical journals and discovers that four percent of people die who have the kind of surgery Kathy will undergo. *You can't die now,* he thinks, *now that I've found you, my love.*

His heart lurches. *My love. God will not be cruel and take you away. Please, God, be there. Be a good God.*

At school the next day, Jeffrey is talking to Kathy when, without warning, she gives him a quick peck on the lips. Jeffrey is in heaven, swooning in the moment when Bill Ricketts, one of the *freaks*, those students who smoke dope, starts singing, "Jeffrey's got a girlfriend, Jeffrey's got a girlfriend." The other students laugh.

Kathy says, "Shut up, Bill," and shakes her fist. Some of the other students say, "Oooohhhh." For the first time in the semester Jeffrey is glad when Mrs. Matson walks in to continue her lesson on basic algebra.

Saturday finally arrives, and Jeffrey awakens to feel his legs twitching, his heart racing and his face hot. He steps into the bathroom, gets the mercury thermometer, and takes his temperature. 99 even – not bad. He decides that after breakfast he will burn off his nervousness. He eats quickly, and before Granny can say anything he's out the door and on his bike, riding back and forth along the gravel drive. He has told Granny that Uncle Frank wants to show him some new beagles he bought. Jeffrey takes a bath later than he's planned, smears on too much deodorant, and splashes on so much Old Spice that Granny says, "Goodness, boy, I can smell you all the way over here in the kitchen. Don't be so wasteful."

"I'm sorry, and I won't," Jeffrey says as he snatches an old satchel, puts his stethoscope inside, and hangs the satchel on the handlebars of his bicycle. It is cooler than normal for early

September, in the low 80s, and he is grateful that he will not sweat as much as usual during his ride to Uncle Frank's.

Finally, at fifteen 'till two, he hops on his bicycle and begins to ride. He moves at a moderate pace, looking at the hardwood trees dotting hayfields, cows standing up and grazing in full sun by a rickety old barn, and a small herd of goats. He hopes the bike ride will burn enough energy to slow down his adrenalin rush.

When Jeffrey arrives at Uncle Frank's and Aunt Lucy's at 1:55, the Smithsons are not there. He worries that something is wrong. He is a stickler for being on time for classes at school, church, and other meetings, and does not understand why the Smithson's do not arrive a bit early so they can be sure to be on time. Uncle Frank emerges from the front door and motions Jeffrey inside. Jeffrey takes his satchel and follows him.

"What do you have in there?" Uncle Frank asks.

"Just some books I'm going to show Kathy."

"Oh, the Smithson girl. You know her already, I see."

Heat rises to Jeffrey's cheeks. "Yes, sir."

Uncle Frank laughs. "You like her?"

Jeffrey nods.

"Does she like you, too?"

Jeffrey's cheeks are hot, and he wonders how red he appears. "Yes, sir. I think she wants to be my girlfriend."

Uncle Frank pats him on the shoulder. "Well I'll be damned! I'm proud of you. Hell, if you were old enough I'd give you a beer to celebrate. Enjoy every moment – you'll remember them the rest of your life, whether or not she turns out to be *the* one."

Jeffrey smiles. "I'll do my best."

Uncle Frank bursts out laughing. "You do that. You get inside and sit on the rocking chair in the living room. I'll greet the Smithsons and let them in the front door. Remember, be polite."

Jeffrey walks around the house to the back door, looking out at scrub brush and trees lining sinkholes in a field across the fence. He greets Aunt Lucy. "I'll be in the living room directly." A pitcher of iced tea is on the counter. Jeffrey prays she didn't make it out of the sulfur water from their tap. He sighs with relief when he sees jugs on the floor with the label, *Distilled Water*.

There is the sound of crackling gravel and a car engine, which stops. Footsteps reverberate on the porch, and Uncle Frank says, "Come on in and have a seat where you'd like. My wife Lucy's already there and so is our grand-nephew Jeffrey." Kathy steps inside first, and blows Jeffrey a kiss before anyone can see her. Mrs. Smithson walks inside next. Kathy has her mother's dark hair, but not the pounds of extra weight. Jeffrey imagines Kathy looking that one day and figures he would still love her anyway.

Aunt Lucy enters with a tray of glasses filled with iced tea, and Mr. Smithson steps inside. He is thin like Kathy, with sandy blond hair a little lighter in color than Jeffrey's, and his face is worn and haggard. Jeffrey thinks that Mr. Smithson is stressed from his daughter's illness and her upcoming surgery. Jeffrey politely introduces himself, and Mrs. Smithson is friendly. Mr. Smithson seems more reserved, though Jeffrey may be reading his own nervousness into him.

The group starts talking, and Jeffrey yawns, but covers his mouth, hoping that Mr. and Mrs. Smithson did not notice. Weather was always the first topic in adult conversations – "It's a nice cool day." "Sure is." *Why do people waste time on trivial subjects*, he thinks.

The conversation turns to politics, and Jeffrey is thankful that his aunt and uncle and Mr. and Mrs. Smithson are both for Nixon. If the group gets along, they will stay longer, ergo, more time for Jeffrey to talk with Kathy.

Mrs. Smithson says, "You two young'uns – why don't you go outside and enjoy the day. No need for you to be bored with politics."

Jeffrey could kiss Mrs. Smithson. He takes his satchel, motions Kathy out the living room door into the kitchen, then out the back door. "What stinks in there?" she asks. It smells like sh..."

Jeffrey interrupts her since he wanted "sh..." to be the last thing on her mind. "That's sulfur water," he says. "I don't much like it."

"Ewwweee. That wasn't in the tea, was it?"

"Oh, no, Aunt Lucy uses distilled water for that."

Beagles begin to bawl like spoiled two-year-olds. "Oh, they're wanting attention," Kathy says. "Can I see them?"

"Sure," Jeffrey says as they walk out the screen door to the back yard and to the dog pen. Jeffrey opens the pen door and step inside to be surrounded by whining beagles – grown beagles, half-grown beagles, baby beagles – all with tongues that love to lick and slobber. Soon they are on the floor getting a bath. "Awww, they're so cute," Kathy says. "Especially the babies."

"Yeah, they call them beaglettes," Jeffrey says.

"Really?" Kathy asks.

"Not really," Jeffrey says, and she hits him on the arm. They both laugh, stumble to their feet amidst dogs churning like washing machine agitators. Jeffrey holds open the pen door barely enough to let Kathy squeeze through. Then he manages to hook the pen door without one beagle escaping. They wander between clucking chickens and a crowing rooster to the rusty gate dividing lawn from field. Jeffrey unhooks the gate, and Kathy and Jeffrey walk into rocky terrain.

"I'm getting tired," Kathy says.

"Let's sit down and rest." Jeffrey locates a large grassy spot under an oak under dark shade, and they sit down to a cool breeze.

Kathy is breathing fast and deep. "Are you okay?" Jeffrey asks. It sounds like you may be wheezing."

"Oh, it's not like I'm dying. I don't have a lot of stamina. The surgery's supposed to help. Don't worry about me. Aren't you going to check me out anyway? I think I might know what's in that satchel."

Jeffrey smiles shyly, opens the satchel, and pulls out the stethoscope. He is about to put the earpieces in his ears when Kathy pulls him close and kisses him - no pecks this time, but tongues touching, Jeffrey's arm stroking her back, his hand reaching up to the back of her neck where his fingers brush Kathy's neck hairs. Her heart pounds against Jeffrey's shirt and he worries that this is straining her heart too much.

"Now listen," she says, and pulls the stethoscope's diaphragm under her shirt and places it, though Jeffrey cannot tell exactly where. All he knows is the heart of the girl he loves is beating loudly and quickly, with a clear "swoosh" murmur every beat. She kisses him again, and her heart races and starts to skip. He releases the kiss, and she takes some deep breaths.

"I'm okay," she says between a wheeze and a sigh. Her voices lowers to a whisper "More okay than I've ever been in my life."

Jeffrey's own heart races and skips, but he says, "I love you." He reddens, coughs, takes a deep breath, and says, "I mean, I'm totally in love with you."

Jeffrey gasps when she cries. He thinks, *Oh, crap, I've screwed this one up too*. Instead of telling Jeffrey to go to *the hot place*, as Granddaddy called Hell, Kathy says, "I'm in love with you, too." She pulls Jeffrey down to the ground, where he lies on his back in soft grass, dappled light and oak leaves above him with sun rays piercing like swords. She rests her head over his heart. As she cries, Jeffrey strokes her hair, stifling a sob.

Kathy stops crying, and sniffles a minute or so until she is able to speak. "I wish I had a heart like yours now. Strong, healthy. Not this bum ticker. I'm so scared of the surgery. I don't want to die."

"You won't die," Jeffrey says. "God won't let that happen. I believe that with all my heart." Jeffrey holds her, kisses her again. She releases the kiss and looks at Jeffrey in silence for a few minutes. Suddenly she grins and asks, "Can anyone see here from inside the house?"

"No, why?"

"Take your shirt off."

I wonder if my heart can stand this, he thinks, and he unbuttons his shirt and takes it off. Kathy rests her head on his chest again. "Your heart's a lot faster now than it was before." Then she says in a playful tone, "I wonder why. I wonder if there's a way you can hear my heart better. I know a way."

Kathy sits up and pulls off her shirt. Jeffrey starts to tremble, and he sits up, folding his hands over his groin to hide the bulge. His eyelids open wider as she shifts her arms behind her back, unhooks her bra, throws it aside as she jostles her hair. She lies down on her shirt and says, "Now listen."

Once when Jeffrey was eight he touched an electric fence down Bramble Road. That shock does not compare to how he feels when he sees Kathy's chest. He trembles so much he figures he looks like Brother Wallace, an old man at church who has Parkinson 's disease.

Kathy's breasts are small, and her nipples pale-pink. Jeffrey's trembling forces him to aim his head to find the right spot over her breastbone. He lands in Heaven. Not even the demon can touch this place. Time has no meaning. An hour could be ten minutes, but he hopes ten minutes can stretch into an hour. His body and hers are one, without the sex and without the risk of killing her by getting her pregnant. Does she know about his fetish? It seems so. Does she share it? It does not matter, although he thinks she does, if not for any reason other than love for him. She, of all the girls in the world, is sharing the most precious, threatened part of herself, the part keeping her alive, with him.

Jeffrey hopes he can listen forever, *world without end, A-men*. Kathy says, "We are one now." She sits up, puts her bra on and snaps it, then puts on her shirt. She says, "We'd better get back before we're banned for life from seeing one another."

Jeffrey sits up and puts on his shirt. Kathy buttons her shirt, smiling in such a matter-of-fact way he wants to kiss her again, but instead they both rise up and walk through the field to the fence and into the back yard. That sets the beagles bawling again. They sit side by side on the concrete steps by the back door. They talk until Kathy's parents tell her it is time to go home.

After that heavenly day, Jeffrey and Kathy meet at least once a week outside of school until Christmas Break. Most of those times they share their hearts, head to uncovered skin. Jeffrey has to struggle to make it home to avoid embarrassing himself afterwards. No matter what Granny or Aunt Jenny wants, he makes some excuse to go upstairs. He figures that tissue paper is one of humanity's greatest inventions.

Christmas break is here, and Kathy is a patient at St. Thomas Hospital in Nashville, getting probed and poked before her heart surgery. Aunt Jenny and Uncle Lawton drove Jeffrey to the hospital the night before her surgery. *Crap – nervous again*. He stills his hands and steps into Kathy's hospital room. Her mother greets him and says, "You have been so good for her. I know how happy she's been since she met you. I'm glad Kathy let you into her life – she's backed away from so many friends the past few years." Mr. Smithson smiles, motions his wife outside, and they leave the room. Jeffrey fears that Mr. Smithson is more skeptical of him. Maybe Jeffrey is being paranoid or letting the stress of worrying about Kathy get to him.

Jeffrey sit by Kathy, and they kiss. He takes her hand and asks, "Are you okay? Ready as you can be?"

"I'm ready," she said. "Whatever happens, know how much I love you."

"Nothing bad is going to happen," he says. "I love you with all my heart."

"I brought something for you," she says. He looks at her face for any sign of quirkiness, but she appears to be serious. The gift is in a small package, and Jeffrey takes it and unwraps it. His fingers grasp a pink stone in the shape of a heart.

Jeffrey cries, his pent up emotions flowing freely. He says, "I'll be holding it – and you – when we see each other after your surgery."

"As long as you don't squish my heart out."

"I'll be gentle."

"Jeffrey," she says, taking his arms into her hands. "Whatever happens, don't hate God. These months with you are more than I dreamed, and I have been happier than I have been in my life."

Jeffrey takes her hand and kisses her one more time on the lips.

The next day Uncle Lawton drives Jeffrey to St. Thomas since Aunt Jenny has to work. "She's a tough gal," Uncle Lawton says. "She's gonna be just fine."

The waiting room is crowded for a busy day of surgeries. Jeffrey sits by the Smithsons and Uncle Lawton. Later they are joined by Uncle Frank, Aunt Lucy and some relatives of the Smithsons. Hours pass like months, it seems, until a nurse motions Kathy's parents outside to talk to the doctor. Ten minutes later they return. Mrs. Smithson looks at Jeffrey and says. "Kathy made it through surgery, but it was more difficult than expected. Her heart was weaker than the doctors thought it would be from beating so long with a bad valve. They think she'll be okay. It will be a rougher recovery than we thought, that's all."

As long as she is alive and keeps living - that is enough for Jeffrey. Mrs. Smithson asks him if he would be kind enough to go down the hall and buy a Coke from the machine, and she gives him the change. When Jeffrey returns and reaches the waiting room door, he notices that Mr. and Mrs. Smithson are having an intense conversation. She sees Jeffrey and motions him forward, and she takes the Coke. "My husband and I both think it would be good if you join us when we visit Kathy. I talked to the doctor about your relationship and he thinks it would be a good thing, too. Isn't that right, honey?"

"Yeah, I'm good with that," Mr. Smithson says in a low voice. Jeffrey detects a tone he does not like in it.

The thought of seeing Kathy in her present condition causes Jeffrey's heart to jump in his throat and a lead basketball to stick in his stomach. He aches to see Kathy, but dread of what the ravages of surgery have done to her body overwhelms him. He remembers Granddaddy, in the hospital after his heart attack, pale, incoherent, and gaunt.

They find Kathy's room and walk inside. Kathy is stirring, but still has the breathing tube in her mouth. Her parents sit by her bed, say a few words, and allow Jeffrey to come forward. He wants to sit on the side of the bed, but monitors and tubes get in the way, so he sits in an uncomfortable plastic chair next to her bed. He takes her hand. She looks at him. What emotion she could show on her face seems to be a smile. She does not look like herself – her hair a mess, her face pale as death (*oh God*, Jeffrey thinks, *get that thought out of my mind*).

Jeffrey takes a look at the heart monitor. The rhythm is irregular. Those lumps of fear in his throat and stomach grow in size, and he bends over to keep from throwing up – the last thing Kathy needs to have in the room is contamination. His interest in the heart led him to read books on EKGs, and he knows her rhythm is dangerous for someone who has suffered from heart disease – multiple premature ventricular contractions, or skipped beats. Plus, the spikes on her EKG, which he knows to be QRS complexes, have very little height, which is a sign of low voltage. The doctor walks in with two nurses, well before their ten minutes is up, and motions the group out. "You can come back next visiting hour. She needs her rest."

They leave the room, sit down in the waiting room. Jeffrey knows that the doctor and nurses came inside because they are concerned about her heart rhythm. He returns to the waiting room, and Uncle Frank and Aunt Lucy tell him they have to get home. A few seconds after they leave a voice rings out over the intercom, "Code Blue, CCU, Code Blue, CCU." Footsteps of doctors and nurses fill the hall, and Jeffrey there is a sound of a wheeled cart being pulled. There are several patients in the coronary care unit – but as the footsteps fade in the hall, Jeffrey knows that they are going the direction of Kathy's room. *Let it be the patient in the room next to hers*, Jeffrey thinks, but then feels guilty about wishing harm on another person. *But it's Kathy – so to Hell with it*. He'll be selfish and hope the Code Blue is for someone other than Kathy. It's not as if Jeffrey wants the Code Blue patient to die if it's not Kathy.

The Smithson's crane their necks to hear better. Jeffrey's heart and stomach are telling him more information than his brain, and he excuses himself and peeks down the hall. *Oh God, it is Kathy's room*, he thinks as two nurses run inside. Now the hall is empty – they must be all helping with the code. Jeffrey steps quietly but quickly to Kathy's room, cracks the door, and peeks inside. The doctor is reaching down inside Kathy's chest. His palms seems to be squeezing something rhythmically.

The truth strikes Jeffrey like a drumstick striking bass drum – Kathy's heart has stopped, and the doctor is trying to squeeze life into it. Jeffrey feels faint, backs away from the door, and hides in a corner of the room behind an unused cart. He looks at the clock on the wall. 3:45. Another doctor arrives, and offers advice on drugs to give Kathy.

Jeffrey realizes that the Smithsons will worry if he does not return, but he cannot to be concerned with that risk when Kathy is...*Christ, when Kathy is dying*. 4:00. He hears a door open and slam in the distance and is afraid that Mr. Smithson is going to check out what is going on. Thank God a nurse is not in the hall.

4:30. Doctors and nurses leave the room, their heads down. Jeffrey struggles to keep from passing out. One nurse cries. The doctor walks into the waiting room. Jeffrey has to see Kathy. "Nurse, you can go for now," a doctor says. "I'll get the family first, and then we can sew her up and send the body to the morgue." The nurse leaves.

Jeffrey thinks that if Kathy's heart would not beat when the doctor squeezed it, surely it will beat for her beloved. It has to. With as much stealth as he can manage he walks over to Kathy's body. He knows time is limited. Kathy's parents will take a few moments to absorb the shock of the news, and that will suffice to keep them out of the room for a short time.

Jeffrey has to bring her to life. God would make that happen. It is fitting for a God of love to let Kathy's beloved save her. Jeffrey pulls down the sheet, sees her small heart lying still and silent inside her chest.

He starts to squeeze it with his palms. He says, "Kathy, it's me, Jeffrey. I love you. You will come back for me, won't you? Remember how you shared your heart with me so many times. Please come back. God, you will let her come back. You love Kathy. You see how good and loving she is. She can do so much for You. Use my touch to move her heart."

He squeezes, prays. Nothing. He hears footsteps and looks for a place to hide. *Crap*. He can't make it to the corner in time. The footsteps draw closer. The door cracks. They will find him. At the last second he spots a cabinet barely big enough to let a person in, opens the door, and squeezes himself inside. He failed Kathy. His hand touched her heart and could not return life to her. *God did not help either. The world means nothing now. A good God would have allowed Kathy to live. He would have let her one true love's touch restore life to her heart. God failed*. Jeffrey failed. Jeffrey hates God. He hates himself.

The Smithson's, a doctor, and a nurse enter Kathy's room. Everyone is crying except the doctor, who paces, looking uncomfortable. Then he stares straight at the cabinet where Jeffrey is hiding, quickly walks over, and opens it. "What the Hell are you doing in here?"

Jeffrey's breaths come in short gasps. "Had to...try and save her...squeeze her heart...like you did. Thought she would live...for me."

The Smithson's stare at Jeffrey. The doctor checks the body, says, "No harm done." He turns to Jeffrey and says, "It's touching in a way, but son, you need counseling." He turns to one of the nurses and says, "Ms. Donaldson, will you walk this young man to the chaplain's office and have them talk?"

"I'll counsel him," Mr. Smithson says. "Jeffrey, you get the Hell out of our lives." Mrs. Smithson puts her hand on his arm and tries to speak, but he pushes it away. "You sick fuck. Desecrating my daughter's body after she dies. I ought to press charges. I will if I see you again. Get that pervert out of here!"

Jeffrey pushes past Ms. Donaldson and runs out of the room and into the waiting room just as Uncle Lawton comes in. Jeffrey runs into him, and he pushes Jeffrey back with his hands.

"Whoa, boy. Where do you think you're going? What's wrong?" Jeffrey takes Uncle Lawton's hand and leads him out the other end of the waiting room into a hall. Waving his arms so much that Uncle Lawton has to stand back a few feet, he explains what happened. "I'm sorry. Lord, I didn't expect this. All that hope…I understand why you did what you did. I understand how Mr. Smithson could be upset in his grief. But nobody, no matter how badly he feels, has the right to hurt you that way. Wait here."

Uncle Lawton returns to the waiting room. A few minutes pass. Jeffrey smells tension, its stench rising like the scent of a demon's claw. Shouting comes from the waiting room, then screaming. The door pops open. Uncle Lawton and Mr. Smithson fly through the door, entangled, fists throwing ineffective punches against one another. Uncle Frank is cursing while trying to separate the men. The pile collapses to the floor. Two burly security guards run down the hall, and Jeffrey leaps aside to keep from getting run over. Then he sees something that chills him to the bone. The demon is between Uncle Lawton and Mr. Smithson, now whispering into Uncle Lawton's ear, now into Mr. Smithson's. It turns its head to Jeffrey with that terrible smile. It widens the smile into a rictus, and Jeffrey swoons. He shuts his eyes tightly, then opens them. The demon is gone. One security guard pulls Uncle Lawton back, the other Mr. Smithson. Uncle Frank staggers back, striking the wall. "You talk to my nephew that way again, and I'll beat the Hell out of you," Uncle Lawton says.

Mr. Smithson reciprocates. "You come after me again, and your ass will lay on the ground by itself after I beat it off your body." Uncle Frank chimes in — "And stay the hell off my property!"

The guard holding Mr. Smithson, a large, middle-aged man with blond hair and bulging muscles, says, "We're escorting all of you out of the hospital and to your respective vehicles. Any trouble, and we'll press charges."

He turns to Jeffrey, points to Uncle Lawton, and speaks gently. "Young man, this your uncle?"

Jeffrey nods. "Okay, come with us, and we'll get you two on the road."

CHAPTER 22
MORE JOY IN AZATHOTH'S REALM

The Antibeing rubs its head with a tentacle, feeling cocky. It says out loud, *You blew it this time, Enemy. Killing poor little Jeffrey's girlfriend. He'll know how sadistic you are, and I will seem so kind, so loving, compared to you. All the pain and suffering in your world - I wonder why you haven't joined me. Surely you know my universe. Don't your philosophers claim you know all possible universes? Maybe they're wrong. Maybe you're a wimpy god. A child god or a sick, senile god, like your old nemesis David Hume said. You won't join me though, stubborn fool. You still insist you're good. I am beyond good and evil. I am greater than der Übermench, greater than your failed creation, the Day Star, greater than you, O Enemy. Soon Jeffrey will belong to me, and I will give him the reward his puny kind deserves after he destroys himself. Then I will stab my tentacles into your face, you weak, skinny young god.*

Zeke and Andy try many times to call Jeffrey or stop by to see him, but he refuses to respond. Granny threatens Jeffrey, and Aunt Jenny and Uncle Lawton lecture him. Jeffrey says he does not want to talk to anyone "who defends that bastard." When Zeke and Andy tell Granny that Jeffrey means "God"

when he refers to "that bastard," she does not believe them and bans them from calling or visiting.

"We've got to help Jeffrey," Andy says. "If we can't and he kills himself, Lord knows how much power that thing will have. God forbid there are others like him."

"There are," Zeke says.

Andy coughs, wheezes, takes a swig of Nehi Grape, and asks, "You sure?"

"I'm sure."

"Shit!" Andy says and turns red. "That's the first time I've said a swear word in years. God forgive me."

"We may both be saying those words a lot more before this is over. I wish I knew how the Bible I gave Jeffrey can help."

"Maybe that's for him to find out. We have to be patient."

"Yeah. Patient as Job."

CHAPTER 23
THE HERETIC

Jeffrey gently lays the journal on the bed in Aunt Jenny's house as if it were as precious as his beloved. He cries openly into the pillow until the pillowcase on one side is wet. His head hurts, but just as the pain becomes unbearable, he stops crying, closes his eyes, allows them to rest. The pain eases. He takes an ibuprofen, and when the pain disappears totally, he picks up the journal and holds it.

The Smithsons never forgave him or Uncle Lawton. Jeffrey is not surprised, and he has not seen them since that long-ago time at St. Thomas Hospital. Twenty years later he learned that they moved back to McNairy County.

Jeffrey did not need a journal to remind him of his relationship with Kathy, but now his emotions are raw once more. *God, you sonofabitch*, Jeffrey thinks, feeling a flush of anger fill his face and clinching his fists. *You stole Kathy when it seemed she would be fine*. "You bastard," he says out loud. "I bet you became incarnate in Christ so you could have a body and whack off at the suffering in the world, especially the suffering of children."

He lies down and cries again, and his headache returns despite the ibuprofen. *Why did I decide to read that damn journal?* Something is making him do this, a force Jeffrey cannot control. *If it is the demon*, Jeffrey thinks, *that may be okay*. The demon now seems infinitely cooler (he laughs at the irony) than God.

Of course the Smithsons do not allow Jeffrey to attend Kathy's visitation or funeral. It is held in McNairy County, a three hour drive, but Uncle Frank or Aunt Jenny - and even Uncle Lawton - would have been happy to take him if the Smithsons had permitted, though they would have to keep his distance from Mr. Smithson.

The night after Kathy died, Jeffrey lies in bed, his mind focused on memories of Kathy, his pillow already soaked with tears. He wipes his eyes as more tears flow, and when he opens them, he stares into the face of the demon, now in his humanoid body. Jeffrey asks the demon if it would cool its claws so he can shake one. The rictus-smile grows wider, stretching its face so much it appears to be turned inside out. "Why yessssss," the demon says, and Jeffrey shakes its paw, which is cool to the touch. Jeffrey says, "We have a common enemy now. I'm on your side. Tell me what I can do to fight God."

The demon's smile now fills its face, like the mouth the serial killer John Wayne Gacy would later paint on his clown face. "I know just the thing," the demon says.

At Sunday school Brother Noland allows Jeffrey to attend the adult class he teaches since Jeffrey still goes to the preaching school. The class is studying the passage in the Gospels about the so-called *Limited Commission*, when Jesus sent his disciples out the first time, before his resurrection, and told them to teach and heal. Jeffrey raises his hand to ask a question.

"Yes, Jeffrey?" Brother Noland says.

"I'm wondering about something. In the story of the Limited Commission in Matthew 10, in verse 10, Jesus is telling the disciples what not to bring with them – he says, "No scrip for your journey, neither two coats, neither shoes, nor yet staves, for the workman is worthy of his meat." Jesus says something similar in Luke. But in Mark chapter 6, verse 8, Mark says that Jesus "commanded them that they should take nothing for their journey, save a staff only; no scrip, no bread, no money in their purse." Then in verse 9: "But be shod with sandals, and not put on two coats." Now why in Matthew does it say the disciples were not to take a staff or wear shoes, while in Mark they are told to take a staff and wear shoes?"

There is a young couple there he has not seen before. *They must be visitors*, Jeffrey thinks. Since they both wear wedding rings, Jeffrey assumes they are husband and wife. When Jeffrey read the passages that contradicted one another, the woman said, "No, no," and pointed to her Bible, looking at the man next to her with panic.

Jeffrey assumes Brother Noland will have some explanation, but instead he says, "Why did you bring up something like this, Jeffrey? Are you questioning God's word?"

"No, Brother Noland, but I want an answer to my question."

"Get out of my class."

Jeffrey raises his voice. "What are you afraid of, Noland! Afraid of the truth? That's what scares you ignorant hicks. Your God is a joke. He isn't real. When you die you'll rot, and your dead loves ones are rancid by now. You might as well eat, drink and be merry."

Aunt Jenny's mouth is wide open as her gaze locks on his face. She follows him out, as does Uncle Lawton and Granny, and Jeffrey opens the outside door and steps on the porch.

Uncle Lawton grabs Jeffrey by the arm and says, "If you were younger, I'd tan your hide."

"You had no business actin' the way you did," Granny says.

Aunt Jenny's is the third voice that chimed in. Tears stream down her cheeks, but she chokes a few words out. "I thought you were raised better than to question God's word. It's all those books you've been checking out at the library."

Uncle Lawton says, "Downstairs I found a book you've checked out called *The Java Ape Man*. I thumbed through it and it says that man came from a monkey."

"Oh, no," Aunt Jenny says. "Don't tell me you believe in evolution."

Granny laughs. "Man from a monkey. I think a monkey must have wrote that book. Jeffrey. What's gonna come of you. I ain't never heard the likes."

Uncle Lawton says, "I'm taking that book back to the library tomorrow and complaining."

"No!" Jeffrey says. "You'll embarrass me!"

Aunt Jenny says, "You should be the one embarrassed, reading lies like that. Scientists don't know everything even if they think they do. I'm ashamed of your behavior. You're getting back in that church for service."

"Please, no," Jeffrey says.

"Yes you are. You'll sit quiet, and then we're going home and we're going to see what books you're reading. From now on, we monitor which books you check out."

"That's wrong," Jeffrey says.

"What's wrong" Uncle Lawton says, "is that you've let the devil get into you and lead you away from the Bible. You upset that poor woman at church. What if she loses her faith and goes to Hell because of you? Wouldn't you feel bad? Don't try to answer me, don't say a word – you ain't got a lick of sense now. Stubborn teenager. Now you're going to sit through the service whether you like it or not."

When Jeffrey sits on the cushioned pew, he wants to lie down and stuff his face into the cushion, an ostrich hiding from the hostile eyes glaring at him. He knows if he closes his eyes, Aunt Jenny will slap his leg, and he has suffered enough embarrassment today. Too often someone turns a head and stares at him, the face red, the mouth twisted and cruel. Jeffrey tries to keep from crying – but he is not sad as much as mad. When Brother Noland walks up to the pulpit to deliver the sermon, Jeffrey imagines beating him in the face until it is black with bruises. Then he realizes the thought is childish, and he stares outside the window at the squirrels playing in the trees. He does not want to think about Sunday dinner. He doubts he will be able to keep any food down or talk cheerfully to any relatives today. Somehow he survives the day on emotional fumes and makes it to bed.

He sleeps late the next morning, and when he wakes up after nine, he glances at the pile of library books on his desk. Half of them are gone. These are mainly books on dinosaurs and on evolution, but there is another book, *How the Bible Came to Us*, that is also missing. Uncle Lawton must have stopped by before he went to work at a little gas station near Randallsville.

Jeffrey thinks that God is now behaving worse than before. *He must really hate me*. He is dividing Jeffrey from the people he loves the most through the ignorant fundamentalist religion God made to fool people and to keep them from progressing. God goes against science to make sure people are ignorant – and sick. God murdered Kathy in cold blood. If Jeffrey is going to be damned by this God and see the demon for eternity, then by God he will make damned sure of it.

"Hey motherfucker," Jeffrey says out loud. "That means you, God. The means you, Father. You, too, Son. You as well Holy Ghost, Holy Spook, Holy Shitface." He starts to laugh. "Holy Ghost. What a dumb assed name. The Holy Spook!"

Jeffrey stands up and begins to dance around the room. He knows Granny might hear him, but he no longer cares. He waves his arms in the air, saying, "Holy Wimp, Holy Coward, Holy Torturer, Holy Murderer of Girls. Holy Asshead. Yeah. I bet you have an Ass's head. Eee-aww, eee-ahh, eee-ahh. What a stupid donkey voice you have."

Jeffrey jumps on the bed, bounces around, jumps in a circle over and over around the bed. God might fry him, but he will fuck God over with words first.

Jeffrey stops when he finds the pink heart stone on the bed. He remembers what Kathy said – that whatever happens he must not hate God. He holds the stone to his heart and sobs. “God,” he says. “Forgive, forgive. Please don’t let me be evil. I have to see Kathy one day.” That silly song from the sixties comes into his head about the boy who lost his girlfriend in a train accident having to be good so he’ll see her again in Heaven. Yet Jeffrey has been doing his best to make sure he will go straight to Hell.

Jeffrey sighs to himself, says, “Whew,” and puts the journal down on the bed. *I haven’t learned much since then*, he thinks. He still throws temper tantrums at God. Although he may not curse the Holy Spirit the way he did as a teenager, God still gets an earful. Jeffrey feels heat rise to his face and says quietly to himself, “Goodness, Lord, how the Hell did you expect me to act?” He had been a lonely teenager, an Asperger’s nerd and not knowing why he was different. He never imagined he would have a relationship with a girl, but he found someone who might have been the love of his life. *You took her, God*, he thinks. Jeffrey is still pissed about that. *I know*, he thinks, *I should be grateful for Lisa. She is good beyond measure and puts me to shame. Yet I wonder - in the midnight dark when sleep seems far away and memories flood my mind - what would have happened if Kathy had lived.*

If there is a Heaven, Jeffrey cannot imagine going there given his tantrums against God, his utter hatred of his Creator. Putting him in the presence of God would be like baking soda meeting hydrochloric acid – Jeffrey would bubble away into steam, leaving nothing behind but a residue to fall away from God and into Hell. There are times Jeffrey prays that everyone will be saved – but there’s that damn free will thing. Jeffrey’s free will is telling him that if he were to meet God he might just tell him to fuck off and return his ticket to Heaven like Ivan Karamazov said he would do in Dostoevsky’s *The Brothers Karamazov*. Jeffrey rubs his aching eyes – they must be so bloodshot that he looks like an alien. He picks up the journal, returning to the passage about the night of his worst tantrum against God.

That night Jeffrey almost dies. As he writes this passage in his journal, he chills thinking of how close he has come either to Hell or to annihilation. He cried himself to sleep, his hand clutching the pink stone heart against his. Sometime during the night he dropped the stone on the floor. Thankfully Granny found it later while sweeping.

Jeffrey awakens, and his chest feels as if something is squeezing the air from his lungs. He struggles to breathe. No air gets in. He opens his eyes to a death's head staring at him, mounted on a python wrapped around his chest, tightening its deadly clamp. Jeffrey cannot speak, cannot scream. A long, thin tongue slithers from the skull-mouth and licks his face. His heart races and he feels its hard beats against the serpent's scales. The beats suddenly slow, and the death's head fades into an image of flames. In the flames stands a tentacled being, not the demon that haunts him but something worse, with a head that is more mouth than anything else. The creature has no lips, but the mouth turns itself upward a complete half circle smile. Long, yellow, sharp teeth fill the mouth, and a tentacle reaches out to take him. He fades and feels himself fall and strike the cool floor. Someone's footsteps echo as if on a drum, and the silhouette of a person stands above him, then stoops down. Granny's voice. Thank God. "Jeffrey! Lordy, Lordy!" The steps become distant. The last thing he hears is Granny's voice yelling on the phone. She is talking to Aunt Jenny. "Jenny, something's wrong with Jeffrey. He's all blue and his chest is caved in. You heard what I said. I don't know how to call the ambulance. Call them and get down here." Dark spots flash in front of Jeffrey. Then everything goes black.

Jeffrey awakens in a hospital room, shirtless and hooked up to a heart monitor. An IV needle is stuck in his arm, and he feels a mixture of itch and pain. Something is in his penis, and it aches so much he thinks about pulling it out but knows that will only hurt more. Later he hears someone call it a catheter. He fixes a stare on the heart monitor. As far as he can tell, the rhythm is regular. A nurse walks in. "You're awake! I'll get the doctor."

His eyes close, and when he opens them a blond woman in her thirties stands over him. "I'm Dr. Gervais," she says. His eyes widen. Jeffrey has not seen many woman doctors except actors playing them on TV. She is pretty, too, so he does not mind at all when she places her stethoscope over his heart. "Sounds good. How are you feeling? Any trouble breathing."

"I don't like this stuff in me, especially that thing down...down there." Dr. Gervais smiles. "I don't blame you. I'll tell the nurse to take that out. The needle in your arm stays. We need to put medicine in you."

"No trouble breathing now," he says. "Last night..."

"You had a rough night, but you're okay now."

"Do you know why this happened?"

"No. Did you fight with anyone at school? You have bruises around your chest and back in a circular pattern."

Jeffrey chills, and she pulls the sheet to cover his chest. "No fights at school," he says.

Jeffrey ponders what to say next. If he says that a demon attacked him, Dr. Gervais would have him committed to Central State. Uncle Lawton once called it an animal hospital, and that's the last thing Jeffrey needs. But animals do get through the door unnoticed – and people keep pet snakes, even big ones.

"It was a big snake. It squeezed me. I pushed and pushed. I found a knife and cut it a little and it crawled off."

"Oh my goodness. People sometimes keep pythons as pets and they get away. I'll tell your grandmother. She needs to call an exterminator to check that out. There's something else that bothers me, too. There are burn marks on your skin. Has anyone at home or at school ever..."

"No," Jeffrey says quickly. "Granny is good to me, and so are my other relatives. Sometimes people pick on me at school but not that way."

"It's okay. I'm trying to figure all this out. Are you sure that bullies at school didn't do this to you?"

"They used to hit me. But their ring leader was killed in a train wreck."

"Was that the boy killed at the crossing last year?"

"Yes."

"That had to be traumatic for you, too, even though the boy killed was a bully. This is a tough case. The snake may be part of the puzzle. I hope I can figure out the rest so I can help you get better and not make another trip here. I'm sure you'd like to avoid that."

"Yes, ma'am. I'd like to figure all this out, too."

Jeffrey throws the journal down and falls back to the bed. He is not tired any more. His mind rebels at what he has read. Was the person who wrote all this down really him? If that were him, what the Hell had gone on? Aunt Jenny had told him that he was in the hospital real sick about that time, but she said he had an asthma attack. Asthma is chronic, right? Yet he never had an *asthma attack* since then.

Jeffrey is a member of the Rhine Research Center in Durham, just north of where he teaches religion at Southeastern North Carolina University. They study psi, which refers to ESP and psychokinesis. ESP includes telepathy in which there is direct mind-to-mind communication, and clairvoyance, or remote viewing, when a person can get direct information from the environment without reading someone's mind. Psychokinesis is mind moving matter. The latter is what may have happened to him. Maybe whatever guilt he felt for cursing the Holy Spirit, guilt that was stronger after he remembered what Kathy had said, caused his mind to temporarily break and caused his chest to constrict. His mind could also have caused the burns. The Death's Head demon could have been his fear of death coming to life, and the demon in Hell and the flames could have been the reflection of his fear of Hell – *or else a damn demon could have appeared in the form of a snake and squeezed me half to death.*

CHAPTER 24
THE CHURCH SPLIT

Another year passes, and Jeffrey moves from eighth to ninth grade, to his freshman year in high school, although he spends it in the junior high school building. The Morhollow High School building only has room for three grades, ten through twelve. The classes count for credits now. In the outside world, President Nixon moves from triumph, when the Vietnam POWs arrive home, to the shame of Watergate. For Jeffrey, the change in Washington is not good since for him change of any kind is traumatic. He has watched the news from fifth grade onward, and it often affected his mood.

At Jeffrey's home, things are pretty much the same. He apologizes to Brother Noland and to the entire church in January. Soon, however, he will be pulled into a situation at church that is one of those turning points in life he will look back upon later – when his church divided into two hostile factions and a split occurred. He is warned about it before it happens.

One day he is walking in the field that borders the back yard. On power lines stand hundreds, maybe thousands, of starlings. That is strange since they usually do that in late fall before flying south. Then a flock of birds flies at full speed toward

Jeffrey. *Oh shit,* he thinks. *Now I am a character in a Hitchcock movie.*

The birds, however, began to coalesce into a figure. *Here we go again,* Jeffrey thinks. *This supernatural stuff is getting old.* This time a humanoid figure with a bird's head appears. *What a surprise,* Jeffrey thinks. "Okay, what do you have to tell me?" Jeffrey asks.

"Beware of Mrs. Massey," the bird croaks. "She is evil and she divides." The bird figure disperses into a flock of starlings that fade into the air.

The Masseys started attending Harrell's Corner a month before. Mr. Massey is a retired grocer from Jackson, and Mrs. Massey is known for her charm. She writes letters to missionaries the church supported. She visits sick church members. When Jeffrey received an award for being one of the students who scored highest in the PSAT, Mrs. Massey congratulated him, patting him on the head so much he was tempted to slap her face.

Jeffrey saw through her right away. Sometimes it takes younger folks to see through a phony. He knew from the start that she is up to something. *So, Bird Man, or whatever it was who warned him, told the truth. She must be up to mischief.* Jeffrey will keep an eye on her.

Brother Miller, Brother Noland and Brother McRae are the elders, which in the Church of Christ means they are the official leaders of the church. Brother Noland is offered a job at a church in Crossville, so the Harrell's Corner Church of Christ is in the middle of searching for another preacher. Mrs. Massey is more charming than ever, and Jeffrey figures she is playing for favor so she can gain support for some evil deed.

Jeffrey listens in on conversations at church. Mrs. Massey (Jeffrey never dignified her with the usual term for female church members, *Sister Massey*) begins to say things like, "I know Brother Miller is a good man and a good elder, but isn't he a bit strict at times? He told his son-in-law to cut his hair shorter." Or, "Brother McRae is such a wonderful man, but my husband tells me he's not as careful with the church's finances as he ought to be."

Jeffrey tries to warn Brother Miller, but he tells Jeffrey it is wrong to gossip. Brother McRae is concerned at Jeffrey's words and says he will keep what Jeffrey said in mind. Jeffrey has a long talk with Jimmy, Brother Miller's grandson, who also realizes that Mrs. Massey is after power and is trying to get the church members to force the elders out so her husband can take power. She will be the real power in that arrangement.

One day Uncle Lawton tells Jeffrey there will be a special meeting at the church the following Tuesday night. Technically Jeffrey could come as a baptized member, but in practice teenagers like Jimmy and Jeffrey are not supposed to come to business meetings. Jeffrey stays home with Granny. After the meeting, Uncle Lawton and Aunt Jenny stop by. Uncle Lawton is red-faced. Jeffrey knows for him to be that mad something bad was going on since he rarely loses his temper (unless Jeffrey makes a scene in Sunday school class). "There's a group that wants to abolish the eldership," he says.

"It's Mrs. Massey!" Jeffrey says. "She's been planning this. Only Brother McRae believed me."

"You're right," Uncle Lawton says.

"What in tarnation can we do?" Granny asks.

"Talk to as many people as possible. There will be a vote two Sundays from now. Millicent Massey has stirred up a group of members – not all bad folks – but misled, and formal charges against the elders will be read."

The following Saturday Jeffrey calls Jimmy and says he is coming over. They agree to split a twenty mile bike ride in the middle, and they meet at a grove of trees on Hangman's Road. "Grandpa's about to have a heart attack over this," Jimmy says. "If the vote goes against him, I don't know what will happen."

"You know we have votes since we're baptized. His cousins are on the other side, but I'll talk to as many people in the middle of this as I can and you do, too."

"What if the vote goes the wrong way?"

"We'll all have to find another church."

The Sunday of the vote arrives, and Brother Milque reads the charges – that the elders never visited the sick, that they misappropriated finances, that they were inappropriate in hugging women. The last charge was so silly that Jeffrey laughed out loud. Millicent of the high-and-mighty-name said, "Brother Jeffrey is disrespectful. Perhaps we should remove him from this meeting. I heard about what he said in Sunday school one day. I don't think he even believes in God. Why should he have a vote?"

Even Brother Milque chaffed at that. "It's okay, Sister. Brother Jeffrey apologized to Brother Noland and to the entire church in public. If he, at his young age, can do that, I have no problem with him voting."

"I respectfully rescind my request," she says.

Respectfully my ass, Jeffrey thinks. He hopes that he and Jimmy convinced enough people to keep the elders, but when the votes are counted, the result is 22-12 in favor of removing the elders. Later that week, Jimmy calls Jeffrey to say that Brother Miller had a heart attack. Jeffrey phones Aunt Jenny, and she and Uncle Lawton take him and Granny to the hospital. By the time they arrive Brother Miller is dead.

Jeffrey cries, as do Granny and Aunt Jenny. Even Uncle Lawton is upset since he stays silent and does not crack a joke to relieve the tension. Jimmy cries loudly in the hall. *This cannot pass,* Jeffrey thinks. *Mrs. Massey cannot get away with murder*.

The following week Jeffrey meets Jimmy at the grove on Hangman's Road. "She has to pay," Jimmy says.

"I agree," Jeffrey says. "We have to hurt her without her knowing it's us. Not kill her, but scare her half to death."

"How?"

"Leave that to me."

Jeffrey rides his bike home, finds a bag that fits on his bicycle handlebars, and fills it with two pairs of gloves, rope, an old rusty knife, a mallet he found in Granddaddy's old garage and two old Halloween masks he found upstairs in a closet. He also put his stethoscope in the bag and a couple of plastic bags used to hold vegetable and fruit fragments to be discarded. He takes the bag upstairs and waits.

It is Saturday morning. They meet at Hangman's Road and ride their bikes to the woods behind Sharon Lane. They pull their bikes into the woods and Jeffrey takes the bag. "Remember the plan." Jimmy nods and smiles for the first time, Jeffrey notices, since his grandpa's funeral.

They emerge from the woods into a cornfield on the Massey property. It ends about thirty feet from their house, a boring two-story brick monstrosity that seems out of place in the country. They walk through corn that is taller than they and reach the border to the back yard. They crawl on the ground to the garage. The door is open and they stealth their way in. Mr. Massey has a part-time job on the old airbase property as a security guard. *Just like Millicent to make her husband work after retirement*, Jeffrey thinks, and feels a surge of hatred for the greedy hag. The boys smile when they see Mr. Massey's car missing. Mrs. Massey's Cadillac remains in the garage. They hear stirring inside and footsteps moving toward the garage door. "Masks and gloves on," Jeffrey whispers. He dons a clown mask and Jimmy slips a skull mask over his face. They put on their gloves. The masks barely cover their faces, but if they are lucky Mrs. Massey will not notice. Jeffrey stands behind the door as Mrs. Massey walks out. He has to take care given the mallet's weight, but he strikes her, he thinks gently, on the side of her head. She crumbles onto the floor, out cold.

"You didn't kill her, did you?" Jimmy asks. Jeffrey checks, and she is breathing. He puts the stethoscope over her chest, and although fat muffles the sound, her heartbeat is regular. "Tie her up," Jeffrey says, and Jimmy wraps the rope around her body, leaving only her chest uncovered so she can breathe. He gags her with a piece of cloth, then takes out the two bags, a main bag and a backup. They wait.

Mrs. Massey stirs and opens her eyes. She moans and tries to speak. Jeffrey tries to understand the words, but all he can sense is her hostile tone. He makes his voice as deep as possible and is proud of the result. He takes the most solemn tone he can. "Mrs. Millicent Massey," Jeffrey says. "We want you to leave Harrell's Corner Church of Christ." She shakes her head, and Jimmy holds it still.

"You will leave," Jimmy says, imitating Jeffrey's solemn tone, "or you will surely die." Jimmy puts the bag over her head and makes sure it is sealed. She struggles like a snake and twists her head, but Jeffrey helps Jimmy hold it tight. After a couple of minutes she passes out, and Jeffrey removes the bag and quickly checks her heart. It is beating rapidly and her breathing is deep and fast. She stirs.

Jeffrey speaks again. "If you do not leave Harrell's Corner, you will die. If you tell anyone about this, you will die. You may die anyway. We may come by one night when you least expect it, long after any police investigation is finished, and find a more creative and painful way to kill you. We know how to haunt your dreams." Jeffrey turns his head slowly, trying to twist it in an odd way like a monster in a horror movie. The skull mask touches her face. She struggles more. He puts his tongue through a hole in the mask and licks her lips. *That is gross but it is a good twist.*

"We have guns, too. If Mr. Massey comes and tries to stop us we will kill him. He must never become an elder at Harrell's Corner. If he does we will kill you both. Understand?"

She nods her head.

"We're going to leave you now. Remember – one word of this to anyone and you will die. We're taking some money from your purse to make this look like a robbery. Make up a description that doesn't match us. Understand?"

She nods her head again. Jimmy opens her purse and finds $100.00 in cash. The boys leave as they hear a car approaching in the drive. They slither back to the cornfield and reach their bicycles. Jimmy puts the bag on the handlebars just as they hear Mrs. Massey's voice. "They went that-a-way!"

"Lying bitch," Jeffrey mutters. "Let's go," he says in a low voice, and they take off down the road. Mrs. Massey probably thinks they have a getaway car, and it will take time for sheriff's deputies to arrive. They watch for a deputy, but none appears, and they make two turns and ride twelve miles before they separate.

They get more lucky because the very day *Brother* Massey was made an elder at Harrell's Corners, a real robber broke into the Massey residence. Mrs. Massey surprised him – but he surprised her, too, and she fell down dead of a heart attack. *All that fat*, Jeffrey thinks. Mr. Massey, grief-stricken, resigned as an elder and moved to Alabama. Less than a year later he died of pancreatic cancer. Since the crowd Mrs. Massey controlled still runs Harrell's Corners, Jeffrey and his family cannot attend there – but Jimmy has his revenge. Jeffrey is glad to have helped him achieve it.

Whew! Jeffrey thinks, putting the journal back down and checking the clock on the table – 2:30 a.m. He does not remember harassing Mrs. Massey. *Was I really that mean?* Yet the more he thinks about it the more he thinks Millicent Massey deserved what she got. His mind turns to Agatha Christie's last Hercule Poirot novel in which it is discovered after Mr. Poirot's death from a heart attack that he had murdered an agitator. *Agitators who harm for sheer spite do not deserve to live*. Maybe it wasn't his call – but he and Jimmy were not the ones who killed *Sister* Massey. The only thing that affected her was fear, and in the end it was fear that stopped her fat-lined heart. Jeffrey realizes he is rationalizing. Revenge remains, as the saying goes, a dish best served...cold. *Perhaps served hot for Mrs. Massey in Hell*, Jeffrey thinks, and he congratulates himself on his cleverness. He smiles as he starts to read again.

Jeffrey assumes the demon will appear to him after Mrs. Massey's death, but that does not happen. Perhaps it is because he never feels guilty about what he and Jimmy did. Regarding the unpardonable sin, he can handle that obsession during spring, summer, and fall – but winters, those cold depressing days after Christmas and into February, when it gets dark at five and his body prematurely tires – those are the times the cursed mantra returns. Sunday evening services at church are the worst times.

The Sunday after Harrell's Corner split, Jeffrey sits with Granny, Aunt Jenny and Uncle Lawton at the Farris Road church for the 6 p.m. service. The song leader chooses *Sweet Hour of Prayer*. Now that's a pretty old gospel song, but when the congregation drags it, it sounds sad and depressing. The song begins:

Sweet hour of prayer,
Sweet hour of prayer
That calls me from a world of care
And bids me at his Father's throne
Make all my wants and wishes known.

Jeffrey's mind races as the congregation drags the hymn slower and slower. *Damn fool devil,* the mantra begins. *Not again*, Jeffrey thinks, and his stomach sinks. *The Holy Ghost is good. The Holy Ghost is good, the devil is bad.*

In seasons of distress and grief
My soul has often found relief
And oft escaped the tempter's snare
"Damn fool Holy Ghost."
At thy return, Sweet Hour of Prayer.

Jeffrey does not remember the rest of the service. When he arrives home, he walks in circles around the house. The lights inside are bright and warm, but all he feels is the chill of winter air and icy wind slicing his face. What remained of God's grace is gone. He is damned.

Two months pass and his mood brightens with the lengthening days. Late in March Jeffrey is at another Sunday evening service at Farris Road. Brother Doty had promised him that he would preach a sermon on the blasphemy against the Holy Ghost. Jeffrey informed Brother Doty of his fears and about the radio sermon that had reawakened them. Brother Doty tells Jeffrey not to worry and to listen to his Sunday evening sermon.

Brother Doty's view is the same as Brother Lowe's, which is a relief. Then he says, "In the religious world today there are ignorant preachers who harm others with toxic religion. They seem to take delight in frightening Christians into an obsessive fear of Hell, and they use the unpardonable sin as a sadistic instrument of torture. One preacher said that he had never heard a curse as bad as blaspheming the Holy Ghost. How many people listening to that sermon, especially young people with undeveloped emotions, allowed their mind to play tricks and said or thought curse words about the Holy Spirit? Then they falsely think they are damned. The unpardonable sin cannot – cannot – be committed by anyone who wonders if he has committed it."

Jeffrey's body relaxes. He knows, and does not doubt from that point on that he has a chance – slight as it may be - to avoid damnation. Hope becomes a balm that cures the wound that has tormented him since that summer of his eleventh year. He still fears Hell, thinks he is too reprobate to enter Heaven, but the sliver of hope builds a home in the back of his mind. When Jeffrey gets home that night he walks around the gravel drive to the scent of spring flowers and the cool of early evening. His legs do not want to stop moving. It is as if his legs themselves are laughing – and sighing – with relief.

CHAPTER 25
A NEW STRATEGY

The Antibeing turns Its mouth downward, twisting it like the mask of Tragedy in a Greek play. Its tentacles flop down as if It is depressed. *Damn preacher, undoing so much of my work.* It wants to swipe that preacher with its tentacles, but figures It can feed enough from killing Zeke. *The preacher – Hell, he's not worth the trouble.*

There is more than one way to skin a human – especially a male. Thank you, Enemy, for giving males a second, smaller brain that can so easily take over from the main brain. An illicit affair - why didn't I think of that before? Jeffrey needs to experience a married woman. His...English teacher. Young. Pretty. Sexually frustrated at home. Itching for more. If only, the Antibeing thinks, *I can influence her to tempt the right boy. If Jeffrey is the hero... who saves her life.* Risky – but It will try out that plan. It is so chaotic it is bound to work.

Zeke awakens with a sudden surge of relief that provokes a sigh. That is followed by an uneasy feeling. A trim, fit blond woman in her mid-twenties appears in the room along with Jeffrey. She and Jeffrey embrace, and they kiss. "No, Jeffrey," Zeke says aloud. "Especially not with a married woman. You're a child, too. Underage."

Zeke tries to get out of bed, but his sixth sense tells him not to interfere, that sometimes permitting an evil can help lead to a greater good.

CHAPTER 26

THE TEACHER

Sex is nice but it can sure get a man – and a woman – into a Hell of a lot of trouble. Mrs. Caroline Davis is Jeffrey's ninth grade English teacher. Unlike many high school teachers, she is a true intellectual and writer who has published articles in scholarly journals and poems and stories in literary journals. Jeffrey knows this because she becomes his first lover. Not his first love – but his first *sexual* lover.

Love is the most distant thing on his mind the first day in her class. She towers over the class and says, "You will speak only when I acknowledge you. If you show me you are not taking this class seriously, you will be removed from class. If you talk to your classmates after the bell rings, you will be removed from class. I expect an orderly class, and I will not tolerate anything less."

When the bell rings at the end of class, sixth period, the last class of the day, Jeffrey is happy to leave to catch the school bus. Ronnie Morton stands in the hall. "What a hateful bitch," Jeffrey says. "Looks like a miserable year in English class."

"They do this to me every year," Ronnie says. "Put me in college-bound English class. I'm going to get out of this class. I'm talking to the principal right now." He laughs since he knows he will pull this off. Jeffrey, on the other hand, does not have the courage to try, and in any case he plans to attend college and needs a difficult class, even if it is with the bitch from Hell.

Jeffrey grows to enjoy her class. She takes them into stories such as Edgar Allen Poe's *The Fall of the House of Usher* and especially *The Tell-Tale Heart*. When she points to her own heart in the center of her chest on her slender but well-endowed body, Jeffrey's eyes pop out of his head. He does not know if she notices, but she asks him to talk with her for a moment after class.

"You seem to really enjoy Poe," she says.

"I like all horror stories. I like that feeling of being scared but not being in real danger."

"That's paradoxical about horror – you know, that you're scared but the story won't hurt you."

"It's a weird thing. It's like there's something erotic about it." He blushes. He did not think that would slip out.

Ms. Davis smiles. "You're right. Why are so many women victims in horror stories? I don't agree with critics who say it's sexist. I think it's a feeling that even some women get while reading. Our hearts beat faster, we imagine the woman threatened, her own heart pounding, the monster at her back. She should not turn around, she should keep running, but then..."

"That's how I feel about it."

"I'll run off some stories of mine for you to read. I have some horror stories published. They're not works of genius, but I think they'll scare you."

"Thank you," Jeffrey says, looking into her blue eyes, her blond hair glistening in the glow of florescent lights.

When Jeffrey gets home, Aunt Jenny is there, and she hands him the newspapers from the last few days. He likes to keep up with local and world events. In the current paper is an article announcing courses in CPR. Jeffrey watches *Emergency* on TV and sees how the paramedics use CPR to revive people, and the connection with his heart interest is obvious. He asks Aunt Jenny if she would take a class one Saturday with him. She says,

"I don't know if I can learn that, but it's something good to know."

The course takes place at an older building with fading wood siding at the college in Randallsville. On the floor are mannequins. Jeffrey's heart lurches when he notices that they are female – the teacher refers to them as *Resuci-Annies*. As the class continues, he picks up the methods so well that he teaches other students the right way to give rescue breaths and do chest compressions. The teacher tells him, "Young man, you are good at this. If you didn't have to be over eighteen, I'd recommend that you take an instructor class."

Aunt Jenny passes, barely, and with much aid from her helpful nephew. Jeffrey hopes he will never have to give CPR to a real person – not after squeezing Kathy's heart. This kind of CPR is on the outside of the body, but it would still remind him of Kathy's death. He thinks, though, that he will be much older before he will have to give CPR to anyone again – if ever.

Jeffrey reads one of Mrs. Davis' horror stories, *Ghost on a Midnight Road*. A man's car breaks down (of course!) and he sees a figure in the distance, a man who offers to help. The man offering the help gives the man with the bum car a ride and drops him off by the side of a filling station. He thanks the stranger, walks inside the store – but there is no store – only a concrete floor and pipes extending from the moonlit ground where a filling station had stood many years before.

The next day Jeffrey feels groggy from lack of sleep. He cannot stop thinking about the story. He figures the man in the bum car must be dead – maybe his car really wrecked and he was killed from the injuries. Who is this stranger? Is this Hell? Purgatory? The story makes him think, which he likes, but thinking is difficult and can keep a boy awake.

Jeffrey walks into English class a couple of minutes early and tells Mrs. Davis as he passes her, "Loved your story. I have some questions for you after class." She smiles, and he admires her deep red lips.

Thunder rolls in the distance and grows louder. Mrs. Davis speaks more loudly as she lectures on Shakespeare's *Julius Caesar*. Lightning flashes and thunder follows within two seconds. Jeffrey thinks they are safe inside even though he realizes that no one can be one hundred percent safe. Then his hair stands on end and he notices that other students' hair as well as Mrs. Davis' also stands straight. There is a bright flash, the odor of floor tile burning, and a crack of thunder that hurts his ears. He is grateful that his hearing is intact. He looks up to find Mrs. Davis sprawled on the floor, an ugly streak on her clothing from her shoulder to her waist. Two students are down but they sit up, dazed. A girl screams "I think she's dead."

Jeffrey points to Scott Miller who seems to be under control. "Scott – go to the office and have the secretary call 911." Scott runs out the door. Then Jeffrey reaches Mrs. Davis and places his ear close to her mouth. No air flow. He checks her pulse in her neck, and even though he is not supposed to, he puts his head over her heart and listens to make sure. In CPR class students were told to bare the chest before doing chest compressions. Jeffrey hates to do that to a woman, but her life is at stake. After he gives her two rescue breaths, He pulls up her shirt and bra. Her skin is corpse-gray. He presses down, one and two and three up to fifteen, then breathes twice. After six cycles he hears an ambulance siren. He is about to give another set of rescue breaths when Mrs. Davis gasps, coughs, and begins to breathe. Jeffrey notices the pulse in her neck resuming. The paramedics come inside and Jeffrey tells them what happened. They slap EKG leads on her chest, check her rhythm. "Good job, young man. You saved your teacher's life."

He sighs, walks toward the door, and rests his head against the wall. Some students pray. Some pat him on the back and say, "Way to go, man."

A police officer arrives and asks Jeffrey if he is the student who gave Mrs. Davis CPR. He offers to drive Jeffrey to the hospital in Morhollow, and Jeffrey agrees. The car moves over rain-slicked roads, and headlights create pale yellow puddles.

Jeffrey stares at them, trying to divert his mind from the horror he's seen.

When they arrive at Morhollow General Hospital and reach the public door to the ER, a newspaper reporter from the *Morhollow Courier* wants to interview him. Jeffrey mutters something about only doing his duty, answers a few questions he will not remember later, and sits down in the waiting room. Other students arrive, some crying, others looking stunned. A doctor comes in and asks to talk to Jeffrey.

"You did one Hell of a job with the CPR. You're a hero," he says. "The lightning stunned the electrical system in her heart, but your help bought her brain time until it recovered. She's going to be okay. You'll be all over the news tomorrow. I'm sure your parents will be proud."

Jeffrey can't find it in him to tell the doctor his parents have passed away, but Granny and Aunt Jenny and his other relatives will be proud. Jeffrey, however, feels shame.

When he saw Mrs. Davis loaded onto the stretcher, her normal color was returning. He had seen her breasts during CPR, but was focused on saving her life. When he saw her alive on the stretcher (her strong heart beating again), he felt a wave of lust flow over him. After the heat reached his groin, when he thought again about the CPR he had done, a picture of her breasts bouncing at each thrust of his palm during CPR appeared in his mind, and the image turned him on.

God, I'm is a freak of nature, not a hero. I deserve damnation, not praise. It does not matter that he felt nothing inappropriate while he was giving CPR. To associate sexual feelings with CPR on Mrs. Davis, even after the fact, horrifies him. The feelings he sometimes has when CPR is performed on a woman on *Emergency* haunt him again. He can try to make excuses, that the women who play in *Emergency* are actresses, that they are attractive, that they are really alive so their color was normal, but those rationalizations do not make him feel any better. Now the sick, twisted feelings have come to real life, though retrospectively. He has to tell Mrs. Davis that he is not a hero, that he is a perverted bastard who lusted, who thought about her heart, her dead heart that started with his touch, and he wants so much to put his hand between her breasts and...*No, obsession growing, please stop*...He feels sick and sits down in the waiting room, head in his hands.

Timing in life can be a pain. It is now, as these obsessive thoughts flow in a circular pattern in his mind, that the doctor comes back in and says, "Mrs. Davis is awake. She wants to see you first."

Jeffrey cannot confess now, not while she is still sick. When she is better, after class one day, he will tell all. That will mark the end of his time in her class, but he has learned so much in the meantime – about English, about him being a super-pervert – that much is useful.

"Hi, Jeffrey," she says as he walks to her bed and sits down. She takes his hand. "You saved my life. I will never forget that. I owe you everything."

"No, ma'am," Jeffrey says. I was doing my duty."

Mrs. Davis smiles. "I admire you even more for saying that. Give yourself credit. Of all the people in that class, you came forward and did something uncomfortable to save another human being. You are always my hero."

"Thank you, ma'am," and the doctor waves him out. "She needs to get some rest. In a couple of days she can go home – once we get that burn healing a little better."

"I'm glad you're okay," Jeffrey says, and he leaves.

The thought crosses his mind that he saved Mrs. Davis, but he could not save Kathy. True, the situations were different, and their problems were different. Yet if he saved Mrs. Davis he should have been able to save Kathy. At least he did not lust after Kathy when he touched her heart, not even afterward. To do so would be sacrilege. He hopes that it was love that fuels his lack of lust with Kathy rather than the fact that she died.

Later, photographers arrive, and reporters from the Nashville television stations ask him for interviews. After he returns home, Granny watches the story on WSM, Channel 4, but he averts his eyes to the side without being obvious and focuses on tuning out. At school he is more popular and does not feel as nerdy as before. All these rewards and he has tainted the good that he has done with lust-filled perversion.

Mrs. Davis returns a week after the lightning strike. The entire class stands up and claps. After class, she pulls him aside. "Jeffrey, why don't you come by my house for an hour after school tomorrow? I'd like to thank you better than I have been able for what you did for me.

"But..." Jeffrey starts.

"No buts. I insist. I'll take you home."

Jeffrey tells Granny what Mrs. Davis said. Granny says, "She's alive. That's the best thanks. Of course if she gave you a new car for when you turn sixteen that would be nice." She wheezes out a laugh through her cigarette. Jeffrey laughs and is glad to see that Granny had a sense of humor even if she does not show it that much.

The next day Jeffrey finds himself in Mrs. Davis' house, a nice three story brick in the middle of Morhollow. He has no idea how she could afford it on a teacher's salary – maybe her husband is rich. He sips iced tea on her couch and she sits beside him.

"You've been looking glum for someone who ought to be happy and proud of your accomplishment."

Jeffrey looked into her eyes, blue sapphires, and half-cries, half-speaks, his voice quavering so much he prays she understands him, "I saw you half naked when I gave you CPR and I didn't feel anything bad then but when I thought about it later I felt something I shouldn't have felt and remembering pushing on your chest was a turn on and I'm a perverted freak who deserves to go to Central State."

Mrs. Davis gives Jeffrey a quirky smile and laughs. He thinks she is making fun of him since she cannot stop laughing. She must have sensed that because she says, "I'm not laughing at you, I'm laughing about your feeling guilty, you hormone-filled teenager. Of course you'll feel something after seeing my, ah, blessings. I would be surprised if you didn't. You are my hero, even if you don't want to take the credit you deserve."

Jeffrey grabs her, hugs her, saying "Thank you, thank you," so much she holds his head in her hands, guiding his face toward hers and says, "Shhhh. You're welcome!" She keeps holding him. His eyes are fixed on those sapphires. She lets go. He moves forward, tilts his head – he has learned something from his time with Kathy. Their lips touch. They touch again. She moves toward him. Then she kisses him full on the mouth and before long their tongues touch, exploring each other's mouths. He pulls her shirt off. She breathes, "Just be careful around the bandages over the burns," and takes off her bra. He pulls off his shirt and their bodies join skin to skin. He touches her left breast, feels her heart speed up, rolls his fingers around the smooth, light pink aureole, touches the tip of the erect nipple and feels her body rise and a sigh escape. His tongue reaches her other aureole and circles it, moving closer to her right nipple. Soon they are naked, underwear off, and she moves his hand down to what feels like a small indentation, places his index and middle fingers on it and said, "Gently now, rub it." He does, and she moans. He sneaks a listen to her pounding heart as he sucks her nipple. Then he enters her, and they are one – he is awkward at first, then thrusts in rhythm, thinking of a heartbeat, up-down, up-down, and she cries out as he thrusts harder. At the same time he feels blessed release and faintness and joy and union and the end of his virginity. She whispers, "Keep going," and he does until she cries out once more, then relaxes.

They lie on their backs side by side. Warmth covers his body, and he slips his arm under Caroline's back, wraps his fingers around her and holds on. Funny how he has to use her first name after making love. "Did you like it?" he asks.

"Nice to have a man who can follow orders," she says. "Your touch, so tender. Young."

"Does it make you feel bad that I'm young?"

"Not at all. I feel no guilt. You're older than your years – what other fourteen-year-old is so intelligent that I can discuss comparing Poe and Hawthorne or genres of horror fiction, and I learn from him? You shouldn't feel guilty either."

"I don't," he lies.

The more the hormone-rush warmth drains from his body, the more guilty he feels. *How old is she? Twenty-five*, he thinks. *Married, too. What if her husband finds out and shoots me? Oh shit! What if she's fertile?* His heart races and Caroline asks, "What's wrong?"

"What if you get...

She laughs. "No, no, no, I'm on the pill."

"That's right – you're married."

"Yes, to Dan. He's away most of the time, but I stay on the pill in case, you know, that feeling comes over me."

Jeffrey feels better that Caroline will not get pregnant but feels worse when he understands the meaning of her last statement – there may have been other guys besides he and Dan. A pang of jealously tries to spoil his mood, but he squelches it and puts his head over her heart. It beats slowly. Calmly. As if nothing unusual has happened. That is odd. Had she planned this whole event – perhaps before the accident? Had she done this for him, for both of them – or for her? Has she been with other students whom she has *fancied* for whatever reason? While he ponders these possibilities, a renewed hardness in his groin blocks his reason – and they make love again, and soon afterward, a third time.

Jeffrey wonders if things will now be different in sixth period. He smiles as he comes in the door on Monday, but Caroline ignores him. On test day, Wednesday, the class has a difficult Shakespeare test, and when the papers are returned on Friday, a "B+" is marked on top of Jeffrey's paper. His usual grade has been an "A" or "A+" on exams. He reviews his answers. There are several minor errors, but no more than he usually has on an A or A- paper. After class he takes the paper to Caroline and asks about it. The other students have left, though Jeffrey can hear their voices down the hall. "Caro..." She interrupts him. "At school, I'm Mrs. Davis. If you meet me in the store, I'm Mrs. Davis. You do not address me by my first name."

Jeffrey stands stunned, staring at her, his eyes watering. "What is it you want?" she asks, her voice like dry ice.

"I'm concerned about my test grade. I think my answers on the test are as good as his earlier tests on which I got A's."

She takes the test, looks it over, pointing out small flaws that she says add up. She returns the test to him, and he looks her in the eye, his cheeks wet, and asks, "Why?"

Caroline sighs and whispers, "You have to be more careful. The way you looked at me during class is too obvious. If anyone hears you call me by my first name and figures out something is going on between us, I could lose my job – and I don't plan to lose my job. I could even go to jail for having sex with someone so young. I don't plan to go to jail either." She smiles, and her eyes relax, the sapphires shining once more. "Not this Friday – too soon – but next Friday, plan to stay after school."

So the love – or was it a lust? – affair continues. By the end of fall semester Jeffrey is in love with Caroline. It is not as intense as his love for Kathy, which fascinates him since he had not been *with* Kathy sexually. Jeffrey learns a great deal during his affair, not only about how to please a woman, but about literature.

He also learns a great deal about how to squelch guilt.

After the first time *with* Caroline, guilt overwhelmed him, and the demon appeared in his dreams, laughing in his face. His guilt worsens when he thinks about Caroline's husband Dan – *but he travels so much with his job and doesn't meet her needs, so he really deserves what he gets*. As for Jeffrey being so young, he is mature for his age. He is eighteen in spirit, and probably older.

The rationalizations work to carve away his guilt. The second time the guilt lessened. By the middle of the semester the guilt is gone. By Christmas Break he begins feel guilty about not feeling guilty.

At the end of the school year, after Jeffrey and Caroline make love, she says, "We're going to have to end this. It's too risky for me, and I don't want your name – and mine - sprawled over the news. If Dan finds out...you do not want to see him when he's angry. Our relationship was truly special, and I hope you remember me in a good way. I owe you everything for saving my life. If when you're out of college and we're both *available*, if you know what I mean, look me up."

Jeffrey should be more heartbroken than he is, but common sense can sometimes crack even a nerd brain like his. He knows he is damn lucky that no one suspects, not other teachers, classmates, nor Granny and Aunt Jenny. He grieves, but that fades over the summer as life improves – and Caroline has helped him to overcome the darker aspects of his fetish.

Jeffrey puts the journal down, feeling aroused, but knowing that if he takes care of that himself he will go to sleep afterwards and not finish the journal tonight. *Lordy, Lordy, Lordy,* as one of Granny's cousins used to say. Yes, he remembers that illicit relationship. He wonders if Caroline had any other relationships with students, but he doubts it. He has no doubt that she had been with men other than Dan. No one suspected her of having a sexual relationship with Jeffrey, and he never turned her in. She no longer lives in the area – he tried to look her up but could not find her – and he still tries from time to time on the Internet. She is probably divorced and remarried with a different last name. It is hard to believe that she is over sixty-years-old. If he sees her again, she would still tempt him. *There is nothing like the first*, he supposes. He knows some people would say that she took advantage of a child, and Jeffrey thinks they are right to some extent, but he knew what he was doing. He is not bitter. He is proud of saving her life and glad she helped resolve his horror at his own strange desires. He takes a short caffeine break before resuming reading.

CHAPTER 27
NOT A GOOD DAY FOR ZEKE

Outside, a thunderstorm rages, and lightning brightens the interior of Zeke's store. He sits in his office after another restless night. "I guess you did it, Jeffrey. Adultery. You did wrong and you're weaker. That thing attacking you will be more aggressive than ever."

Zeke tenses as another message comes into his mind. Jeffrey is about to confront the demon. Zeke is about to call Andy so they can visit Jeffrey when something falls from a counter. He turns around, but nothing is there. He dials another number, and several cans of soup crash to the floor. The entire shelf rocks. Zeke pulls out a gun from under the counter, points it toward the area of the fallen cans. "Get up. If you try to rob this place I'll blow your head off."

Cans of oil fly through the air, one striking him on the head. He swoons and fires his .38. The bullet strikes a window and it shatters. Sheets of rain blow through the window, and the floor by the window collects a pool of water.

Someone's - or something's - hot breath singes the hairs on the back of Zeke's neck. He twists around and fires at – *what the Hell is that? An octopus? Shit, it must be the demon – but this thing's not from Hell. From...some other bad place.*

Zeke's shots sink deep into the thing's flesh, but it keeps moving toward him, stretching out its tentacles as Zeke empties the final round into the Creature. Tentacles wrap around Zeke, and images from every bad nightmare he or anyone else has experienced flood his mind. Heat overwhelms his body, and the world fades into blackness as Zeke and the earth part for good.

CHAPTER 28
THE BATTLE

Jeffrey puts his pen down after writing down the latest entry in his journal. He may not continue his journal much longer. Ninth grade is coming to an end, and with it the evil obsessions that have haunted his life for four years. He dealt with the unpardonable sin and can accept, at least in part, his heartbeat fetish. There is one last matter to which he has to attend – one round-mouthed bastard to kick out of his life with the Good Lord's help – *and*, he thinks, *with Zeke's as well*. This story begins in horror and sadness.

R. J. sneaks over to Trash Hill, and Jeffrey asks him how Sherry is doing. He says she has a boyfriend who is a lot like Jeffrey – nerdy, but not quite as *bad* – whatever that means. R. J. asks him, "Wanna take a bike ride to Zeke's?"

"Zeke!" Jeffrey says. "Strange. I got a call from his friend Andy early this morning – he wants us to take a ride down there. He's been visiting relatives in New York and can't reach Zeke at the store. I'm thinking that storm three nights ago knocked out his phone. Can we avoid getting caught?"

"Sure, if we can make it to Farris Road without being seen. My folks hardly ever drive that direction."

"I'll tell Granny I'm taking a ride. I'll meet you back here."

"I'll stay out of sight for now," and R. J. ducks his bike behind some giant pokeweed plants.

Soon they are on their way. The day is overcast, with low stratus clouds floating amidst pockets of blue sky. They reach Zeke's store without passing a single car. As they approach the building, R. J. says, "Geez, there must be road kill close. Something smells rotten."

"I don't see any buzzards," Jeffrey says. "Whatever it is must be nearby." He opens the door, and the odor strikes him like a whiff from a rotting cow on a hot summer day. That old feeling of dread fills his gut, and he tells R. J. to stay behind him. Every item in the store seems in order, and the cash register on the counter sits undisturbed. Then they look behind the corner of the counter. R. J. screams.

Flies circling his head, worms crawling over the body, Zeke lies dead and decaying, his mouth wide open, frozen in a terror cry, his arms stiff and extended as if trying to ward off whoever – or whatever – attacked him. Jeffrey brushes the flies away, looks at Zeke's neck, and passes out.

When Jeffrey wakes up a paramedic is checking his pulse. He tried to raise himself up, but the paramedic says, "Whoa, whoa, stay down, young man. You passed out. I can understand why, but we have to make sure nothing else bad is going on."

Jeffrey nods, trying to push away the image of Zeke's neck and those claw marks from a creature not of this earth. The paramedic secures Jeffrey's head, and he can only look straight up. He overhears the deputies talking.

"Sheriff Newton coming?"

"Yep. Looks like his car's pulling up now."

There are footsteps as a heavy man walks inside.

"Sheriff, we've secured the scene. Two teenaged boys found the body. Deputies have talked to one of them. The other passed out and just woke up. He's over there. Paramedics loadin' him on the stretcher. Doc's gonna check him out in Randallsville to make sure he's okay."

"Deputy Carter, you follow them and as soon as he's cleared to talk, interview him. Where's the body?"

"Over here, sheriff. Look at the neck."

"Holy shit. What the Hell? Damn, I thought you were taking cop humor too far. I suppose those footprints are real, too."

"The boys' footprints mixed with them, but there's a path in the dust to the back door. Forensics is going to preserve those prints, and they've taken photos. Take a look." There are more footsteps.

"*Shee-it*. We need to call somebody who knows about animals. I've seen wildcats, badgers, mad dogs, and in the last year or so coyotes 'round here. Never seen a print like that."

"Deformed goat?"

"With a hand that grabbed a man's neck? Come on."

"Sheriff, maybe the suspect dressed up in some kind of costume to throw us off."

"Now that's an idea. I sure as Hell hope you're right. Make sure to search for any fabric that could have come from a costume."

Jeffrey wants to keep listening, but he is now secure on the stretcher and being loaded into an ambulance. He remembers the shape of those claws from Granny's basement the day the tornado passed over. His mind is awhirl, and he barely concentrates enough to answer all the paramedic's questions. Whoever/whatever murdered Zeke was not wearing a costume. A surge of anger and fear moves into Jeffrey's chest, and he forces himself to calm down so the paramedic will not notice.

Jeffrey's prayers were answered with a *No.* He hoped the demon would not turn out to be real. He prayed it would be a personification of Jeffrey's guilt. Guilt, however, does not make footprints. Guilt does not take a man by his throat, squeeze and leave burn marks. Whatever guilt Jeffrey suffers is for not visiting Zeke after he saw him for the first time, and for losing the sheet of Latin Zeke placed in the Bible he gave Jeffrey.

At the hospital the doctor briefly checks Jeffrey and releases him to Granny. Deputy Carter wants to talk to him first, and Jeffrey takes care to describe only the bare facts, if there can be such things in a case like this, when he discovered the body. Deputy Carter thanks him, puts his notebook away, and gives him a card with the sheriff's office phone number. "Call the sheriff's office if you remember anything else. The smallest detail could be important."

Granny hugs Jeffrey in the hall as do Aunt Jenny and Uncle Lawton. Uncle Frank has come along as well.

"Damn," he says. "I saw ol' Zeke last week. Said he felt dread about something. He wouldn't tell me what was scaring him, but by God he was scared shitless. I saw that look in Europe in World War II. We'd be in combat in a rough spot, and some of the men would have that look in their eyes that said, *I am going to die today*. That's the look Zeke had. Hell, nobody saw Zeke for three days while he rotted in that hot store. Wish I could have done something."

"I wish I had gone to see him three days ago" Jeffrey says.

"Hell no, you don't. You'd be dead, too. Zeke at least had a chance with that .38 pistol he owned. If only he'd hit what bit him. That would teach somebody not to hurt ol' Zeke."

Jeffrey does not tell him that the .38 would not have done any good. From overhearing the police conversation, Jeffrey knew Zeke had fired the pistol four times. Not even the AK-47s and the M-16s used in Vietnam combined would have helped – a hydrogen bomb probably could not kill what murdered Zeke.

Sometimes, Jeffrey thinks, *something creeps through into this world from some other place. Another dimension. Heaven. Hell. The Void. Who knows how many portals there are to worlds that no human would want to see, but where creatures live who would love to see – and harm – humans. These beings thrust their way into the world in dreams, when the seams connecting realities are torn*. Jeffrey hopes that he is not the person who rent the veil since he would have indirectly killed Zeke. More likely it was that the demon that haunts him, this angelic being, once so beautiful that its light would blind human eyes, twisted its will and its twisted form followed – if it is a demon. Now he hopes it is one rather than some mysterious transdimensional being. A demon he can understand to some extent from his religion. If the thing is something else...it is evil, and evil tends to be the same everywhere it exists. There is a chance, then, that Jeffrey can use his understanding of evil to defeat the creature.

What characterizes evil? Pride. Hatred. Spite. Ultimately, it is self-centeredness that desires to demean everyone but the evil person. Evil twists the physical form of a being. Sometimes you see a mug shot of a known criminal and notice that the face is different – turned out of shape. The mouth is not right, something about the jawbones is not aligned the way it should be, the angles are off. When this angel became a demon, or when this creature was corrupted, the angles imploded into a monster, the lips, once rich and full and beautiful, rounded into a parody of a circle and a mockery of a smile.

The creature searches for the vulnerable, those people haunted by despair, and it feeds. Zeke gave him the key to overcome the demon. Jeffrey fears that the thing tormented Zeke, that thing that visits in the dark, that fills dreaming and waking with horror, finally feeding enough to materialize, clutch and burn Zeke's throat, leaving his body to rot.

Now Jeffrey has added more meat for the demon to eat – the sin with Caroline. It may have set up the situation that led to Jeffrey's relationship with her, and Jeffrey chills when he remembers the lightning strike.

At home before supper, Jeffrey drops a book he is reading, *The Exorcist* by William Peter Blatty. The book captures fears of annihilation after death that he thought only he experienced. Jeffrey is not Roman Catholic and does not know whether a Catholic exorcist will be able to help. As Jeffrey searches for the book under the couch, the ends of his fingers feel a folded piece of paper. He pulls it out, unfolds it, to find the Latin text that Zeke gave him. Grace arrives from a place and time unexpected. Jeffrey phones Aunt Jenny and asked her if she can pick him up at the Morhollow Public Library the following day an hour after school.

"You're making me drive to Robin Hood's Barn lately. You know that Lawton and I have to keep an eye on you when you're in the library."

"There's a book by J. W. McGarvey on Bible lands I'd like to check out. He was Church of Christ, you know. There are some other books by Church of Christ people I want to read."

That works – end of conversation.

The next afternoon the bell rings at school and Jeffrey walks to the public library which is a couple of blocks down the street. He checks the reference section in the 400s and finds the Latin dictionary he had located earlier. He begins to translate the prayer literally: *humbly majesty glorious your pray...* and so forth. He cannot yet refine the translation, but since the text is not from the Bible, it must be from a worship book, and Catholics like to pray from a book. Jeffrey slips the paper into his pocket, sets the dictionary down, and walks to the 200s, the religion section. There he locates a large book entitled, *History of the Western Catholic Liturgy with Primary Texts*. Normally the library does not carry lots of books about the Catholic Church, but this book is old – it was published in the 1930s – and maybe the library keeps it for that reason. Jeffrey thumbs through it for a half hour, knowing that every minute that passes draws him closer to when Aunt Jenny will arrive to pick him up. He will have to rush to check out some Church of Christ books before he leaves.

Frustrated, he throws the book open and finds a prayer that seemed to fit the Latin.

We humbly entreat Thy glorious majesty to deliver us by Thy might from every influence of the accursed spirits, from their every evil share and deception, and to keep us from all harm. Through Jesus Christ our Lord. A-men.

A prayer of deliverance from evil spirits – can that help Jeffrey? Surely it would not would work like some magic charm, but who knows? The cliché is correct that God works in mysterious ways.

Somehow the key to his deliverance – and to others who might be haunted by this demon – may be in the Latin phrase at the bottom of the sheet: *Desperatio accit Exterminans*. This phrase is easier to decipher, and after a few stops and starts he arrives with a translation that fits: *Despair brings the Destroyer*. The dictionary contains a reference to *Exterminans* from the *Latin Vulgate*. From looking over the first page of the Catholic Bible that Zeke gave him, Jeffrey knows that the passage is translated from the *Vulgate*. The reference is to Revelation 9:11. Jeffrey pulls the Bible from his book bag and reads, *A king, the angel of the bottomless pit, whose name in Hebrew is Abaddon, and in Greek Apollyon, and in Latin Exterminans.*

Jeffrey sighs – the answer is there – and he returns the book to the shelf and finds some Church of Christ books. He checks them out just as Aunt Jenny steps through the door with an "I'm proud of you" smile on her face.

There is one more set of questions he must answer before a final confrontation with the demon. He wants to know more about Zeke, and the obvious person to ask is Andy Davis, Zeke's friend. He lives down Farris Road just a few miles on the other side of the railroad tracks. On Saturday Jeffrey carefully crosses the New Randallsville Highway, glad that Granny or Aunt Jenny cannot see him or they would tan his hide. Once on the other side of Farris Road he rides his bike to a small wood frame farmhouse with a large vegetable garden behind it. Beside the driveway is a pear tree coming into bloom. He climbs the creaky wood stairs onto Andy's porch and knocks on the door.

Creak; creak – footsteps sound on the old floor and the front door opens to reveal a slender, white-haired man in overalls. "Jeffrey Conley. Welcome, cousin. You know your granddaddy and I were double first cousins." Jeffrey does not correct him – they were actually double first cousins – once removed. He guesses that makes him and Andy double first cousins, third degree.

Granddaddy's old guitar sits in a corner. Andy bought it for fifty dollars a couple of years before Granddaddy died.

Grandfather clocks and clocks of all description dot the room. They all ran, and only a fool would miss that Andy Davis repairs clocks – and from the parts on a desk lit by a bright lamp Jeffrey realizes that he repairs watches, too.

Andy motions Jeffrey to sit down and surprises him when he says, "Reckon you're here about Zeke."

"What do you know about him?"

"He was my cousin too, on my mama's side, so he was your distant cousin. Kept to himself – even when he was a child. Told me my mama would die when I was twelve, and when it happened I stayed away from him – most other folks did too. At the time I thought he was workin' with the devil. Haven't thought that for years, though."

"What changed your mind," Jeffrey asks, as he studies an old grandfather clock that reminds him of the one on *Captain Kangaroo*.

"Back in the late forties, a bunch of girls lived down Allenville Road disappeared – never found. Some of us thought Zeke had somethin' to do with it, but the sheriff didn't find anything on him. In fact he was talkin' to a deputy about the mess when one of the girls disappeared. Happens that one day Zeke runs into the sheriff's office and says, *Bessie Roland. Allenville Community. She's next. Get there!*

"Sheriff thought he was drunker than a skunk, but one of his deputies named Potts figured he'd better show up there just in case. He got there, and of course Bessie's mother, Mabel, didn't know what he was up to – thought he might be tryin' to hurt her – but he convinced her to leave and let Bessie be the bait. Deputy Potts hid in the closet. Door opened in the back and a man wearing a potato sack with eyeholes for a mask came in and grabbed Bessie, holdin' a knife to her throat. Said, 'We're goin' to a real good time together, girl.' Potts jumped out of the closet, pulled his gun, said 'No you ain't,' and the masked man threw Bessie to the floor and let that knife fly right at Deputy Potts. He ducked, fired his gun, and must have hit the man since he ran off and there was a trail of blood goin' to the back door. They never found the guy, but no more girls disappeared. Reckon he bled out somewhere and died. Now Zeke was a hero and police came from 'bout everywhere in the South for his help. I think he may have helped them solve some murders way up in Louisville. He got tired of people botherin' him, bein' shy and all, and stopped helping police. Boy, you're lookin' thirsty. Want some iced tea?"

"Yes, sir," Jeffrey says, and Andy fetches some from the fridge and pours it into a glass of ice. When he returns, he continues his story.

"Zeke didn't withdraw totally from most folks right away. He tried to help locals, especially in life and death matters. But his timing was off. He told the sheriff that Jacob Sprigg was going to kill himself in his barn. Sheriff believed him this time, and drove himself and two deputies down Allenville Road to the Sprigg farm. Jacob was meaner than a cornered badger, but I don't enjoy what happened – he was hanging from a rope in his barn, eyes gouged out."

"Gouged out?" Jeffrey says. "By whom? Or what?"

"His boy Sheldon said goats did it. Nobody believed that, of course."

The iced tea is not the only thing chilling Jeffrey. Andy continues.

"Poor Sheldon. Don't know what it does to a boy to see his daddy hangin' up like that. He's still living with his wife and daughter in the same place."

"How old is his daughter."

Andy laughs. "Too young for you – nine or ten. Anyway you wouldn't be doin' yourself a favor goin' there. Sheldon's a real piece o'work, I'm tellin' you. In any case Zeke's reputation dropped, but what killed it was Bernie Curley's hangin.' That wasn't Zeke's fault."

"I've heard the name somewhere."

"You granny or aunt or your granddaddy may have said somethin.' Everybody loved Bernie – he attended Harrell's Corner every Sunday. Led singing there. Zeke said he was goin' to kill himself. Nobody believed him since they knew Bernie as a devout churchgoer. After Bernie's sixteen-year-old son found Bernie hangin' in the barn, people blamed Zeke."

"That was unfair," Jeffrey says.

"You're right. People are funny. Zeke knew that, too. What really broke his spirit, though, was when a boy 'bout your age – Charlie was his name - killed himself. Hung himself on a tree. People were mad that Zeke didn't predict it, as if they believed him last time, and Zeke felt bad because he knew Charlie and tried to help him. He kept tellin' folks, 'I tried to help, I gave him what he needed. I should have made him understand.' Sheriff's office found a note – I knew Deputy Potts and he told me it said something about him having cussed the Holy Ghost and goin' to Hell."

Jeffrey gasps, swallows hard.

"Are you feelin' okay? Lookin' peekid. Anything you'd like to tell me?"

Jeffrey takes a deep breath and says, "I'm fine."

"Zeke bought that store in the middle of nowhere, made a little money, but stayed away from locals. Most folks stoppin' were strangers, and he was fine with that. Hate that somebody killed him – seems like something worse than a *somebody* killed him. Strange rumors about, and I believe them, but I'm too old to fight dragons. That's for young folks to handle."

"Like me?"

"You're a little young. Enjoy yourself before you get too old. Keep hope. More than anything else, keep hope. That's the best way to stop dragon fire in its tracks."

"I've been thinking along those lines myself," Jeffrey says.

"Zeke talked about you. For years."

Jeffrey starts. "For years?"

"Before you and your buddies rode up on your bikes, he had a dream 'bout you and a demon."

Jeffrey starts to swoon. Andy catches him, lays him on the couch, and puts a pillow under his head.

"Easy now. Don't get bent out of shape. You know how Zeke is. Way back in '48 we tried to help a boy like you — the one who hung himself."

"We?" Jeffrey says. "I thought it was Zeke by himself."

"No," Andy, and he jerks his head as if struggling with overpowering emotion. "No. He told me about Charlie, who was eleven when he started having trouble."

"That's how old I was..."

"Yes, I know - that's when Zeke called me. We talked to Charlie over the three years he struggled. He saw a demon, too - lips swollen, an oval smile, claws, heat."

"The same demon I've been seeing?"

"Guess so. We tried to keep Charlie's spirits up. It didn't work. We didn't try any kind of ritual other than our own personal prayers. You know our church says that demons don't attack or possess people today."

"They're wrong," Jeffrey says.

"Yes, and so were we. The boy needed an exorcism of some kind. We should have given him advice on how to fight a demon instead of assumin' the demon was his own mind.

Years later Zeke had a dream about a bookstore in Nashville on Church Street. He drove there, and seemed to be guided to a copy of the Douay Version of the Bible. Inside he found that old folded sheet. He knew he had to keep it. When he saw you in his store, he knew he had to give the Bible and the sheet inside to you. Somehow the key to defeating the demon is there."

"I think I know what to do. I could get a Catholic priest, but this task is something I must do alone. I don't know if this is a demon from Hell or not. It may be some other evil monstrosity from another dimension, or it may be working with some being from that realm. I have a feeling that this is something more than an ordinary demonic attack."

"I think you might be right. Be careful. I don't want to have another child's life on my conscience."

"You won't," Jeffrey says.

After Jeffrey returns home, he thinks about Zeke and wishes he could tell him that he had given Jeffrey what he needs to fight off the demon. Tonight Jeffrey will be ready.

At midnight he sits in his chair and recites the prayer against evil spirits. The demon rises from the floor and says, "No hope for you, boy." Then the demon takes on Caroline's voice. "Oh Jeffrey. I enjoyed having sex with an underage boy, especially one who knows better. I even called Dan and he wants you and him to do me at once. Wouldn't that be fun? You'll be in great shape to meet God on Judgment Day."

"I will not despair," Jeffrey says. "The affair is over with Caroline. Yes, I was wrong. Good came out of it, too. God is merciful to bring good out of evil. I trust God will forgive me."

"You do not deserve to see God, boy. Your blasphemies stink in His sight."

"I have no choice but to rely on His grace. I trust that it will be sufficient."

"It won't be," the demon hisses, turning into a snake. It wraps around Jeffrey's chest and starts to squeeze. Its face changes into a skull with rotted flesh hanging down. "This is you in a year," it says. "Look in the mirror if you have the courage to know who you are now. Or are you a coward?"

"I'm not afraid," Jeffrey says, although he realizes he is lying. He stands up, steps into the bathroom, turns on the light, and looks into the mirror. Instead of his familiar body stands a body full of scales, a face with features formed at odd angles, an oval, wide-lipped mouth turned upward in a perpetual sneer. Jeffrey is the demon; the demon is Jeffrey.

A voice emerges from the black hole inside the mirrored mouth. "We are one. We are damned. You made me and I made you."

The mouth spews out a song in a woman's voice that reminds Jeffrey of the people on TV who wear beads, read horoscopes and think people might be reincarnated as possum, badgers, weasels and other animals. "We are not iso-lat-ed, we are all con-NEC-ted."

Jeffrey sings to the same tune, “Then you are connected, to Jesus and to GA-AD.” The creature turns from drab brown to red – and its face changes back to Jeffrey’s. “We are separated only from God, but connected to everything else,” Jeffrey’s voice says. The thing in the mirror laughs.

“Do you ever watch television?” Jeffrey asks.

“Of course I do,” his own voice answers.

“Sometimes on a show the voice comes before the mouth moves,” Jeffrey says. “If you’re going to pretend to be me, at least you can sync the voice with the mouth. And when I laugh, you at least need to make the mouth move on the face, you fake piece of shit.”

The face changes into the skull draped with flabs of rotting flesh. “You are dead in your sins, and in a year…”

Jeffrey interrupts. “You’re boring me. But even if I were dead,” he says slowly, “even if you kill me, I still will not despair, Exterminans.”

The snake body starts to melt into a stinking jell. The rotting death’s head says, “Damned, damned, you’re damned, no hope, unpardoned.”

“You are unpardoned, Apollyon, Abaddon, Exterminans, Destroyer. Despair yourself, demon.”

A long death’s gurgle escapes through the skull’s teeth and the snake melts into a putrid liquid that evaporates in a grey steam. The flesh melts off the skull, and the skull fades into nothingness.

CHAPTER 29
GOING BACK

Jeffrey will not yield, the Antibeing thinks. Why a silly prayer to the Enemy weakens the Antibeing is something It finds to be a mystery – but it always works. Damn Its weakness in this dimension.

If the boy does not fall into despair, the Antibeing will weaken, perhaps to the point that It is thrown back into Its native dimension, never again gathering enough strength to visit this one. The Antibeing curses the boy's stubbornness.

Still, the boy does not yield, the Antibeing thinks. *He calls me Exterminans. Not technically my name but close enough to drain my power every time that boy says it. Why I don't know. Some spell by the Enemy.*

The Antibeing hears the voice of the human boy say, "Exterminans, I shall not despair. I will not kill myself."

Power drains from the Antibeing, and the false form It has taken unravels. It reverts to Its tentacled, squid-like form. It feels Itself pulled, stretched to the point of breaking, and it pops back into the Circle of Azathoth. It tries to cross over to the planet called *Earth* but cannot. A flute flies into Its hand, and the Antibeing plays pure dissonance. It dances with other monstrosities around the blind god of Chaos, pulled by Fate Eternal, never resting, dissonance slowly unraveling what remains of Its Being.

The Antibeing begins the process of fading into a hateful ball of spite. It will flash in the middle of the monstrous dancers like a perverse Antilight radiating Its hatred in Antispace until It disperses into nothingness.

CHAPTER 30
THE WRAP UP

Jeffrey closes the journal. Now he remembers everything – "Despair brings the Destroyer." Not despairing drives away the Destroyer. The journal ends at that point – fitting, he thinks.

Jeffrey considers burning the journal, but decides instead to place it in a fire box and bury it. Perhaps God will find some use for it or a new Zeke will find it and give it to someone who needs it.

Jeffrey knows what to do about the mantra the next time it invades his mind. Instead of fighting it, he will let it do its will, for it is merely a mind trick. Mind tricks will not send him to Hell.

At times Jeffrey desires to return to the area where he was reared. At other times he fears that possibility since the portal connecting worlds remains. He read about hyperspace in some popular books on physics he owned. He understands the notion of a wormhole. This area, though, may be a space that is *thin* between two – or more – worlds. *May God keep the naïve and the curious away from demons that stand at the gate, eager to invade.*

Recently a sinkhole collapsed in the field bordering the back yard of his grandparents' house. He had visited the old place yesterday morning and did not see any bottom when he shined two LED flashlights into the hole. Jeffrey assumes there is one and that that sinkhole is not the bottomless pit of the book of Revelation. He does not know whether the sinkhole is connected to the portal or whether is it part of the Karst topography of middle Tennessee, where carbonic acid eats into underground limestone and sandstone to form caves, and the ground collapses into sinkholes. What he knows is that strange events continue. In 1982 he read in the Randallsville paper that Sheldon Sprigg had disappeared without a trace. Now that property on Allenville Road is overgrown, house torn down, barn covered by bushes, strange lights seen there at night. As much as Jeffrey enjoys ghost investigations, he refuses to touch that place with a ten foot pole. Developers have pursued Ginny Sprigg Marshall, Sheldon's daughter, to buy the property, but she and her husband Paul have thus far resisted.

At Southeastern North Carolina University, whenever Jeffrey teaches a university Biblical Studies class, he mentions the unpardonable sin. He tells the students the proper interpretation of the passage and that even if they have cursed the Holy Spirit, that is not what Jesus meant by the blasphemy against the Holy Spirit. Who knows whether at least one student in class is struggling with despair over the unpardonable sin? Perhaps the lesson helps someone, and if not, Jeffrey thanks God for every student who learns not to fear Hell-mongering preachers who use the *unpardonable sin* like Torquemada's rack.

With the journal as a cue, Jeffrey remembers the final battle with the demon – or the trans-dimensional being or whatever the Hell that thing was. "Despair brings the Destroyer." Not despairing drives away the Destroyer. The only thing Jeffrey knows for sure about the thing that attacked him is that it was real and not merely a part of him. It was evil in the worst possible way. It did not reflect the ordinary evil in some punk that murders someone to cover up a robbery. It was spiteful evil, the kind of evil C. S. Lewis wrote about in his novel *Perelandra* when a demon-possessed man keeps calling the hero Ransom's name over and over with his sole motivation to irritate Ransom. It is the evil of an agitator, a Millicent Massey who divides for the thrill of watching the hate. It is the evil of a preacher who misuses a passage in the Bible as a tool to fulfill his sadistic desire to drive people to madness, to suicide and to Hellfire.

Every account Jeffrey has read of a child thinking he has committed the unpardonable sin is by a *he* – a male. *Why? Are there not females who get obsessed with the unpardonable sin, allowing their minds to slip and falling into despair?* He thinks it has to do with boys' embarrassment and guilt over pubescent sexual desire. Perhaps the guilt of girls is expressed in other ways.

Every child who is not abused or in deep poverty gains a glimpse of Eden. For him Eden was swinging across the gravel road with a breeze cooling the sweat off his face or enjoying Sunday dinner and the banter of relatives after church. For another child it might be going to a Yankee's baseball game with his dad. A girl might go to a concert of someone on whom she has a child's puppy crush.

Puberty makes us face our flaming sword, driving us east of Eden into adulthood. Puberty is our Rubicon from which there is no turning back. Jeffrey's Rubicon flowed from him while climbing a tree branch. A twelve-year-old girl's Rubicon may flow red, her blood boiling out the news of her emerging womanhood.

Children under twelve do know right from wrong, despite the informal teaching of the church. Young children can be cruel, as my cousins were when they told me about Santa's unreality early, but until the sexual serpent comes all but the worst behavior has an air of innocence. His journal chronicled how sexuality tied all his struggles – with a fetish and with religion - into one. *Sexuality is good, but so powerful it is easy to turn aside from the good.*

Jeffrey sets the journal aside, take a legal pad from his briefcase, and writes down a list of words:

Puberty	*Sex*
Asperger's Syndrome	*Heart*
Fetish	*God*
Demon	*Church*
Guilt	*Despair*
Change	*Stability*

The patterns come quickly, like a clinical diagnosis. As a child with Asperger's Syndrome, something he did not discover until he was forty, he wanted the world to remain unchanging with no death, sleeping in the same bed, never outgrowing it, never throwing away toys. He would personify toys, even the rubber balls he liked to bounce, and cry when they disappeared as if they were beloved pets. Change was bad. Change meant death – of time, of possessions, of animals, of people, of all that he loved.

Death and sex poured into the mix seasoned by Asperger's – his twin brother Michael's death haunted him so that he was aware of death far earlier than most children. Death became associated with the heart stopping, and later, sex and death became combined in his mind. Fascination with the heart, the organ that beats to keep a person alive and whose failing causes death, became an obsession. With the little death on the maple tree branch and the associated pounding of his own heart, the heart and sex were connected, and thus the heart and death. As someone with Asperger's Syndrome, obsessions come as a second nature and are exaggerated, and when sex is involved, an obsession easily becomes a fetish.

Death includes spiritual death which is connected in Christianity with Hell. Fear of Hell as well as fear that religion was bullshit and that he will be annihilated after death coalesced. Fear of damnation in Hell became a form of self-fulfilling prophecy when he was eleven and read that passage in Matthew 12:32 about blasphemy against the Holy Spirit and the unpardonable sin. Obsession with the Church of Christ and with God made his relationship with God more emotional than his relationships with other people. For Jeffrey, extremes of love and hatred associated with deep relationships are more intense with God than with anyone else.

The demon was an exception. Its reality challenged Jeffrey's world view. It still does. Yet Jeffrey learned the damage despair could do to the soul to the point of pushing a person to suicide. *If demons exist, then God most likely exists, unless the demon is some being from another dimension that enjoys playing with us, as in the fiction of H. P. Lovecraft. Even then, God may still exist and have power over the most vicious of Lovecraftean gods.*

Today Jeffrey is married to Lisa who accepts his heartbeat fetish and will let him play – to a limit. That is fine by him. He is a ghost investigator today, and a good one – it seems that he opens a permeable barrier between what is seen and what is unseen. As long as ghosts are involved and not demons that is a good thing.

Seventh through ninth grades marks a living Hell for many teenagers entering puberty and early adolescence. God bless them, Jeffrey thinks, and he prays they may they have an easier time than he.

Some religion is toxic. Jeffrey knows that guilt is essential to a good life – he wishes he had felt more guilty about Caroline. Too much guilt drills a hole that lets hope drain out. All that remains is a shell that barely survives emotionally from moment to moment. *Some preachers, if there is a Hell, will roast with lawyers and politicians at the lowest level. Damn their sadism.*

The mantra that fills his mind on cold dark evenings at church services remains as a residual, like those houses haunted by a brutal murder. Somehow that information replays itself again and again like a recording. *The Holy Ghost is good, the devil is bad* followed by the cursing of the Holy Ghost is a residual that remains dormant in his mind until a song, a sermon or something he sees on TV reminds him and the manta replays again. Like a residual in a haunted house, the mantra is like the remains of abandoned goat skeletons left in rocky areas that Jeffrey collects from time to time. *They are worth collecting. The mantra is not worth the time wasted in worry.*

Jeffrey trusts that one day he will see Kathy again – and all his beloved relatives, friends and pets.

Jeffrey thinks, as he drifts into sleep and falls into pleasant dreams, *Life is good. God is good.*

ACKNOWLEDGMENTS

A writer's development would not be complete without exposure to the good teaching and advice of other writers. I wish to thank the Writers' Loft program at Middle Tennessee State University, in particular David Pierce, a fine mentor who was always kind to fledgling writers. His death this year is a sad loss to the literary community in Tennessee, and I will miss his friendly voice at Writers' Loft workshops. I would also like to thank Jean Cavelos and the Odyssey Writing Workshop, a fine workshop on writing science fiction, fantasy, and horror. Many thanks are due also to my colleagues at Methodist University, Michael Colonnese and Robin Greene, whose teaching and encouragement have been of supreme value to me in improving my writing. I thank Mike Parker of Wordcrafts Press for all he has done for me and other authors as they share their best work with the world. Finally, I thank my wife, Karen, who has the often thankless task of putting up with a husband who is a writer.

28862393R00138

Made in the USA
Columbia, SC
25 October 2018